THE DEVIL'S WINCHESTER

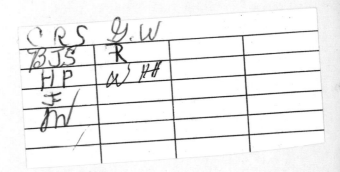

5-11

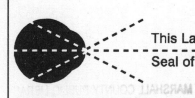

THE DEVIL'S
WINCHESTER

PETER BRANDVOLD

WHEELER PUBLISHING
A part of Gale, Cengage Learning

GALE
CENGAGE Learning™

Detroit • New York • San Francisco • New Haven, Conn • Waterville, Maine • London

LIBRARY OF CONGRESS CATALOGING-IN-PUBLICATION DATA

Brandvold, Peter.
　　The devil's Winchester : a Lou Prophet novel / by Peter Brandvold. — Large print ed.
　　　　p. cm. — (Wheeler Publishing large print western)
　　Originally published: New York: Berkley Books, 2011.
　　ISBN-13: 978-1-4104-3747-1 (pbk.)
　　ISBN-10: 1-4104-3747-7 (pbk.)
　　1. Large type books. I. Title.
　　PS3552.R3236D49 2011
　　813'.54—dc22　　　　　　　　　　　　　　　　2011003261

Published in 2011 by arrangement with The Berkley Publishing Group, a member of Penguin Group (USA) Inc.

Printed in the United States of America
1 2 3 4 5 6 7 15 14 13 12 11

In memory of my aunt Ellen,
who always enjoyed a good, racy yarn.

1

With two long, furry black legs, the tarantula probed the eye that was still stretched wide in horror and disbelief at the owner's premature demise.

The spider drew back as though in distaste at what it found in the eye socket, then scuttled around the edge of the bloody bullet wound in the bone-white forehead and crawled down the length of the dead man's sunburned nose to his brushy brown mustache. Clinging to the mustache, the spider bent all eight of its black legs slightly and lowered its beadlike head atop its conelike thorax as if to investigate the man's mouth, back from which the man's lips were spread in a grisly death grin.

The yellow teeth were crooked, with bits of dried food and tobacco caked between them. The right eyetooth had been broken off during a fight in the Venus Saloon in Julesburg, Colorado. It was the jagged edge of this tooth, to which remnants of the man's recent breakfast still clung, that the spider seemed to probe with interest before freezing suddenly at the sound or possibly the vibration of oncoming riders.

As the thuds grew louder, the tarantula scrambled down over the dead man's chin and spade beard and across his right shoulder before leaping to the ground and hiding inside the collar of his calico shirt. Meanwhile, fifty yards down the trail, Lou Prophet checked down his ugly, hammeredhead dun which he appropriately called Mean and Ugly, and reached down to slide his Winchester '73 from the cracked leather saddle scabbard jutting up from under his right thigh.

The big, sun-seared, broken-nosed bounty hunter cocked the rifle one-handed as his blond partner, Louisa Bonaventure, reined her brown-and-white pinto pony to a halt beside him. Prophet stared out from beneath the dusty, funneled brim of his battered Stetson at the dead man lying in the brush left of the trail, about ten yards from a scraggly mesquite shrub.

Spying the dead man as well, Louisa unsheathed her own Winchester carbine and looked around cautiously, squinting her hazel eyes beneath the flat brim of her

8

brown felt hat with its braided leather band. The hem of her dusty wool riding skirt brushed her tall stockmen's boots, the spurs of which glinted in the late afternoon sun.

When Prophet had scrutinized the scrub around him and spied no bushwhackers skulking behind the rocks and cedar trees that stippled the sandy apron hills of western New Mexico's No-Water Mountains, he grunted, "Back me," and swung down from his saddle with a grace unexpected in a man of Prophet's size — his brawny, frontier-seasoned frame weighed 230 pounds desert-dry, and he stood well over six feet tall in his stocking feet.

Louisa levered a cartridge into her Winchester's breech. Remaining atop the pinto, she looked around cautiously. Strands of her honey blond hair were blown by a light, cool breeze around her smooth cheeks that, despite the sun and wind of the hundred trails she'd been dusting since being orphaned by a gang of cutthroats in Nebraska Territory three years ago, still owned the texture of fresh-whipped cream. Her lips were full and rich — what some might call bee-stung — though her hazel eyes were tough and practical if a little on the snooty side.

She wore two pearl-gripped Colts around

9

her slender waist, her striped serape pushed up to expose their handles. Though she looked as though she belonged in the piano room of a middle-class midwestern house with four or five gables and gingerbread latticework under the eaves, she knew how to use those guns. In fact, a good many men had been planted heel-down in Boot Hills all across the frontier by those fancy shooting irons, as well as by her carbine.

Lou Prophet stooped over the dead man lying belly up in the scrub and gravel, blood still oozing from the fresh wound in the stiff's forehead. Another, older wound in the man's high right side — the wound he had received a day earlier, after he and his gang of six cutthroats from the surrounding hills had robbed the bank in nearby Corazon — was blood-matted and fly-blown. Prophet and Louisa had by chance ridden into the town a couple hours after the robbery and quickly booted their horses onto the outlaws' trail though only the leader, Blanco Metalious, had a bounty on his head — a mere $250 one at that.

"Junior Pope," Prophet said.

"The one the druggist wounded."

"Yep." Prophet kicked Junior Pope onto his belly to expose the entrance wound in Pope's left shoulder blade and spied the tarantula scuttling away from the carcass and under a rock. "Too bad for Pope." The big bounty hunter allowed himself a dry chuckle. "The druggist said he'd been aiming for Metalious. Now Pope's lyin' out here with the black widows and the tarantulas, likely gonna be wolf supper later."

"Looks like one of his own drilled that nasty hole in his worthless head."

Prophet nodded. "Appears one of his amigos decided Pope had suddenly become more trouble than he was worth, likely slowin' 'em all down. So they — probably Metalious his own nasty self — drilled one through Pope's noggin."

"One less to share the loot with."

"Uh-huh."

Louisa said behind Prophet, "If you're gonna say a few words over him, Lou, say 'em and let's shake a leg. It'd be nice to catch up to the other five before they're on the other side of the No-Waters and headed for Texas."

"Nah, I see no reason to waste words on the likes of Junior Pope." Prophet turned sideways to shoot his blond partner an incredulous glance. "You know, I do believe the man's been an outlaw since he was old enough to heft a shootin' iron, and I've never heard of a single bounty on his head.

Now, that there is the very definition of a wasted life."

Louisa canted her head to one side. "Do you think we could discuss the tragedy of Junior Pope *after* we've run down the rest of his gang?"

"Don't you worry your purty head," Prophet said, resting his Winchester on his right shoulder and strolling back to his horse. "They're likely holed up snug as spiders in rocks at Nugget Town up yonder."

As Prophet swung up into his saddle, Louisa frowned into the distance, toward the steepening slopes of the No-Waters. "Nugget Town?"

"Little boomtown that went bust about two years ago. Sittin' up against the base of that ridge." Prophet pointed with his rifle. "It's the end of the trail. I was through there when the town was boomin', just before the bust. Plenty of owlhoots hole up there, on the run from posses, and tank up on water before they cross the mountains. They'll rest up there a day or two. No point in us hurryin', now that I'm sure that's where they're headed."

"If there's a reason to drag your feet, you'll find it."

"You got a point there, Miss Bonnyventure," Prophet allowed with a chuckle, nudging Mean and Ugly slowly ahead.

"It's Bonaventure, you Southern repro-bate," Louisa said, pooching out her lips and furling her blond brows. "There never has been any *y* in it."

Prophet chuckled again as Louisa came up beside him and they rode up and down the rocky hills, rising gradually toward the base of the bald crags looming before them. The clay-colored range, moderately high, was eroded, boulder-strewn, and nearly treeless, with a deep crevice here and there filling with shade now as the sun sank. The peaks were as sharp and as evenly spaced as the teeth on a whipsaw blade.

"Whoa," Prophet said, drawing back on Mean's reins when they'd ridden another half hour.

Prophet sniffed the breeze, staring straight ahead toward the mountain ridge that glowed copper now as the sun sank lower. "Smell that?"

Louisa lifted her chin, drawing a breath. "I was wondering when you were going to smell the smoke. Cottonwood. Maybe a little pinyon pine."

Prophet scowled at his comely partner, who turned to him with challenge in her clear, hazel gaze. "You're wrong about the pine. That's mesquite."

He gave a caustic chuff, then booted the dun into a shallow ravine off the trail's right side. He stepped out of his saddle, looped Mean's reins over the branch of a small ironwood, and grabbed his sawed-off, double-barreled shotgun that had been secured to his saddle horn. He looped the leather lanyard over his head and right shoulder, then slid the weapon — none the less savage-looking for being so short — behind his back so that the double-bores peeked up above his shoulder.

As he grabbed his rifle and ran his fingers along his cartridge belt, making sure all the loops were filled with brass, Louisa stood beside her pinto, checking the loads in each of her pearl-gripped Colts, narrowing an eye to inspect each oiled cylinder in turn.

When she'd twirled the second gun on her finger with customary flourish, then dropped it into her holster, Prophet said, "Show-off."

He started following a game path up the northwest side of the wash. Behind him, Louisa said, "Remind me, and I'll show you how to do that sometime."

"Don't wanna know," Prophet grumbled. "Don't *need* to know less'n you're plannin' on throwin' in with Buffalo Bill Cody's Wild West Show."

Hearing Louisa give a snort as she slipped a cartridge through her carbine's loading gate and softly seated a shell in the chamber, Prophet tramped along the faint game trail, holding his Winchester in one hand and keeping his head low as he stared toward the base of the high ridge.

He and Louisa followed the trail well wide of the horse trail they'd been following, amidst large boulders that had fallen from the ridge above and that offered good cover. When Nugget Town rose before them on a slight plateau at the base of the No-Waters and fronted by a deep, brush-choked ravine, Prophet dropped to a knee behind a boulder.

Louisa dropped down behind the boulder's far end, staring out across two shallow arroyos at the town comprised of a half dozen sun-silvered, false-fronted business buildings flanked by squat log hovels and stock pens. A large wooden water tower stood between Prophet and Louisa and the town proper. Sluice boxes on high wooden pilings ran down from the tower, disappearing into a ravine about fifty yards away from it.

The tower would offer good cover, Prophet thought, for him and Louisa approaching the town straight out from where

15

they were now.

He shifted his gaze just beyond the tower to the opposite side of the street from the business buildings. There, a large corral abutted a broad wooden livery barn topped with a rooster weather vane that, while penny colored with rust, brightly reflected the golden rays of the falling sun. Five horses stood statue-still in the corral while a sixth rolled on its back, kicking up dust that the light touched with pink and salmon. The air was so still that Prophet could hear the horse's satisfied snorts and grunts, the scrapes of its hooves against the ground.

Directly across the street from the corral was a broad, three-story structure that Prophet remembered as the Gold Nugget Saloon. It had a broad front porch around three sides. Although the porch was vacant, the inside of the saloon was not. Gray smoke unfurled from a broad, brick chimney that ran up the building's near side.

The ghosts that had mostly populated the town over the past several years, since the gold disappeared, didn't need fires to stand off the imminent high-country chill. And they'd have no use for the horses in the corral yonder, neither.

Louisa said, "Okay, you're right."

Prophet glanced at her. Her pretty brows furled.

"I think it is mesquite they've mixed with the cottonwood," she said.

"Told ya."

Prophet narrowed an eye at the saloon that lay a good hundred yards away from his and Louisa's position. "When we get down to the water tower, we'll split up. You move to the front corner. I'm gonna work around the corral, try to draw 'em all out into the street."

"You think they have a lookout posted?"

"If they do, he's well hid. I'm bettin' there ain't any. Judging by how this bunch stuck to only one trail, without so much as one little detour to throw a posse off, they're pretty confident they ain't been followed."

"*Haven't* been followed. God, your English is awful, Lou."

"That's another thing I'll remind you to teach me one of these days. Good English. Comes in right handy in our line of work." Prophet looked at her. "You be careful. The only seasoned outlaw of the bunch is Metalious, but Dusty Willis is right handy with a six-shooter, too. The other three are amateurs, but they can be just as dangerous as professionals."

Louisa looked at him askance. "This ain't

17

the first bunch of owlhoots I've brought down."

"Don't let it be your last."

A faint smile pulled at Louisa's mouth, and her eyes grew soft. She glanced toward the town. Then, seeing no one outside the saloon, she walked crouching over to Prophet, tipped her hat back off her forehead, tipped his back with the barrel of her carbine, and pressed her warm lips to his.

"Just for that I'm gonna curl up in your blankets tonight. Stark naked by a hot fire."

"Am I gonna be there?"

She pulled his hat brim back down over his forehead. "I have a feeling."

Prophet swallowed the dry knot in his throat and raked his eyes from her velvet pink lips and creamy neck toward the ghost town aglow in the waning light at the base of the ridge. Slowly, quietly, he levered a fresh round into his Winchester's breech.

2

Keeping their heads low, Prophet and Louisa moved with little sound across two dry washes, weaving through brush and around boulders, both keeping their eyes skinned on the terrain around them as well as on the town.

When they gained the base of the water tower, they each hunkered behind a creosote-slathered piling. The saloon was only fifty yards away, and the street before it was bathed in shadow. A shingle chain under the saloon's porch roof, announcing nickel beers and a fresh lunch plate, squawked faintly in a rising breeze.

Prophet glanced at Louisa, nodding. She rose from behind her piling and began to head toward the saloon's near side.

"Wait!" Prophet rasped, gritting his teeth.

Louisa dropped behind a piling just beyond the one she'd left, pressing her back against it as she squatted in the gravel, knees to her chest. Her cheeks flushed with apprehension.

Prophet doffed his hat to peer around the piling in front of him. He'd heard voices and a muffled clomp of footsteps, and now he drew a slow, anxious breath as a man walked out of the saloon's front door onto the porch. A tall man in a long, spruce-green duster and carrying a sixteen-shot Henry repeating rifle from a lanyard around his neck and right shoulder. From the man's mustached mouth protruded a long, black cigar. He had a spade beard and he walked with a slight hitch in his right leg.

Dusty Willis.

As Prophet peered out from behind his piling and Louisa watched from over her right shoulder, Willis stared straight out across the rugged hills and washes bathed in a golden, late day haze. Willis lifted his head slightly as he drew deep on his cheroot. Then, letting the Henry hang barrel down at his side, he turned away from Prophet and Louisa and blew the cigar smoke into the street.

There was a low rumble from inside the saloon. Willis glanced over his left shoulder and said something that Prophet couldn't hear. Then Willis turned full around toward Louisa and Prophet, and the bounty hunter jerked his head back behind the piling, hoping the post concealed him, wide shoulders and all.

He stared at the coated wood before him in which someone had carved a heart between the letter *L* and the letter *J*. His heart thudded anxiously. The breeze sifted through the pilings, blowing the pungent tang of the creosote.

After a long, slow minute, Prophet leaned slightly left, peering out from behind the post. Dusty Willis had stepped to his own right along the porch and was leaning slightly back at the waist as he sent a piss stream arcing into the street while continuing to puff the cigar in his teeth.

Louisa softly but insistently cleared her throat. Prophet glanced at her. She looked at him with a question in her eyes. She didn't want to poke her head out from the piling and risk being seen.

"He's shakin' the dew from his lily," Prophet said just loudly enough for Louisa to make out above the breeze and the creaking platform high above.

He cast his gaze toward the saloon once more.

Willis faced him but his head was down as he tucked himself back into his pants, bending his knees and clamping his Henry

21

repeater under his right arm. When the outlaw had strolled back into the saloon and out of sight, Prophet said, "I do believe Dusty is feelin' better, and so am I. Let's go."

While Louisa ran out from the right side of the water tower pilings, Prophet ran left. A glance in her direction as he rounded the rear corner of the badly sun-bleached and splintered livery barn told him that she'd gained the first of the main street structures and was starting to make her way past a boarded-up drugstore on her way to the Gold Nugget Saloon.

She strode quickly, her skirt swishing around the tops of her boots, her rifle held up high across her chest. Even from this distance he could see that her expression betrayed not the least bit of fear.

Only resolution. Eagerness.

The Vengeance Queen, Prophet had dubbed her long ago.

She had nothing personally against these men they were hunting. Only, as they were riding out of Corazon in the wake of their robbery during which thcy'd killed a teller and the bank president who'd tried being a hero with a double-barreled, gold-chased derringer no longer than a pencil, one of their stray rounds had clipped a sandy-haired boy in faded dungarees and left him sprawling dead in the dirt, blood oozing from both ears.

That had been personal enough for Louisa, who'd watched her own young siblings die bloodily at the hands of Handsome Dave Duvall's gang a few years back. As Prophet ran along the back wall of the livery barn, he almost felt sorry for Blanco Metalious and Dusty Willis and the three other poor, unsuspecting sons o' bitches who'd been unfortunate enough to cross paths with Louisa Bonaventure.

Prophet ran out from behind the barn and along the stock corral in which the gang's six horses milled. A blue roan that had been standing nearest the barn gave a start when it saw the big bounty hunter, and the other horses swung their heads around to inspect the intruder.

"That's all right — go ahead," Prophet said quietly, as he dropped to a knee behind a corner post. He kicked a tumbleweed away from the post and growled, "Go ahead — git a fuss up, damnit!"

All six horses regarded him sullenly. The blue roan walked toward him cautiously, slowly lowering its head and twitching its ears.

"Shit! When you *want* horses to keep their

damn traps shut, they summon half the owl-hoots south of the Arkansas River. When you want 'em to go ahead and *give the alarm*, they look at you like you're some harmless angel that done dropped out of a pink puffy cloud and is here to feed 'em carrots and sugar cubes!"

The roan stopped suddenly, dust lifting from its shod hooves. It stretched its neck out a little more, its black, seed-flecked nostrils working daintily.

Prophet pushed off his heels and strode down the corral's far side toward the front corner, where he'd have a good view of the Gold Nugget. As he walked, he whistled softly, trying to get one of the horses to sound the alarm.

They only watched him, twitching their ears. A black with one white sock gave a moderately loud blow, rippling its withers, but then turned its head to nip an itch on its side.

"Useless critters."

Prophet dropped to a knee behind the corral's front corner post and stared toward the saloon with its broad front gallery on which two old wicker chairs sat in the thickening shade. On one sat a tumbleweed. The saloon's windows were boarded up, so it was impossible to see inside. He could

24

hear the low rumble of voices emanating from behind the saloon's batwing doors, but the only movement was a small, charcoal cat slinking around in the shadows under the porch that was set on low stone pilings.

Prophet looked at the saloon's front corner but saw no sign of Louisa. She was likely keeping herself hid until the curly wolves scrambled out of their den. Glancing over his right shoulder, he saw that three of the cutthroats' horses were standing within ten feet of him, heads down to inspect him with typical dull-witted curiosity while the other three were slowly walking up to join them.

Prophet snorted and grabbed a rock, intending to bounce it off the porch's ceiling to summon Metalious's men. He cocked his arm and froze as movement at the saloon's far front corner drew his eye.

Dropping the rock, he hunkered low behind the corral's corner post, quickly doffed his hat, and edged a look around the porch. He sucked a sharp breath. His knees turned to putty.

Louisa was walking out from behind the saloon. A rough-garbed rider with a cinnamon beard and a billowy red neckerchief held himself tight against her back, one of his brawny arms hooked around her neck while his other hand held a cocked .45 Colt Army against her left temple.

"Goddamnit, girl," Prophet heard himself grumble as he continued to hunker low and edge his right eye around the side of it, squeezing his Winchester in both his gloved hands. "What the hell have you gone and got yourself — ?"

He stopped as the man behind Louisa said loudly, "Blanco! Hey, Blanco, get out here! Look what I found!"

The man kept his head close to Louisa's as, gritting his large horse teeth, he slid his cautious gaze along the street fronting the saloon.

Prophet stared, hang-jawed and sharp-eyed. He couldn't believe what he was seeing.

Louisa had eyes in the back of her head. How could she have let herself get snuck up on? Hell, on his worst, most hungover days with buxom whores still dancing around behind his eyes, he wouldn't have let . . .

The echoing thumps of several pairs of boots echoed inside the saloon, growing louder until a short man in a yellow duster pushed through the batwings and onto the porch. He was flanked by Blanco Metalious, who wore a dusty, flat-brimmed black hat over his stringy, pale blond hair and was

26

holding a Henry repeater in one hand, letting it dangle negligently down along his right leg that was clad in cheap orange-and-brown-checked wool.

Two more men followed the short man, whom Prophet didn't recognize, and Metalious onto the porch, where they sort of spread out as the bearded hombre shoved Louisa out farther into the street.

Metalious stopped on the porch's top step, leaned against a post, and grinned, showing his white, even teeth under his white mustache that stood out against the redness of his sunburned face. In town, Prophet had learned the man's infamous father was a big Greek, though Blanco had been dropped from the womb of an albino whore somewhere in Alabama. Blanco's yellow-gray eyes narrowed down to the size of steel pellets.

"Well, goddamn, Santee — I thought all the gold was done pinched out of these hills!"

Santee continued to hold Louisa in his firm grip and look around carefully. "I thought the same thing, till I spied this little golden-haired beauty skulkin' around out here when I was headin' back from the shitter. You think there's any more of her ilk out here?"

27

"What the hell is her ilk?" asked the short man standing to Metalious's left and fingering the two matched Remingtons positioned for the cross draw on his narrow hips.

He wore a bowler hat and brown wool trousers. A wood-handled bowie knife was sheathed on his chest, dangling from a braided rawhide cord around his neck.

"A whore? Is that what she is?" The short man raised his voice. "Is that what you are, little girl? You come out here to give us each a squeeze off'n your titties for the price of a whiskey shot?"

"She was carryin' a carbine like she meant business with it," Santee said. "And she was sneakin' around real catlike. If I didn't know better, I'd think she might have meant us harm." He lowered a hand to Louisa's striped serape, feeling around. "And she's got more than two mosquito bites inside this poncho — I'll tell you that." He reached down and lifted Louisa's skirt high, exposing both her pale, supple legs and the brown leather knife sheath strapped inside her right thigh. "And lookee here!"

Louisa did not struggle but only gazed up at the men on the porch blandly as Santee slipped the razor-edged Mexican pigsticker from her hideout sheath. He held the knife up for the others to see, then tossed it into the dirt.

"Why, she's armed herself for 'Paches," intoned the stocky man dressed in deerskin slacks behind the short man with the matched Remys.

The men on the porch, including Metalious, had become tense and defensive, raising their weapons and looking around the street. Holding his rifle in one hand, barrel up, Metalious thumbed the hammer back as he strode slowly down the porch steps. The others followed until they were all in the street, looking around, swinging their pistols or rifles this way and that, wary of an ambush.

Metalious walked up in front of Louisa and, staring up the street beyond Prophet and the corral, cupped her chin tightly in his gloved left hand.

"What's your game, miss? There a posse out here?"

Louisa swiped his hand away from her face. "No game. And there ain't no posse. I came to find a bottle for Pa. Ma made him give up the firewater on account of him sleepin' all day instead of diggin' for gold. But he's been seein' snakes for nigh on three days now, and Ma and me is done tired of it. We don't care how much he sleeps as long as he pipes down about the

29

snakes. So, I come to Nugget Town to see if I could rustle up a bottle. Then I seen your horses and the smoke in the chimney." She shrugged. "I was just bein' cautious, that's all. You never know who's on the lurk amongst these hills. Besides, ghost towns give me the willies. You fellas have a bottle you could spare for Pa?"

Blanco Metalious narrowed an eye at her. "A bottle for your pa, huh? You sure that's all you're doin' out here?"

Behind the corral post, Prophet caressed his Winchester's cocked hammer with his thumb and watched Louisa nod her head while feigning an expression of wide-eyed, girlish innocence.

"What else would I be doin'?" she said.

"She's lyin', Blanco," said Santee, continuing to hold his cocked Colt to Louisa's left temple. He lifted one of her matched Colts from its holster and tossed it into the dust. Reaching for the other one, he said, "This purty little thing is armed for bear."

"In these hills, one can't be too careful." Metalious's head was turned away from Prophet as the outlaw leader studied Louisa, probably running his eyes up and down and all around her delectable frame. "Especially little girls on their own and away from home."

30

The gang leader slid her hair back away from the right side of her face with the back of his free hand. "What you got to buy a bottle with, young lady?"

"Don't have no money," Louisa said. "What'd you have in mind?"

Prophet stopped caressing the Winchester's hammer with his thumb. Tensing, mentally calming himself, he prepared to start shooting.

The three men in the street besides Metalious and Santee were all looking at Louisa now, lusty leers showing on their hard, weathered, belligerent faces. Prophet could take those three easily enough, but Santee still had his Colt pressed against Louisa's temple. And Metalious was partly blocking his view of the pistol-wielding cutthroat.

"Steady," Prophet told himself. "All in good time. The fool girl done got herself in a peck of trouble, but she's obviously got an idea about how to get herself out of it."

Above the slow thudding of his heart, Prophet heard Metalious ask Louisa her name.

"Louisa," she said with mock schoolgirl innocence.

Metalious didn't say anything for a time. He just continued to stare down at Louisa, who looked up at him coolly, her hair ruffling in the cooling breeze.

"Fellas," he said finally, turning to the three men between him and Prophet, "take a good long look around. I mean a *long* look around."

Suddenly, Metalious grabbed Louisa's hair and jerked the girl out of Santee's grip. Louisa gave a startled grunt and went sprawling into the street near the bottom of the saloon's porch steps. "Me and Miss Louisa here gonna climb up on top of this woodpile here and do us a business transaction!"

Metalious reached down, shoved his hands under Louisa's shoulders, and tossed her brusquely atop the wood stacked on the right side of the porch steps. He drew her wool skirt and white petticoat up around her waist and, laughing savagely, stepped back to unbuckle his cartridge belt.

3

Louisa looked dazed as she sat back against the porch rail, her naked rump propped on the woodpile. Her hat was off, and her mussed hair screened her face. Prophet's heart hammered as he watched Metalious drop his checked trousers down around the cartridge belt he'd thrown at his feet and step between Louisa's bare legs, laughing louder.

Santee stood near Metalious, enjoying the show. He still held his cocked Colt in his hand, and the gun was still aimed at Louisa.

The other three were sidestepping along the street toward Prophet. Prophet was waiting for them to get good and clear of Louisa and Metalious before he showed himself, so his own lead wouldn't take out his partner.

Waiting wasn't easy. Not with his heart pounding bile through his veins and rage resounding like a smithy's hammer in his ears.

Just as the last of the three men moving toward him stepped clear of Louisa and Metalious, Prophet jerked his head up, rising to his knees and snugging the butt of his Winchester against his right shoulder. Normally, he gave even the most black-hearted cutthroat a chance to give himself up. But Santee was holding that cocked pistol a little too close to Louisa, who was groaning and grunting against Metalious's savage thrusting.

Boom!

In his haste, Prophet had punched his Winchester round a hair south of Santee's heart.

For a quarter second he wasn't sure if he'd hit the man at all. But then, as the other men jerked their heads toward Prophet, Santee gave a little shiver and stepped back, impulsively triggering his Colt into the ground beside him, blowing up dust and rocks. Dropping his chin, he looked down at his chest where a patch of something dark and wet shone, though it was hard to see against the cutthroat's brown wool vest and in the wedge of barn shadow the man had stepped into.

There was a moment of crystal silence.

Prophet ejected the spent brass from his Winchester's breech, and the empty casing clinked to the ground behind him as he levered a fresh round in the chamber. Dusty Willis and the other two cutthroats stared fierce-eyed toward Prophet, but, taken aback by the sudden, unexpected rifle bark, they held as still as stone statues.

A scream broke the silence, and Prophet wasn't sure where it was coming from until Blanco Metalious jerked his head up, hang-jawed, and staggered bare-assed away from Louisa while thrusting a hand at his crotch.

Dusty Willis and the other two glanced at Metalious and then, as though their heads were all tied to the same string, whipped their gazes back to Prophet. Willis brought his Henry repeater up, bellowing, "Fuckin' bounty hunters!"

But before he could get the barrel of the sixteen-shooter leveled, Prophet drilled him in his upper left chest, and then, shooting from his right hip, punched both the other two hard cases back against the raised saloon porch. While Metalious continued to bellow like a poleaxed bull, Dusty Willis brought his Henry up once more while clutching his bloody chest, and managed to trigger a round three feet to Prophet's right.

Several of the horses whinnied and

lurched toward the corral's far end.

Prophet's Winchester roared. Willis grunted and staggered straight back, dropping his Henry in the dust, then setting his boots and buckling his knees. He grabbed his belly from which thick red blood oozed and hit the street with a curse, stretching his lips back from his teeth, lifting his chin, and yelling a raspy curse at the sky.

Prophet heard gunfire to his right and more bellows from Metalious. He kept his eyes ahead, as the other two cutthroats behind Willis were still alive and trying to get their own weapons raised.

Stepping out away from the corral's corner, Prophet raised his Winchester and dispatched first the man on the right and then the man on the left, shooting quickly but purposefully and feeling the Winchester buck against his shoulder.

He shot the first man through his right ear while he tried to push himself up against the porch. He drilled the other man through the chest and, as the man reached for a big Dragoon jutting from behind the buckle of his cartridge belt, screaming and spitting blood from his lips, Prophet drilled him through the dead center of his forehead.

The man's head whipped back so hard that his black derby hat, which already bore what appeared to be a bullet hole in its crown, turned a somersault in the air before hitting the dirt at his quivering feet.

At the same time, a pistol barked to Prophet's right.

Levering the Winchester but finding it empty, he swung around in time to see the top of Santee's head burst like a ripe tomato. Somehow, the man had managed to scramble over to the front wall of the livery barn. Louisa was ten yards away from him, lying twisted in the middle of the street, one leg curled beneath the other.

"Son of a *bitch!*" the girl bellowed as she dropped her hand and smoking Colt down by her bloody right thigh.

Prophet ran over and dropped to a knee beside her. "How bad?"

She hardly ever cursed — cursing lacked nobility, she'd explained time and again — so it must be bad.

"It's nothing," she said, gritting her teeth and glaring at Santee, who'd taken a good three or four shots to the torso and his own left thigh before Louisa's head shot had finally blown his wick.

He slumped slowly sideways, leaving a long arc of red on the gray barn door behind him.

Louisa pitched her voice with exasperation — another rarity for her, who was usually as composed as a Lutheran preacher bright and early on Easter Sunday. "I couldn't get the bastard to die!"

"Where's Metalious?"

"Back there — running like the yellow-livered devil he is."

Louisa canted her head to indicate the saloon along the side of which the outlaw leader ran, shuffling awkwardly while trying to pull his pants up. He had his cartridge belt thrown over one shoulder, a gun in his hand.

Prophet set his empty rifle down beside Louisa and shucked his walnut-gripped Colt from the holster thonged low on his right thigh. "Wait here."

"Don't do him any favors. Let the mangy dog bleed to death, Lou!"

Prophet was already striding around the front of the saloon. Metalious had left a scuffed, bloody path behind him. Louisa must have stuck him good with one of her hideout knives, two of which she kept hidden on her lovely person. Never one to walk around armed for anything but bear — that was Louisa.

And she'd always taken a risky satisfaction in luring men under her skirts for just such punishment as she'd given Blanco

Metalious. One of these days, it was going to get her killed — and it almost had a year ago in Mexico, before they'd taken on a town called Helldorado up in Wyoming. You'd think she'd learn.

Metalious had just gotten his pants up around his waist with a grunt and a jerk, and disappeared around behind the saloon, when Prophet broke into a run.

"Hold up, Blanco," he ordered. "From as much blood as you're paintin' the gravel with, you ain't goin' nowhere."

He ran around the back of the saloon and stopped suddenly. Blanco Metalious was down on his butt, sort of twisted around at his waist, anguish pinching his beady yellow-gray eyes. Sweat streaked his fleshy, freckled face and patchy, colorless goat beard.

"Help me, Prophet. For chrissakes, that crazy bitch damn near cut my balls off!"

He'd barely gotten that last out before his eyelids drooped, and his head began to sag backward. Prophet hadn't seen the nasty gash in his temple. Apparently, Louisa had drilled him in the head as well as cut into his nether regions.

Metalious groaned. Then the back of his head hit the ground, and he was out.

To Prophet's left, something thrashed around in a snag of cedar and chokecherry

39

shrubs. There was the flash of what appeared to be a gun between the branches and the click of a hammer. Prophet wheeled and, crouching, squeezed off two rounds with his .45.

A high-pitched groan. A thud. The clatter of a gun striking gravel.

Prophet glanced at Metalious, whose eyelids were fluttering. Otherwise, he lay still.

The bounty hunter went over and relieved the unconscious cutthroat of two pistols, a double-barreled derringer in an ankle sheath, and two knives. Then he stole over to the shrubs and, moving slowly, began parting branches to peer inside the snag. Holstering his Peacemaker, he lifted his shotgun up over his shoulder and, clutching the gut shredder in both hands, thumbing the rabbit-ear hammers back to full cock, stepped farther into the snag.

The dusky salmon light glistened off an old revolver that lay at the base of a mossy boulder. A hand lay beside the gun, palm up, fingers curled, unmoving. A delicate hand.

A female hand.

Prophet moved forward, holding the shotgun out from his right side, and soon found himself standing over the body of a brown-haired girl, blood leaking from the back of her head. Blood also spotted the boulder. Prophet saw no other wounds on her. He placed two fingers on her neck, found a steady pulse. He gently shook her shoulder.

"Miss?"

He scowled down at her. Imagine a skinny little waif out here at the backside of Nugget Town. A white girl, too — suntanned face lightly freckled, with a little girl's nose and close-set eyes. A small brown mole off the right corner of her nose. A beauty mark, some would call it. A comely face. Comely body, too — a calico blouse drawn taut against the ripe bosom of a well-developing seventeen-, eighteen-year-old. She wore fringed deerskin leggings, stockmen's boots, and a leather brush jacket. There was a gold locket around her neck, looking about as out of place with the rest of her attire as Prophet would look behind a preacher's pulpit.

She also wore an old holster on a plain leather belt, both the holster and belt the color of butterscotch. The gun was an old cap-and-ball .44. A Civil War model Colt Army.

He scrubbed a hand across his jaw. She must belong to one of the men in the gang.

Funny, though — there were only the tracks of six horses. She was either riding double with one of the men, or waiting here, with a horse maybe stabled elsewhere or picketed off in the brush.

"Hey, miss."

Prophet slid his right hand beneath her head and gently lifted it a couple inches above the ground. Her dark, wavy hair was blood matted in one spot no larger than a silver cartwheel. She must have fallen against the boulder when Prophet had fired into the brush, hit her head on a pointed knob protruding from the rock, and knocked herself cold.

She was alive, though with a head clubbing like that, there was no telling for how long.

Louisa called his name from the other side of the saloon.

"I'm on my way," he yelled back at her.

He shoved his ten-gauge back behind his shoulder, wedged the girl's old horse pistol behind his cartridge belt, then gently lifted her up in his arms and bulled back through the branches, screening her head with his own. When he surfaced from the bushes, he glanced once more at Metalious, who was slowly shaking his head, coming around.

Prophet carried the girl up along the

saloon and stopped when he saw Louisa standing with one leg propped atop a stock tank in front of the barn. She'd slid her skirt and fringe-hemmed petticoat up tight against her waist, revealing all of her bullet-creased right leg above her dusty boot. She was wringing out her red neckerchief when she looked up and saw Prophet standing there at the corner of the saloon with the girl in his arms.

"What do you have there?" she said, wincing as she pressed the wadded, wet neckerchief to the bloody tear across the outside of her well-turned thigh.

"Found her in the brush behind the saloon. Don't ask me what she was doin' there, but I got a feelin' she was fixin' to shoot me. Smacked her head on a rock."

Louisa frowned as she straightened a little at the waist, holding the wet neckerchief against her thigh. "Do you think she rides with these killers? Or . . . rode."

Prophet shrugged. "I'm gonna take her inside, get her warm." He glanced at his partner's leg. "How bad you hit?"

"It's nothing, I said."

Prophet grinned. "Don't want no nasty bullet wounds marring them purty legs of yours."

"A gentleman would avert his gaze."

43

"You see any gentlemen around here?"

"I certainly do not."

He carried the unconscious girl up the porch steps. At the top, he turned back to Louisa. "When you're done there, go back and keep an eye on Metalious. I think he's comin' around. That trough you carved across his head laid him out nearly as cold as this little miss."

Louisa lifted her gaze from her leg. "I didn't carve any trough across his head. I was too busy trying to kill Santee after that missed heart shot of yours."

Prophet stared back at her, brows furrowed. "Well, someone gave him a nice tattoo." He glanced down at the girl in his arms.

But she'd had only the big horse pistol, which was only good at close range — say no more than ten feet. Prophet knew that from experience, as he'd fired such unwieldy, hard-to-load, inaccurate beasts during the War of Northern Aggression.

"Musta been a ricochet."

Swinging around, he pushed through the batwings into the big, cavernous saloon that had already filled with night shadows. The fire was merely a mound of glowing coals in the hearth in the southeast wall, flanked by a horsehair couch on one side, a green velvet settee on the other. Both pieces of furniture were dusty and shabby, and the settee had two nickel-sized holes through its back inside a dark bloodstain as big around as Prophet's head.

Prophet walked around a table cluttered with playing cards and shot glasses. A cigar stub sent smoke curling into the air. The stolen money hung over a nearby chair back — two swollen saddlebag pouches bleeding greenbacks. Most of the money had come from the bank, the rest from a stage the gang had robbed a few hours before riding into Corazon.

Prophet kicked another chair out of his way and eased the girl onto the couch. He smoothed tendrils of dark hair back from her face and took another hard look at her.

She was too young and pretty to have been riding with this bunch of curly wolves. The rough trail garb said she was from the high and rocky — maybe a prospector's daughter like the one Louisa had been pretending to be. She might have been from a ranch around here. On the other hand, Prophet had been on the frontier long enough to know that how people looked and how they really were could be flip sides of the same coin.

It was important to know who and what

she was. He wouldn't turn his back on her until he did. And if she'd had some part in the robbery and killings in Corazon, she'd have some explaining to do before a circuit judge. If she lived.

Prophet went over to the messy stack of wood and torn catalogues near the hearth and chunked some logs onto the grate. Someone was grumbling outside. He turned as Louisa, limping only slightly, rifle-butted Blanco Metalious into the saloon through the shuttering batwings.

Metalious cursed and ground his teeth. He'd lost his hat. He was crouched slightly forward, holding a bloody bandanna to the right side of his crotch, where the blood from the pigsticker Louisa had poked him with was spreading a nasty, dark red stain.

"You two don't understand," he said, after roundly and nastily cursing Louisa. "I pretty much do as I please around here. You know Sam 'Man-Killin' ' Metalious? Well, that's my old man."

"The sheriff in town done told me that. Told me your old man has a price on his head, same as you. If we can get him, too, that just about makes this trip out here worth it."

"He didn't have no part in this job."

"How come?"

46

Blanco just stared at Prophet, one nostril curled.

"Well, he still has a price on his head." Prophet jerked his head. "Come on over here, Blanco. Take a look at this girl."

"What girl? Who?"

Louisa rammed the butt of her carbine against the cutthroat's back. He stumbled forward, spurs ringing raucously, almost dropping to his knees before setting his boots once again. He whipped around toward the blond bounty hunter. "God-damnit — you hit me with that thing again, so help me I'll take it away from you and do things with it to you . . . !"

Metalious had let his voice trail off. He just stood facing Louisa, so Prophet couldn't tell what had made him think twice about threatening the comely, deadly lass known far and wide as the Vengeance Queen. But he knew what Louisa could do with her eyes. Especially after what she'd done with that pigsticker.

Grumbling, Metalious turned back around and strode daintily, setting his right foot down easily and far wide of the other, over to Prophet near the fire and stared down at the girl. He looked like he'd just chugged a gallon of bad milk, but his eyes acquired a leering cast.

"Nice. She one of yours, too? How many you got, Prophet?"

Louisa, standing beside him, buried the butt of her carbine in the outlaw's belly. Metalious crumpled, took mincing feet straight back, then looked from Louisa to Prophet, stricken.

Prophet shook his head. "She don't like you, Blanco. That's how Louisa is about ugly sons o' bitches like yourself that try to rape her atop woodpiles thinkin' she's the innocent schoolgirl type and is just so ripe for the pickin's."

Louisa gritted her teeth. "She ride with you?"

"Hell, no," Metalious groaned, still crouched so low that he was almost to the floor, knees bent toward each other, boots out. "Never seen her before in my life." He gasped, tried to straighten, then decided his current position was the best one for the time being. "Where'd you find her?"

"You sure she didn't ride with you?" Prophet urged.

"Hell, I'm sure! Wouldn't I know if some purty little filly was ridin' with me? It ain't like I had that many folks on the roll that I'd forget about a *girl*." Metalious jerked his fearful eyes at Louisa. "Don't do nothin'

48

else to me now! I just called her a purty filly. It was a fuckin' *compliment!*"

4

While Louisa stayed with Blanco Metalious and the unknown girl, Prophet went out to fetch his and Louisa's horses from the ravine they'd tied them in. When he left the saloon, the light was sand colored. When he returned, leading both horses, it was purple. The abandoned, eerily silent town was slowly being swallowed by the night tumbling down the high southern ridge.

He unsaddled both horses and gave them each a good rubdown while they fed from feedbags and drew water from a stock trough. When he'd turned them into the holding corral off the side of the barn, hoping Mean and Ugly didn't start any fights with the others, as he was likely to do to prove his dominance over all, the weary bounty hunter dragged the dead men out of the street by their heels. He rolled them into a ravine at the far end of town, hearing the coyotes yammering from the ridges.

He knew they were eagerly watching and awaiting a rib-sticking meal.

When Dusty Willis had rolled down the bank with the others, Prophet walked, dragging his boot toes, over to a rock, and sagged down on it. He dug his cigarette makings out of a shirt pocket and slowly, pensively built himself a smoke. He smoked the quirley, habitually shielding the glowing coal with his palm, and watching the stars, wondering about the unknown girl and Metalious's old man.

Prophet did indeed know Sam "Man-Killin' " Metalious's reputation. Every bit the outlaw he'd raised his son to be, Sam Metalious ranched — if you could call an outlaw hideout with a few cows nibbling the range around it a ranch — about fifty miles from Corazon. There'd be trouble with the elder Metalious unless Prophet and Louisa could get Blanco the hell out of town pronto and on the road to see the circuit court judge in Albuquerque.

The Corazon town marshal, Maxwell Utter, wouldn't be much help in keeping Blanco behind bars. Utter had been confined to a wheelchair for the past two years, after getting backshot by rustlers late one night on the desert, but he'd been too stubborn to turn in his badge. And, anyway, no one else had wanted the job, so it had remained Utter's.

Utter was sided by his Mexican deputy, Ivano Rubriz. It was said that Utter and Rubriz had ridden the wrong side of the law down in Mexico twenty years ago and more, and while Rubriz still wore the bark of an old border bandito, he wasn't much of a lawman. For one thing, he was old. Even older than Utter, who was pushing sixty. For another, he drank the worm off the bottom of a tequila bottle every night on the Mex side of Corazon.

No, Prophet and Louisa would find little help in Corazon after Sam Metalious learned of his son's capture. Prophet would just as soon skirt the town altogether, but since Blanco had robbed the bank there and killed several of the town's citizens, that was where he belonged. For official arraignment and so the mothers and widows of his victims could spit on him, anyway. Then Prophet would convince Utter that it would be in his and his town's own best interest that Blanco be taken to Albuquerque for trial.

Prophet mashed his cigarette stub in the dirt and strolled lazily back along the dark main street to the saloon, a couple of the downstairs windows of which shone with candle and firelight. He'd set his and Louisa's gear on the porch. Now he hauled it all inside and found Louisa kicked back in one chair, boots crossed on one another, sipping from a tin coffee cup. A black pot chugged on a rock in the fireplace, fronting the flames.

Louisa had Blanco sitting on the floor, his back against a ceiling joist from which a lantern with a blackened mantle flickered. His ankles were cuffed together, the chain of the cuffs in turn cuffed to a table. Blanco sat on his saddle blanket, which was bloody from the nasty hole in the extreme inside of his ass, about two inches shy of Louisa's target area. He had a bottle of whiskey in one hand, head tipped back against the post, groaning.

The mystery girl remained on the couch, only now she had a sack of cracked corn beneath her head. Louisa had also thrown a blanket over her. The girl's face was tipped to one side, and she had a slightly pained look on her waifish young face.

"Nothing out of her yet?"

Louisa shook her head and held her smoking cup to her lips. "Just him." She tossed her head to the groaning, grunting Blanco, who seemed to be staring at the wall above the fieldstone hearth. "I'm fixing to shoot

53

him, put him out of all of our miseries."

"Tempting," Prophet admitted. "But the hangman needs to eat, too."

"I won't hang." Blanco tipped his bottle back, jerked it down, and swallowed hard. "You two are the ones gonna hang . . . soon as my pa and his boys get wind of what you done to me."

"I came a good six inches of giving you what you deserve, Blanco." Louisa's voice was liquid smooth. "If you hadn't jerked when Proph shot Santee . . ."

Blanco scowled at her, apparently thinking that over. He gave a shudder, as though chilled. "Speakin' of which, I hate to be a pest an' all, but I could use some medical attention. My old man's gonna be doubly piss-burned if you bleed me out."

As he kicked a chair out and sagged into it, Prophet said dryly, "Louisa, you want the honors?"

"No, no — just forget it!" Blanco said, his odd gray-yellow eyes snapping wide. "I reckon I'll live till we make it back to town." He stared drunkenly off, a cunning light entering his gaze. "Question is, will you two?"

Prophet scowled at him. He wondered if Blanco had been intending on meeting up with his old man here in Gold Nugget.

Probably not. If Sam "Man-Killin' " Metalious had been in on this scheme, he'd likely have been in on it from the get-go. And, since Sam's bunch had no fear of the Corazon law, they'd have likely headed for the Metalious Ranch, which, Prophet had learned, was appropriately called the Triple 6, with the sign of the devil blazed into the hindquarters of its beeves. When it had beeves, that was, and the place's sole purpose wasn't as an outlaw headquarters.

While the pie-eyed Blanco stared dreamily into the fire, Prophet grabbed one of the two whiskey bottles off the table and filled a shot glass. He threw back the shot, enjoying the burn in his belly and the instant filing of his weary edge, and refilled the glass.

He sat back in his chair, saw the bloodstain on Louisa's skirt.

"You need ole Doc Prophet to take a look at that?"

She looked tired, depressed, which is how she often looked after a hard day of tracking and killing. It wasn't the killing that depressed her. It was having it done and over with. She shook her head.

"Come on," Prophet said, leaning forward and patting her knee. "Let me see."

Louisa rolled her eyes toward him. Then she glanced at the finally quiet Blanco before shuttling her gaze to the ceiling and lifting her boots from her chair. "Upstairs."

Prophet looked at the mystery girl. Still sound asleep. Likely would be till morning at the very earliest. Even if she was partnered up with Blanco, she hadn't feigned that bleeding goose egg on her head. Blanco himself wasn't going anywhere, and if he tried, Prophet would hear the chair skidding around the worn floor puncheons.

"All right."

Louisa grabbed her saddlebags. Prophet grabbed his own and those that contained the loot, closed and locked the saloon's outside doors, and followed her up the broad, splintered stairs at the back of the room.

On the second floor, Prophet struck a match on his holster, and held it out until they found a room that hadn't been stripped bare. There was only a bed, one leg propped on a Sears & Roebuck catalogue, and a stained mattress. Louisa tossed her bedroll onto the bed. As she sat gingerly down, Prophet set one pouch of the moneybags beneath her head.

"Might as well make use of the loot. Lord knows we ain't gonna get much else out of it."

"We don't need money for every job,

Lou." Louisa eased her right leg onto the bed with a sigh. "Just the satisfaction of retrieving it, and bringing to justice those who stole it, is enough for me."

"You don't have gambling debts. I racked up quite a bill, last coupla months we was in Denver."

"You were in Denver. I lit out — remember?"

"Yeah, I remember. You couldn't stand the noise. And your delicate stomach couldn't stand the stench of cow shit wafting up from the stockyards."

"Fetid place. When a town gets that big, all the people should be run out of it, and it should be burned to the ground. Let the prairie claim it for ten years before anyone's allowed to return."

"Now, that's forward thinkin'."

Prophet removed a whiskey bottle and a clean, calico bandanna from his saddlebags, which he'd set with his rifle on the floor near his feet, and sat down on the edge of the bed. Outside, the coyotes were yammering much closer to town than they were a few minutes ago. The smell of death had drawn them to Blanco's friends. Prophet gave a wry snort as he heard them out there, snarling and fighting over the carrion. A couple of the older ones were really giving the what-for to the pups.

Prophet uncorked the bottle, took a long pull, then propped the whiskey between his legs. He grabbed Louisa's right boot by the toe and heel, jerked it off, and dropped it on the floor. He did the same with the left.

"Take my socks off," she ordered.

"No. Your feet stink."

"Not half as bad as yours. If you wanna play doctor with me, Mr. Prophet, you gotta do the dirty work, too."

When he'd removed her socks, exaggerating the smell by breathing through his bicep, he lifted her right foot and pressed his lips to it. She gazed down at him benevolently, like a princess thoroughly enjoying the ministrations of her servant boy.

Prophet set her tender, white foot back down on the bed and slid the hems of her skirt and petticoat slowly up her slender right leg until he'd exposed the bloody bandanna she'd wrapped around the wound. The bloody wrap contrasted with the long, clean perfection of her leg that was neither too skinny nor owned a scrap of excess flesh.

A more perfect appendage, Prophet had never seen.

He untied the wrap and lowered his head to scrutinize the wound. It wasn't exactly a graze, but the bullet had gone all the way through, leaving ragged entrance and exit wounds. It had plowed through about three inches of Louisa's flesh, and Prophet burned at the thought of a man's bullet harming this woman-child he'd taken under his wing so long ago and whom he felt protective of, as though she were his woman — but he doubted Louisa would ever belong to any man, least of all him.

Prophet rolled his eyes up to her face. Resting her head back against the money pouch, she was staring at the ceiling as though trying to decipher words written there in a foreign tongue.

"That hurts, don't it?"

Louisa kept her eyes on the ceiling and hiked a shoulder.

"Well, this is gonna inflame it some."

"I'm ready."

"You sure you don't want a shot first?"

Louisa shook her head.

"All right, then." Prophet touched the lip of the bottle to the ragged edge of the wound and poured a shot's worth into the hole.

Louisa sucked a sharp breath and stiffened, pointing her chin at the ceiling, curling her toes and hardening her eyes. Corking the bottle, he picked up the clean calico bandanna and began dabbing gently at the wound with a corner, soaking up the blood that the whiskey had thinned out. He re-dampened the cloth from the bottle, and touched it to the wound once more. Once more, Louisa sucked a breath and stiffened, keeping her wide eyes at the ceiling, steeling herself against the burn.

When Prophet had cleaned the entrance hole, he had her lift her knee so he could begin cleaning the exit wound, first soaking it with the whiskey-drenched bandanna, then carefully dabbing until the blood was gone and only the ragged hole, about as big around as the tip of his index finger, remained.

"Ain't gonna stitch it," Prophet said, lowering his head to inspect both wounds in turn, glad he'd gotten the bleeding stopped. "Best to let it breathe. But we gotta keep it clean, and that means a whiskey bath regular-like."

"How 'bout twice a day?"

"Three times. Any arguments, we'll go to four times a day." Prophet winked at her, then reached under her skirt, grabbed the hem of her cotton petticoat, and ripped off a foot-long strip.

When he'd wrapped the bandage around her leg, knotting it tight enough to keep the wounds closed but not tight enough to cut off her circulation, he kissed her knee.

"Good as new."

She reached down and fingered the collar of his buckskin shirt. "You learn about doctorin' in the war?"

"Nope. I didn't learn about nothin' in the war except killin'. I learned doctorin' on the runnin' scout out here, west of the Miss'ippi, after I went home to Georgia and found there wasn't nothing there but one-legged cousins and burned fields."

"Come up here."

Prophet, who'd propped himself over her bandaged leg, now crabbed up until his head was six inches from hers and his chest was pressed against hers. Her hazel eyes held his. They were varnished hard with concentration, with want, old-fashioned carnal need. Clutching the front of his shirt with her left fist, she removed his hat with her right, held it out away from the bed, and dropped it onto the floor.

She ran both hands brusquely through his hair, staring at him with that stubborn need, pulling his ears, grinding against him, grunting softly. Prophet lowered his head to hers, closed his mouth over her own. He kissed her hard for a long time, urgently, entangling his tongue with hers, reaching under her serape, pulling her calico shirttails up out of her skirt, and caressing her firm breasts until her nipples ridged against his palm.

He lifted the serape and her shirt to her neck, baring both tender, white orbs, and kissed the fully budded nipple of each.

Groaning and squirming around beneath him like a bobcat in season, murmuring hotly in his ears, she continued to run her hands urgently through his hair and across his neck, wrapping her legs tightly around him. After a time, when neither could wait longer, he stood and quickly shucked out of his clothes including his wash-worn balbriggans, dropped down between her spread, quivering knees, and entangled himself in her limbs.

They moved together with a near-savage fulfilling of their physical urges until, exhausted, they lay slumped together breathless, naked, and sweating.

Downstairs, someone screamed.

5

Prophet was out of bed like a human lightning bolt, stumbling around in the candlelight to find his hastily discarded balbriggans. From downstairs came the sounds of sobbing and pounding boots, all dwindling until there was a metallic rattle and then the rasp of the door being opened across swollen floorboards.

Louisa dropped her bare feet to the floor too quickly and grabbed her right thigh, gritting her teeth.

Prophet was hopping around on one foot as he poked the other one into a leg of his inside out long underwear bottoms. "You stay here. I'll find out what's goin' on."

"You think Blanco's off his leash?"

"Not unless she helped him."

Prophet crammed his other foot into his underwear bottoms, quickly pulled on his socks, then his boots, and wrapped his cartridge belt and .45 around his waist. He grabbed his sawed-off twelve-gauge from the chair he'd set it across, donned his hat, and glanced at Louisa, who sat on the edge of the bed with her blanket thrown across her lovely nakedness, one of her pearl-gripped Colts in her hands, looking anxious.

"Stay here — I'll yell if I need you," Prophet said again and went clomping on out the door and into the hall, spurs ringing raucously in the suddenly too-quiet, ghost-haunted hotel.

He hurried down the dark hall, then descended the stairs two steps at a time. The fire was still popping and snapping in the broad hearth, and the smoky lantern was still flickering a wan tongue-sized flame, outlining Blanco sitting beneath it, his back against the post, leaning slightly forward and shaking his head as if to clear it.

"What in tarnation?" he said as Prophet clomped toward him, shotgun in his hands, its lanyard swinging loose.

The bounty hunter glanced at the couch where the girl had been, then swung his gaze back to Blanco.

"Where is she?"

Blanco snorted wryly, quirking his thin lips to show a fanglike eyetooth. "Stuffed her down my pocket. Turn me loose an' I'll pull her out for ya."

Prophet shoved his gut shredder's menacing double bores toward Blanco's head and thumbed both hammers back.

"Hell, I don't know!" the outlaw cried, jerking sideways, away from the savage-looking popper. "She just gave that coyote yell and lit a shuck on outta here. Couldn't leave fast enough!"

Prophet looked at Blanco's ankles. They were still cuffed and secured to a chair leg. He wasn't going anywhere. He hadn't gotten his hands on any weapons, either. That settled, the bounty hunter hurried on to the front of the room, out the double doors standing open, and stepped to one side, instinctively avoiding being backlit in case someone was drawing a bead on him.

He looked around.

The moon was behind a large whale-shaped cloud that hung black before it while the sky around it was lilac. The street was dark purple, with buildings limned in indigo. There wasn't a breath of wind. The coyotes, which he'd heard yammering even while he and Louisa had been coupling like alley cats, had fallen silent.

There was a soft crunch of gravel. Prophet looked toward it, up the street on his right. Just beyond the holding corral where he could see the white streaks on a couple of horse faces, a shadow moved. One of the horses nickered softly.

Prophet rasped, "Girl?" What the hell was her name, for chrissakes?

Getting no response and having lost the shadow against the thicker shadows beyond, he shoved off the saloon's front wall, leaped down the steps, and paused in the street, crouched and aiming the cocked double-bore out from his right side, waiting to return possible gunfire. He continued to hear gravel crunch under quick moving feet, the sounds dwindling gradually.

There was a wooden rasp above his head. Rusty hinges squawked. Prophet jerked his head up quickly, swinging around and raising the shotgun slightly. A blond head jutted from a window above the porch roof.

"Fifty yards ahead on the other side of the street," Louisa said in a low, dull voice.

Prophet headed in that direction, muttering, "Obliged, Miss Busybody."

"Don't mention it," came the quieter response beneath the crunching of Prophet's own boots in the silent street.

He'd walked on past the holding corral, evoking another soft nicker and a blow from the horses, and was passing an old gray shed sheathed in spindly brush and tumbleweeds when a thin voice said behind him, "Who am I?"

Prophet wheeled. He saw a slender, dark outline against the dark wall of the shed. Keeping his thumb on the shotgun's left hammer, he squinted into the shadows though it helped him see her no better.

"Say again?"

"I don't know who I am!" The mystery girl sobbed and lifted her hands to her face.

Prophet lowered the shotgun and, depressing each hammer in turn, walked slowly toward her until he could see her more clearly standing slumped against the shed wall.

She gave a little gasp, and he stopped. She said, a trill of fear in her voice, "Who're you?"

"Lou Prophet. You got no reason to be afraid of me. I'm a friend. At least, as of a couple hours ago."

The girl cried. He could see her mostly even white teeth between her fluttering lips.

"Ah, there, now, miss." Prophet held his ground three feet away from her. She was severely disoriented and trusted no one. "It'll be all right. You just bumped your head, ain't quite right from it. Let's go on back into the hotel and get you warm,

maybe get some food in you. You'll feel better."

"My head hurts," she said, sobbing, pressing her fingers into her temples.

"I don't doubt that a bit. That's a nasty
gash and a good-sized goose egg. Easy,
now." Prophet stepped closer and turned so
that he was beside her, his own back to the
shed wall. Very slowly and gently wrapping
an arm around her quivering shoulders, he
said, "Come on, now. Let's get you back
close to the fire, get you warm. You
shouldn't be out here."

"I woke up and looked around," she said,
no longer sobbing but in a pinched, anguished voice. "I didn't realize where I was."
She let Prophet lead her around the front of
the shed, heading toward the hotel. "At first
I thought I was dreaming. Then I tried to
remember who I was and what I was doing
there in that room with that man chained to
the chair, and I couldn't remember anything!"

She broke down again, the tears flowing
freely, resembling quicksilver now in the
moonlight angling out around the potbel-
lied cloud.

"Even now you don't remember?" Prophet
asked her as they continued making their
way to the hotel.

Shaking her head, she continued crying. "You don't know, mister?" The girl stopped and looked up at him with miserable beseeching. "You don't know who I am?"

Prophet felt helpless. The girl's own anguish was catching. He couldn't imagine how lost she must feel, not only clueless as to where she was and what she was doing here but as to *who* she was. He didn't for a second suspect that she was acting. Her desperation was poignant and real.

Prophet shook his head. "I'm sorry. I don't know who you are. Let's go on inside and get you warm, and I bet it'll come back to you real soon, just as soon as the cobwebs clear."

He led her up the hotel porch. Louisa waited by the front door, wrapped in a couple of wool blankets and wearing her boots and hat. "What is it?" she asked. "What happened?"

The girl stopped in front of her. They were roughly the same height, almost the same build. Prophet guessed the unknown girl was two or three years younger than Louisa, which, as he'd figured, would make her seventeen or eighteen.

"You don't know, either?"

Louisa's moonlit eyes slid from the girl to

Prophet and back again. "Don't know what?"

"Who I *am?*"

The girl continued sobbing. Prophet led her inside, sharing a perplexed look with Louisa, then ushered her across the room and back to the couch where she'd been lying before.

"What's goin' on?" Blanco said from his floor seat against the post. He ran a hand across his whiskey-damp, colorless chin whiskers that added to his resemblance of a human billy goat. He was working on his bottle again. "She see a mouse or somethin'?"

Prophet eased the girl onto the sofa. "Shut up, Blanco."

"Who's he?" the girl asked, frowning at the gray-eyed outlaw, who was slumped back against his post, uncorked bottle in one hand.

Blanco looked at her drunkenly and arched his brows. "What's the matter, Mary Louise? Don't you remember your old Blanco?"

The girl stared at him.

"Sure, you remember," Blanco said. "You didn't hit your head all that hard — now, did you?" He chuckled. "Come on. Jig's up. Quit pretendin'. Ole Proph here don't look much smarter than a wagonload of three-cent bricks, but he ain't that stupid."

The girl continued to stare at the outlaw. Prophet shuttled his gaze between them, apprehension rippling along his spine. Louisa had come into the saloon now, too, and she stood near the table littered with cards and coins, frowning curiously as she held her blankets closed across her chest.

The girl's voice was tremulous, weak. "Do you know me?"

"Sure, I know you. You're Mary Louise Lockhart. You're from Trinidad, New Mexico, and you done rode with me and the boys out here to Nugget Town after the robbery. You got tired of bein' a whore, though you were a right fine one — sure enough." Blanco laughed. "You were holding our horses in the alley across the street from the bank. When we burst outta there, six-guns poppin' like Mex fireworks on All Saints' Day, you hustled 'em into the street for us. You an' me" — he grinned lasciviously — "was ridin' double."

The girl looked stricken, horrified, as she stared at Blanco.

"Forget him," Prophet said, squatting in front of the girl, placing a hand on her knee. "Don't listen to him. He's bullshitting you."

"Am I?"

"Shut up, Blanco."

"How could I be riding with you?" the girl asked.

"Why not?"

"Because you're ugly." She shook her head slowly. "You're ugly bad. Mean and stupid. A killer. I wouldn't ride with the likes of you." She looked at Prophet, whom she seemed to be trusting. "Would I?"

Blanco scowled with mock indignation. "That's no way to talk. No way to talk at all, Mary Louise. Now, I admit I ain't the best-lookin' fella right now, on account of this trail dust and three-day growth of beard. But, hell, give me a bath —"

"Shut up, Blanco," Louisa said.

Blanco cast his look of manufactured indignation at Louisa flanking his right shoulder, then turned back to the girl. He showed his chipped crooked teeth as he grinned, pale, sun-mottled cheeks dimpling. "Speakin' of baths . . . you used to like to take 'em with me, Mary Louise. Surely you remember that?"

The girl grimaced, appalled, and drew her shoulders in. Louisa walked over to Blanco, drew her right foot back, then hammered the toe of that boot into his rib cage. Blanco yelped, recoiling sideways from the blow and pressing his arm against his ribs. "You

72

didn't have no call to do that, you — !"

Staring up at Louisa, seeing the hard, threatening look on her stony face, Blanco cut himself off. He turned away from her and squeezed his arm to his side, groaning and cursing under his breath.

"Any more out of you, and I'll lay you out with my pistol butt," Louisa warned him.

She walked over to the sofa and placed a hand on Prophet's shoulder. When he'd gone over to the table and sat down with a sigh, pouring himself a drink, Louisa removed one of her blankets from her shoulders and draped it over the mystery girl, who sat slumped on the sofa's edge, staring at Blanco, likely wondering how much of what he'd said, if any of it, was true.

As Prophet sipped a shot glass of whiskey, he wondered the same thing.

"I don't even know my name," the girl said, looking down. "I haven't the foggiest idea where I got those boots. I don't even remember putting them on."

"Don't think about it anymore," Louisa said. "After a long night's rest, you'll likely remember everything. It'll be a bright, fresh new day. Your family's probably up on one of the ridges around here, waiting for you. We'll find them."

The girl looked at the blond bounty

hunter, narrowing her eyes. "What do you think I'm doing here alone?"

Louisa smiled and shook her head. "We'll find out."

"It's a very lonely feeling, not knowing where you come from." The girl's eyes were clear, but tears streaked her cheeks. "I got no memory of anything. I don't even know what I had for dinner. I've lost my mind."

"Memory's not such a terrible thing to lose." Louisa drew the girl's head down against her shoulder, smoothing her hair back from her left ear. "Sometimes I wish I'd lose mine."

6

The unknown girl had trouble falling asleep. She was restless, tossing her head and sighing.

The physical as well as emotional pain of not knowing where or who she was must have been like the cruelest form of Indian torture, Prophet knew. He tried to find something amongst his possibles to give her some relief from the throbbing pain, but it was Louisa who found some tea amongst her own gear.

They set a small kettle of water to boil while Blanco, passed out drunk once more, snored deeply with his chin on his chest. When the water boiled, Louisa steeped the tea, then poured it into a tin cup, to which Prophet added a jigger of whiskey. The girl took the cup in her hands and drank, not curling her nose at the snake venom that Prophet had bought in a dusky little saloon in Socorro, when they'd passed through the town several days ago.

The detail did not go unnoticed by either Prophet or Louisa. The girl had obviously imbibed before. What this meant, however, neither could have said. But it was the little details that would eventually add up and draw a clearer picture about who the girl was. Or, if not who she was, then what she was like.

Could they trust her? Prophet had found her with a loaded pistol. He didn't think Blanco had been telling the truth, only taunting them as well as the poor girl herself about a possible alliance. But there was a part of Prophet that wasn't sure, and he could tell from a few dark, questioning looks from Louisa that his partner wasn't sure, either.

The girl may have imbibed before, but she hadn't made it a habit, as the whiskey and tea went to work on her before she'd consumed half the toddy. When she'd drifted off, Louisa drew the blanket up tight around her, then banked the fire.

"You go on to bed," Prophet told her. "I'll sit up, keep an eye on things."

"Cold upstairs without you." Louisa sat down in a chair across the poker table from Prophet. "I'll snooze here. The sun will be up in a couple of hours anyway."

Prophet was sitting back in his chair, thoughtfully rolling a cigarette in his large, brown, callused fingers. "How you wanna play it?"

"The girl?"

"Yeah, the girl. We already know what to do with Blanco. Box him up purty for the hangman."

Louisa poured what was left of the tea from the smoking kettle into her fire-blackened tin cup and took the cup in both her hands as though to warm them. "She must be from around here — don't you think?"

"I don't know what to think."

"Meaning?"

Prophet stuck the quirley between his lips, fired a stove match to life on his thumbnail. "Meaning I'll try to backtrack her come daylight, see if I can see how she entered them shrubs. If she didn't ride in with Blanco, she must have a horse around here somewhere. Unless she lives here for some reason, all by herself."

"Even then, she'd likely have a horse."

Prophet touched the match flame to the quirley, puffing smoke. "I'll look around."

"And if you don't find anything?"

Prophet blew out the match with a smoke puff, drawing deeply on the cigarette. "Then

77

I reckon we take her back to Corazon. Closest town around. Someone there will surely know her."

Louisa sipped her tea and looked at the girl curled on her side beneath the blanket, flanked by the popping fire. "And if she really was with Blanco's bunch . . ."

"Someone from town'll know. They'll have seen her, most like. Metalious holes up not far from here."

Louisa turned to look across the table at Prophet, keeping her voice low. "What if she was?"

"Then we do with her what we do with Blanco." Prophet let smoke dribble from his nostrils and turned to parry Louisa's gaze. "Bein' a scared little girl don't make her innocent of what she took part in earlier."

"Might have taken part in."

Prophet shuttled his gaze back to the girl asleep on the sofa, his hard bounty hunter's eyes not betraying the conflict inside him. "All right."

Prophet and Louisa dozed in their chairs and rose at dawn the next morning. While Prophet rode out, trying to backtrack the girl from the shrubs he'd found her in, Louisa made tea for her and the girl and tossed

Blanco a couple of pieces of jerky for breakfast.

Prophet's mission ended disturbingly.

Judging by the scuffmarks that disappeared in the snag, the girl had come from the direction of the saloon. He saw what he thought were tracks the size of her boots near the saloon's back door, though it was hard to tell as the ground there was rocky. He looked around but could find no other clear sign. Most of the boot prints were overlaid or wiped out entirely by what may have been a brief sprinkle a few hours before he and Louisa had arrived in Nugget Town. There was no one to track from the saloon, much less back to wherever she had originally come from.

An hour later, Prophet had saddled Louisa's and Blanco's horses. He'd also saddled a mount for the girl. There was little to do but bring her back to Corazon and see if someone could identify her. Prophet hoped she was some innocent daughter of a desert-dwelling family, either prospectors or jackleg ranchers, and not part of Blanco's bunch.

She seemed innocent enough. A cute kid with a good heart. Could a person forget how to act hardened or depraved?

Prophet had ordered Blanco into his

saddle and was finishing tightening the latigo strap on the girl's horse when she and Louisa walked out of the saloon. The sun was climbing, and the western ridges were silhouetted against the blossoming, buttery glow. There was a chill in the air, and Louisa wore her heavy, striped serape and buckskin gloves against it.

The girl wore her brush jacket with a brown wool blanket draped over her shoulders. Her pixielike, pug-nosed features with large, dark brown eyes and a light spray of freckles across her suntanned though fair-complected cheekbones appeared slightly gaunt, with a white, pinched look of pain around her mouth.

Mostly, she looked worried.

Louisa had told her where they were headed; likely she was wondering herself if she would be recognized in Corazon and was facing the prospect of learning who she was with trepidation.

The night's rest had done nothing to bring back her memory.

"Well, good-mornin', Mary Alice," Blanco said as Louisa led the girl to her horse. "How'd ya sleep? Or don't you remember?"

The girl scowled at him with unfeigned derision.

"I thought it was Mary Louise," Louisa said.

"So it is," Blanco said. "I was just checkin' to see if you were on the mark today, Louisa. You don't mind if I call you Louisa, do you? Seein' as how close we've been an' all."

Louisa ignored the remark as she turned the piebald toward the girl.

"If you haven't got the drift yet," Prophet told Blanco, sliding his rifle into his saddle boot, "let me give you one last piece of advice that might just keep you from singin' soprano the rest of your life, short as it may be." He grinned darkly up at the outlaw leader whose wrists were cuffed and tied to his saddle horn. "Don't fuck with my partner."

Blanco looked at Louisa, who strode past him without returning his gaze. "Damn," he said to Prophet. "She's way too purty to be so *mean*."

Prophet sighed as he reined his horse away from the hotel, the east side of which was bathed in golden sunshine while the rest remained in shadow. He booted Mean and Ugly back out of the ghost town the way he and Louisa had come, his partner hanging back to ride drag behind Blanco, the girl flanking Prophet.

She'd swung easily up into the saddle, as

though she was well accustomed to horses. She was riding well also — straight-backed, light-butted, and with a light hand on the reins. These were automatic things she didn't need to remember. They were ingrained in her. Her rough-hewn range garb and suntan made none of that surprising. And her hands, Prophet had noticed, were not a town girl's hands. Wherever she was from, she worked hard, and mostly outside. She'd worked a water pump plenty and likely split wood.

He continued to think about her as they rode down out of the rocky apron of the No-Waters. There was no need to push the horses as it was an easy day's ride back to Corazon, which sat nestled between the No-Waters and the San Mateos.

As they rode, Prophet and Louisa kept a close eye on the terrain around them, as bushwhackings in this country were common. From Socorro westward to the Mogollon Rim in Arizona Territory was prime outlaw country, where badmen of every stripe outran posses and lawmen and disappeared in the No-Waters, the San Mateos, in the Blade Range slightly south, or on the Plains of Saint Augustine farther north.

It being prime outlaw country made it a

lucrative hunting ground for bounty hunters. That's what had brought Prophet and Louisa up here from Las Cruces, after they'd run down a passel of train robbers and hung around to watch the cuffed and shackled hard cases led up onto a gallows and dropped through trapdoors with a gun-like pop of snapping necks.

Afterward, there'd been a celebration to rival the annual Fourth of July festivities in Cheyenne.

"Hey, did you two bury Junior on your way through?" Blanco asked.

"Why should we have buried him?" Louisa said from the rear of the string. "He was your partner."

"Just wonderin'." Blanco was looking around curiously. "I think this is where we left him."

"It is." Prophet checked Mean and Ugly down and looked off into the brush beyond the mesquite near which they'd found Junior Pope with a bullet through his forehead. "Nature's been treatin' him no worse than you did."

Blanco drew up beside Prophet and followed the bounty hunter's gaze to where a carcass clad in Junior Pope's torn, bloody clothes lay nearly concealed in the mountain mahogany and Spanish bayonet. Deep scuff marks showed where the bobcat — Prophet had seen the sharp-nailed tracks when he'd first ridden up — had dragged Junior off into the brush.

Judging by the several sets of overlaid coyote tracks mingling with those of the bobcat, there'd been a dustup over the carrion. The bobcat had likely won out and begun dining on Junior in earnest.

In the morning quiet there was the buzzing of flies that showed in a foggy dark cloud over the glistening carcass.

"Nature," Blanco said, scowling at the remains of his partner. "You can have it."

"Someone's gotta clean up our messes." Prophet glanced back at Louisa and the girl, both staring into the brush. Louisa was stone-faced. She'd seen plenty of death before. More than her fair share. The mystery girl scowled in revulsion. There was no telling how much she'd witnessed of the gang's doings.

"Come on," Prophet said, booting Mean and Ugly ahead. "Let's get a move on."

They continued along the winding trail through the low, rolling hogbacks, their dust sifting in the brassy sunlight. In the early afternoon, they rode up a steep, broad bench to see the little town of Corazon nestling in the sage and pinyon of the broad valley below. The town's mostly rough wooden buildings — a motley collection scattered around the doglegging main drag called Brush Street — looked stark and forlorn.

It sat in the valley between the No-Waters behind Prophet and the vaster, higher San Mateos beyond the town to the east. The population was a little over five hundred — Mexicans as well as Anglos. A supply town for the surrounding ranches, mostly, was Corazon. The stage trail wound in from the sage-covered hills to meet Brush Street at its southern end and continued on out beyond where the town stopped abruptly at its northernmost fringe, curving toward Springerville, Show Low, the Fort Apache Agency, and the even more remote camps along Arizona Territory's Mogollon Rim.

The trail that Prophet's party was traveling bisected the town's southwest side, becoming a street of sorts sheathed by chicken coops and goat pens, a few humble little houses. It intersected Brush Street in the town's center.

Near the intersection, a stoop-shouldered gent with coarse gray hair hanging down from his bald, sun-darkened pate stepped out of his shop holding a broom. He glanced at Prophet and shook his head anxiously, holding the broom beneath his chin. He tossed his head toward the intersection on his right, where there was apparently a dangerous ruckus building.

"What is it?" Prophet said, drawing Mean and Ugly to a halt before the small, narrow pink-painted CRUMB'S ROOTS, SUNDRY NATURAL ELIXIRS, AND FORTUNE TELLING shop.

"Law business," Crumb said quietly, thumbing his small, wire-rimmed spectacles up his nose. "It's Marshal Max Utter. Please don't distract him. He's all the law we have!"

Just then a raspy, slightly hoarse voice yelled from the main street ahead, "Get on out here, Roy Devlin. You, too, Johnny Reeves. Get on out here before I come and blow you outta that whore's crib with my shotgun!"

The man guffawed, sending echoes pinwheeling over the otherwise quiet town.

7

As the hoarse laughter continued to echo, Prophet nudged Mean and Ugly a little farther forward until he could see around the corner of the woman's hat shop to his right. Town Marshal Max Utter sat his wheelchair about fifty yards up the main street, in the street's dead center, facing down past Prophet's left.

Utter was a big man with skinny, near-useless legs in black broadcloth, and an enormous belly pushing out his white shirt and black wool vest trimmed with a gold-washed chain. Two big Colt pistols jutted from holsters strapped to his chair arms, up high and in easy reach. A long, double-barreled shotgun rested across the crippled lawman's lap.

Prophet swung his gaze to his left, where a man was slinking slowly out of a whore-house on the far side of Brush Street. Another slunk out behind him, one dressed in a top hat and a clawhammer coat, the other in a cream duster and with a big, silver-trimmed Mexican sombrero tipped back on his head.

Both were Anglos. The man in the top hat was a redhead with the purple-lensed glasses favored by cardsharps. The other had long sandy hair hanging to his shoulders and a clean-shaven, pockmarked face.

One after another, they sidestepped off the whorehouse's porch and into the street, looking bleary-eyed from drink. They'd both been holed up in the crib for a time, it appeared, and hadn't exactly been ready to rise and shine. The bespectacled gent's fly was unbuttoned, the tail of his white-striped pink shirt poking out the opening. The long-haired gent was still tucking in his shirttails and smacking his lips, narrowing one eye against the sun, which the sheriff had wisely positioned in his favor.

The crib they'd just left was a rough-hewn side shed sloping off the north wall of the Nova Saloon, a three-story structure that wasn't much wider than its whorehouse addition. It abutted the San Mateo Bank & Trust — a boxlike adobe hovel with a plank door and one front window. The insubstantial saloon building, propped on low stone pilings, looked as though it could tumble into jackstraws at the first chill winter wind whistling down from the Rim.

"What the hell you want, old man?" the man in the purple glasses asked as he wandered out to the middle of the street, folding the right side of his clawhammer coat back behind an ivory-gripped Smith & Wesson.

"It's been brought to my attention, Mr. Devlin, that you and your scoundrel sidekick, Mr. Reeves, have not only been cheating at cards for the past three days here in Corazon, but that you cut one of Miss Betsy's girls. Cut a finger off her right hand."

Devlin glanced at the long-haired Reeves walking out to join him and stopping about ten feet away from him.

"That you not only cut off the poor girl's finger, but that you chopped it up and ate it in front of her." Utter paused, tipping his gray-hatted head to one side like a preacher waiting to see how his message had been received by his congregation. "After which," the marshal added, "Miss Betsy asked you to leave her premises, and you refused."

"Well, hell, Marshal," Reeves said, turning to face the lawman and sliding the left flap of his duster back behind his short-barreled Remington and also revealing a second pistol jutting up over his flat belly from the waistband of his trousers. "We was fixin' to leave this mornin' just as soon as we drowned the worms in our throats and had a bite to eat."

"You was, was you?"

"We was," agreed the bespectacled Devlin. "And that's a bonded fact. Now, if you'd quit caterwaulin' out here like a damn catamount, we'll just do that and be on our way. If you like, I'll even apologize to Miss Betsy for the finger episode."

"Too late for that. I'm haulin' you both into the hoosegow where you'll wait and see what the circuit judge has to say about your less-than-poor behavior here in my fair city. And, in the meantime, you'll be relieved of all of your misbegotten poker winnings. They'll be returned to the men you fleeced with the use of a card file and by adding weights to the Nova's roulette wheel. Anything left over will be paid to the whore whose hand you mangled."

Devlin jerked a finger at the marshal. "I was drunk when I mangled that hand, Sheriff!"

"Yeah, a man ain't responsible for what he does when he's drunk," said Reeves, hitching his shell belt up his hips and adjusting the handle of his belly gun.

"Get your hands away from them hoglegs, Reeves." Marshal Utter gave them both the devil's stare, propping his elbows on the arms of his wheelchair, just behind the upward-jutting Colts. "Now, very slow, unbuckle them belts and let 'em drop to the street."

Devlin grinned mockingly. "Make up your mind, Marshal. Do you want our hands near our hoglegs or don't — ?"

He cut himself off abruptly as his left hand snaked across his waist to cover the butt of his cross-draw Smith & Wesson. His friend reached for his own weapons an eighth of a second later. Another eighth of a second after that, the big Colt filling Max Utter's right fist popped. Then the one in his left fist, extended straight out in front of him and angled toward Devlin, stabbed smoke and fire.

The reports sounded like two tied-together firecrackers.

Prophet had jerked with a start at the first report and shuttled his incredulous gaze between the marshal and the two hard cases in the street only a few yards to his right. Devlin was the only one who grunted and bounded back a step as Utter's .45 round tore through his paisley vest, causing Devlin's string tie to leap. Devlin had his gun

91

only half raised. As he staggered farther backward, groaning through gritted teeth, he raised the gun slightly higher and swung it toward Utter.

Utter's right hand gun roared again, but the slug flew slightly wide and plunked into the street behind the purple-spectacled hard case.

Utter fired again quickly, hardening his jaws in frustration, and watched as Devlin was punched straight back to hit the street spread-eagle on his back. Blood pumped through the hole in the dead center of his chest.

Meanwhile, Prophet wondered if Reeves had been hit at all. The long-haired outlaw just stood staring blank-faced toward Max Utter. Both his hands, each clutching a cocked revolver, hung straight down at his sides.

Was he giving himself up?

Suddenly, the gun in the man's left hand roared, blowing up dust in the street about six inches from Reeves's spurred boot. Then the hard case made a bizarre, high-pitched sighing sound and sagged straight back on his heels, hands continuing to hang straight down at his sides, until he, like Devlin, had smacked the ground hard on his back.

Obviously, he'd been dead before he hit,

because he'd done nothing to break his fall.

Prophet glanced at Louisa, who'd ridden up beside him to watch the show. She arched an appreciative brow. Prophet shuttled his gaze back to Max Utter, who was holstering his Colts inside his chair arms and wagging his head in frustration.

"Nice shootin', Marshal," Prophet said as he booted Mean and Ugly slowly forward.

Utter jerked his head toward him with a start, the surprised light in his eyes softening when he recognized Prophet.

"Ah, shit, Lou — I tell you it's no damn fun getting old!"

"What're you talkin' about? You just took down a pair of veteran cold-steel artists. I know Devlin was, anyway. As for the long-haired hombre — I never seen him before."

Prophet was riding along beside Utter as the sheriff wheeled himself toward the two dead men. Utter had no trouble hauling himself through the six inches of churned dust and horse shit of Brush Street. He kept his wheels well-greased, and his arms were stout as fence posts.

When he needed a rest, his deputy Ivano Rubriz gave him a push. Prophet saw Rubriz walking out from the bank on the street's right side, holding an old Spencer repeater down low by his side as he angled toward the dead men, half dragging his gimpy left leg.

Rubriz was a whipcord-lean, nut-brown Mexican with some Indian, or mestizo, blood and a cloud-white mustache brashly crowning his upper lip. He'd been quite the cold-steel artist in his day, about twenty years ago, but story had it he'd taken a Lipan Apache knife in his back and had never been the same since. He could handle the drunks and the slower gunnies, but even in his wheelchair old Max Utter presided over the curliest of the curly wolves who wandered into Corazon.

"Reeves is from around here," Utter said as he, Prophet, and Ivano Rubriz met at the spread-eagled carcass of Devlin, whose glasses hung down over his mouth and whose dead, dung-brown eyes stared skyward. "As you can see — he wasn't much good. That's likely why Devlin drew first."

"Still, damn good shootin'," Prophet said. "A clean brisket shot."

"Yeah, but shit, my second bullet flew two feet over his damn head!" Utter stared down at the dead gambler who was bleeding out from two holes in his chest. "I never used to miss from that distance."

"The point is," Louisa said, "you gunned both these well-deserving privy scum from a distance of sixty yards, and from a wheel-chair, no less. Even I would have a hard time making a shot like that."

Utter looked up at Louisa. His dark blue eyes softened in their withered sockets. Louisa had that effect on men, no matter how old. Prophet thought he could feel the marshal's heart melting in his chest.

"Why, thank you for that, pretty bounty-huntin' lady. You're right sweet!" His eyes shifted to Blanco Metalious sitting slumped on his horse behind Louisa, head down as though he were trying to make himself as small as possible. "Hey," the marshal intoned, bright eyes widening with glee. "You got Blanco!"

"Yeah, they got me," Blanco grumbled, curling his upper lip. "When you're done celebratin', you suppose you could fetch me a doctor, Marshal? That blond bounty-trackin' polecat damn near cut my balls off. If I can't procreate and continue the Metalious line, see, my old man's gonna be even madder than he will be when he finds out where I'm at."

"Shut up, Blanco!" Utter said. "You'll see a medico when I'm good and ready to send for one." Utter summoned his deputy with a jerk of his head. "Right now, damn your ugly eyes, I gotta see to these two men I done gunned, get 'em stripped of their stolen cash, and turned under before we draw that bobcat back to town. You know the one, Ivano — the one that kept runnin' off with chickens and our smallest children for two months last winter."

"Si, si," said Rubriz as he pushed the marshal over toward Reeves, who lay closer to the whorehouse side shed.

"That damn painter ran off with two toddlers and a four-year-old, not to mention about six tomcats that was doin' a real nice job of keepin' down the rat population!" As Rubriz halted the marshal near Reeves's boots, Utter stared down at the gunman's face, which was already turning chalky in death.

Prophet, who remained atop his horse near Devlin, heard the marshal ask his deputy, "Where'd I hit the son of a bitch?"

Neither man said anything for a moment. Then Rubriz pointed. "There. See? Blew a tooth out when you shot him through the mouth."

Utter leaned slightly forward in his chair to inspect the body. Chuckling, he sat back. His chuckle grew to a deep guffaw, which sailed high over the street as he threw his head back on his shoulders.

"Hey, Prophet, can you believe this? I shot

96

this poor bastard through the mouth." Utter roared. "I was aiming for his heart!" He roared some more.

Then he turned his wheelchair around to face the three newcomers. "I tell you, it don't pay to get old." He frowned as he canted his head to see the girl riding behind Prophet and Louisa and off the hip of Blanco's steeldust gelding. "Hey, who's that? Didn't realize you had another girl with you?"

Before Prophet could say anything, Blanco leaned forward and shouted, "Will someone please get me a goddamn doctor! My crotch has done opened up again, and all my blood which has been dribblin' down my leg the whole way here will soon be fillin' my boot!"

Utter glared at the young killer. "How 'bout if I call for the mother of that boy you killed on your way out of the bank — Delwyn Harris? Have her come out here and tend your oysters for you?"

Blanco fidgeted and dropped his eyes to the street.

Utter gave a disapproving chuff, then glanced over his shoulder at his Mexican deputy. "Take Blanco on over to the jailhouse, Ivano. Lock him up, then fetch the doc. Lock up the loot in one of the cells. The judge'll want a look at it."

97

Rubriz limped over to take Blanco's reins from Prophet, as well as the saddlebags stuffed with the stolen money, then led the horse and the hunched outlaw past the several townsfolk who'd wandered out of their shops to tentatively investigate the killings. The man who had taken charge of the bank stood on the bank's ragged stoop, fingertips in his vest pockets, scowling.

"Will we be getting our money back soon, Marshal?" he asked in a tentative voice.

Utter didn't look at the man as he barked, "I'll be holdin' it for evidence till the judge gets here, Howard. Don't bother me about that now. You'll get your money back!"

Utter cranked his chair close to Prophet's group to stare curiously up at the girl.

Prophet shuttled his gaze between them. "You know her, Marshal?"

"Rose Tawlin, ain't it?"

The girl stared down at him apprehensively. She looked to Prophet as though for help.

"She don't know. She come to hit her head on a rock before we found out who she was. Jarred her memory — in the wrong direction, if you get my drift."

"Amnesia," Louisa said.

"Say what?" asked Utter.

"Memory loss," Louisa explained with a

faintly haughty air, looking off in disgust. "Usually caused by a sharp blow to the head."

"Well, hell . . . she don't remember *nothin'?*"

"I don't remember anything, Marshal," the girl said weakly. "This Rose Tawlin — are you sure I'm her?"

8

As a tall man in coveralls and a boy dressed the same meandered over toward the two dead men fallen in the street, Marshal Max Utter poked his gray Stetson back off his forehead and massaged his receding hairline with two chubby fingers. He stared critically up at the girl from his wheelchair, balling his cheeks in hard thought.

"Well, I think you're Rose Tawlin. I mean, the last time I seen Rose she was a whole head shorter than you." Utter's scowl deepened almost painfully. "Your pa didn't bring you to town much. I reckon if you don't know . . . hell, I reckon I couldn't be sure, neither."

"She looks pretty close to this Rose Tawlin, though?" Prophet said.

"Well, hell, now you got me doubtin'."

"Please, Marshal," the girl said. "Look at me close. Could I be Rose Tawlin? I gotta know. Not knowin' who I am has got me feelin' all hollow inside and just plumb scared!"

The girl's dark eyes acquired a golden sheen, and tears began to dribble down her sun-browned cheeks. She was terrified, and Prophet didn't blame her. He'd never lost his memory, but he could imagine how doing so would make you feel like a very small boat lost in a vast ocean during a big storm.

"Well, sure," Utter said uncertainly, continuing to stare up at the girl, narrowing one eye. "You sure do look like Rose. I reckon about the only way to find out is ride out there."

"Out where?" Prophet asked.

"Out to Silver Creek. A half day's ride north of here. Out near the Plains of Saint Augustine. The Tawlin family has a gold claim out there on the creek, and they run a few cows. Haven't seen ole Roy Tawlin in a month of Sundays, though. Him and Sarah might have pulled their picket pins. Last I heard, they were so poor they couldn't afford the ammo needed to keep themselves fed."

Prophet looked at the girl, who was thinking hard on what the marshal had told them. Then he asked Utter, "Is there anyone else in town who'd know Rose?"

"I doubt anyone has seen her since I have.

Roy and the little boy came in about nine months ago for dry goods and to report some cattle rustlin' out their way. The dry goods has switched hands since then. But the doc might have been out to the Tawlins' in the past few months or so. He'll likely be over at the jail in a few minutes, tendin' Blanco."

Utter's mind switched gears, and he glanced from Louisa to Prophet. "Blanco the only one you brought back?"

"The rest are some bobcat's easy lunch," Prophet said as Louisa gestured for the girl who might have been Rose Tawlin to follow her on over to the jailhouse at the other end of Corazon.

When they were a good distance away, Prophet looked at Utter and chewed his lip before saying, "Blanco was probably just greasing our gears, but his story about that little gal is she was runnin' with him. Could she have been holding their horses while the men robbed the bank?"

"If so, I didn't see her."

"Who would have?"

Utter glanced up the street on Prophet's left, toward a small wooden building whose tall false front identified it as LUNDQUIST'S DRUG EMPORIUM. "Knut Lundquist's the one who popped off several shots at the

102

gang before they galloped outta town. I reckon he had the most to lose. His store don't look like much, but you can't believe what he's made sellin' headache powders and red-striped candy. Probably the biggest stockholder in the county."

"He got a good look at 'em, did he?"

"I'd say so. It was pretty early in the mornin' when they hit the bank. Most folks were still havin' breakfast."

"Let's ride over an' chat him up," Prophet said, reining Mean around.

Utter nodded, then turned to where the overall-clad man and boy were hefting the dead Devlin onto a wheelbarrow. "Lester — them boys have poker winnin's on 'em, and I want every cent of it in my office, you hear? I'll pay you out of the town fund for buryin' them jackals. Understand?"

The undertaker and the boy shared a sullen glance before the man threw up his hands in supplication, then continued lifting Devlin onto the wheelbarrow.

Prophet was dismounting Mean and Ugly in front of the drug emporium as Utter wheeled himself up to the building's front steps, then spun himself on his back wheels so that his back faced the covered porch.

"Help me, here, will you, Prophet?"

The bounty hunter tossed his reins over

the hitchrack, then grabbed the porcelain-knobbed handles jutting from the back of the marshal's wheelchair and hauled the heavy man up the three porch steps. Clumsily negotiating the door, he pushed the portly lawman into the shop rife with the discordant though not unpleasing smells of camphor, chocolate, and licorice. A girl with short, jet-black hair was sweeping the floor to the room's right, near a display of Burmeyer's Scented Lye Soap and a barrel of red rock candy.

"Yellow Feather, is Mr. Lundquist in?"

She'd had her back to the front door as she tidied up the edges of a pile of dust, candy wrappers, and mouse droppings with a broom. Now she turned. Her sullen brown eyes, high-tapering cheekbones, and cherry-tan complexion bespoke Comanche. She rolled her eyes toward the back of the store. "Behind the curtain. They've been having trouble with the little one."

Her low-cut bodice billowed as she glanced at Utter and gave a little, oblique smile. She continued sweeping, and her deep bosom jostled, the dark valley of cleavage opening and closing alluringly. Prophet glanced at Utter, who was staring admiringly at the girl.

"What can I help you fellas with?" came a

man's voice.

Prophet jerked with a start, as did Utter. Both men turned away from the girl sheepishly to see a thin, bald-headed man with watery blue eyes standing behind the plankboard counter at the back of the room.

"There's our druggist now!" intoned Utter, his ruddy, craggy cheeks flushed with embarrassment.

Prophet followed the marshal down a broad aisle to where the druggist waited, bony fists on his counter. He appeared fifty or so, his eyes red-rimmed, gaunt cheeks sprinkled with gray beard stubble. Through the curtained doorway behind him emanated the fussing of a small baby and the nervous cooing of a sleep-deprived mother.

There was also the vinegary stench of urine and scorched milk.

"Little Emma's got the colic. Kept both me an' Evelyn up all night. What can I do for you fellas? Unless, uh . . ." Lundquist shifted a wily glance toward where the Indian girl was sweeping unseen near the front of the store. ". . . You came to see my hired girl?"

"Came to see you, Knut," said Utter, jerking a thumb at the big man flanking him. "This here's Lou Prophet."

"I know," the druggist said with mild

distaste. "Bounty hunter. That him shootin' up the town a few minutes ago and wakin' up little Emma soon as we finally got her bedded down?"

"No, no, that was me. And I do apologize. However, it should please you that Devlin and Reeves are both about to be kicked out with Lester Hedges's shovel."

"That does please me. Since them two been in town, the good folks of Corazon been reluctant to walk the streets. And when they don't walk the streets in fear their womenfolk'll be ogled or far worse, they don't walk through my door and buy my merchandise."

Prophet heard the snicks of the broom grow louder behind him. He glanced over his shoulder to see the Comanche girl sweeping about ten feet away, slowly making her way toward him and Utter. The sheriff looked at her, too. She cast the local lawman a sidelong glance, then turned to let her hair slide down and cover her face as she continued sweeping, her movements making her rich bosom jiggle.

The druggist sighed, and Prophet turned back to him as he said with a frustrated headshake, "You know, ever since I hired that girl to sweep and stock my shelves, I've been getting all kinds of traffic through here. Mostly men. And do you think men buy anything in a drugstore? Nope. They just come in to moon around like school-boys!"

Prophet glanced reprovingly at Utter. "I do apologize, Mr. Lundquist," the bounty hunter said, though it was the sheriff who seemed especially taken with the girl. "If it'll make you feel any better, I'll buy some of that red rock candy over yonder."

"Don't do me any favors, bounty hunter!"

"All right, all right," Utter said, holding up his pudgy, hairy-backed hands. "We didn't come here to argue over Yellow Feather. We came to ask you, Lundquist, if you happened to see a dark-haired girl in town the day the bank was robbed across the street. It's been mentioned, albeit by an unreliable source, that she might have been holding the Metalious gang's horses between your place here and Randall's harness shop next door."

"Dark-haired, you say?"

"Dark-haired," Prophet said. "Dressed in range garb — calico blouse, fringed buck-skin slacks. Had a cap-and-ball pistol when I found her. Pretty little gal." He glanced once more at Yellow Feather, who'd stopped sweeping to listen in on the conversation.

"White girl," he added, turning back to

the owly druggist.

"Ah, hell," Lundquist said. "It all happened so fast. I think there was someone milling around with horses between my store and Randall's, but I was busy mixing some powders for Emma's colic. I didn't look out the window till the shootin' started."

"Did you see a girl with the gang?" Utter asked.

Lundquist dropped his gaze and narrowed his eyes thoughtfully. "I reckon one of 'em mighta been a girl. Yeah . . . now that I study on it, one of 'em did look sort of slight." He looked at Prophet. "I think I remember that calico shirt, too."

Utter and Prophet shared an uncertain look.

"Who is she?" Lundquist asked. "You bring her in?"

"Prophet brought a girl in with Blanco. Not sure who the girl is, though."

"Or if she was with the gang," the bounty hunter added, feeling less than satisfied by what he and the marshal had learned so far.

Lundquist gave each man across the counter from him a wry, mocking look. "Did you think of asking her who she is?"

"Did that." Prophet hooked his thumbs behind his cartridge belt as he stared absently out the window to his left, off the end of the counter. "She don't remember."

"Likely story," the druggist chuffed.

"Smacked her head," said Utter. "Don't seem to be fakin' the aneesha."

"Amnesia."

Prophet and Utter swung around to the Indian girl, who stood holding her broom behind them, regarding them with one arched brow.

"Memory loss," Yellow Feather said. "The medical term is amnesia." Her chocolate brown eyes danced between the surprised bounty hunter and town marshal of Corazon. "I went to a mission school in Las Cruces . . . before I was adopted by a doctor."

She glanced at Utter once more, her mouth corners rising coquettishly before she crouched to sweep some dust out from behind a wooden tub of flavored soda water. The sheriff's face reddened, and he swiped a fist across his nose in embarrassment.

"I don't care who you was raised by, girl, you just keep sweepin'. That's what you're good for — sweepin'." To Prophet and Utter, the druggist said, "If you got that girl to town, someone'll surely recognize her."

"Looks to me like the Tawlin girl," Utter said. "I couldn't say for sure, though, as I haven't seen her since the last blue moon."

"Me, neither." Lundquist winced as the baby in the backroom began yowling in earnest. He raised his voice to be heard above it. "Last time the family came to town, she wasn't with 'em. Don't think I seen the boy, neither. If she's from around here, someone'll surely know her. It just goes to reason."

He glanced regretfully at the curtain behind him. "If you two don't want nothin' else, I'd better get back and see if Evelyn needs some help. I swear, if this colic keeps up, she's liable to throw that little one down the privy hole."

Utter waved him off. "Luck to you, Lundquist."

When the man had disappeared through the curtain, the marshal glanced at Prophet, who grabbed his wheelchair and turned him toward the door. "I told him not to marry that Evelyn Snyder. Bad family. Germans by way of Dakota. The whole family was likely born with the colic and died from it though not before they reached a good eighty years and gave the pure sanctified hell to them they married!"

The marshal laughed as Prophet pushed him toward the door, which Yellow Feather held open for them. On the way out,

Prophet pinched his hat brim to the girl. "Sorry if we caused you any trouble, miss."

Prophet headed on out the door, easing the marshal down the steps to the street.

Yellow Feather came out behind them, closing the shop door, still holding her broom.

"If that is Rose Tawlin," she said, "keep a close eye on her. I've never met her myself, but I worked for a farmer out near where her family has their claim. I heard she got wild over the past couple years. You know —" She hiked a shoulder. "After she filled out and got the tomcats prowlin' around the Tawlin place. Tomcats of the bad stripe."

Prophet and Utter gazed at the girl standing atop the porch steps. She took her broom in one hand, raised the other one to an awning support post, and threw her shoulders back, pushing out her breasts.

The top of her cleavage was dark and inviting. Her eyes and round hips to which the skirt of her dress clung tightly said she'd spoken of prowling tomcats from personal experience. Neither Prophet nor Utter doubted that experience a bit.

"Much obliged, Yellow Feather," Utter said thickly, giving his hat brim a pinch.

She narrowed her eyes slightly. Apparently, she enjoyed staying on the good side of the local law. "Anytime, Sheriff."

9

"Find another one to charm out of her bloomers, Mr. Prophet?"

Louisa was walking toward the jailhouse at an angle from the other side of the street and glancing toward the drugstore, where the Indian girl was sweeping the porch steps.

Prophet sat atop Mean and Ugly. The marshal sat his wheelchair in front of the jailhouse, a dilapidated wooden building with a porch whose roof was missing most of its shingles. The green paint on the vertical, whipsawed siding boards had all but weathered away, and what was left hung in sausage curls.

Prophet hipped around to look behind him. The Indian girl dropped her head abruptly, but he thought he could see a smile tweak her mouth corners behind the dark screen of her dancing hair.

Prophet looked at Louisa, who planted her right boot on the porch steps, to take some weight off her wounded leg, and cast him a smart look. They had an agreement that, despite their occasional bedroll tussles — it got damn lonely out on the stalking trail of a night — neither of them was now or ever would be short-roped to the other. That didn't keep Louisa from riding him for his easy ways, however.

"Nope," the bounty hunter said. "That one there's the sheriff's girl."

Utter chuffed with embarrassment. "Ah, hell — Yellow Feather'll flirt with any man with a steady paycheck. Even a crippled, old lawdog!"

A wooden ramp ran up and down the jailhouse porch steps. Over the ramp, a stout rope hung from a hook. The end of the rope was latched to a nail in a post at the bottom of the steps. Marshal Utter grabbed the rope and used it to haul himself up the ramp, grunting, red-faced, then he wheeled himself around to look toward the drugstore.

"Watch out for her, Lou. She ain't been in town long, but already she's got a good half dozen men in trouble with their wives."

"Don't doubt it a bit," Prophet said with a wry chuckle as he swung down from Mean and Ugly's back. To Louisa, he said, "Doc inside with Blanco?"

The blond bounty hunter nodded. "He

114

said if we put Blanco in the saddle again before that wound heals, he'll bleed out inside of six miles."

"He's gotta ride," Prophet said. "If he bleeds out, he bleeds out."

Louisa doffed her hat and ran a hand through her thick blond hair. "It won't do much good to trail him out of here if he's gonna die on us."

Utter looked indignant. "Where the hell you plannin' on takin' him? I'll pay the reward on him right here. The stock association that hung the bounty around his neck is known for speedy reimbursements."

"You know we won't be able to hold him here, Utter," Prophet said. "His pa bein' 'Man-Killin'' Sam Metalious an' all. Why, he probably has twenty seasoned hard cases on his roll, and they'll all ride into town in a big, hump-necked group as soon as they learn we got Blanco."

Utter's face was still red from his ride up the ramp. It turned even redder now, and he bunched his lips at Prophet. "He stays right here. Right here is where he done held up the bank and killed four citizens of Corazon. This town has every right to see him hang, which he for certain-sure will about ten minutes after the circuit judge rides into town next week."

Louisa cast a quick look at Prophet, then, setting her hand carefully on her head, turned to Utter. "When's the judge due?"

"Middle of next week."

"Even if we can keep Blanco in the lockup that long," Prophet said, "Metalious won't let him get here. His gang'll dry-gulch him along the trail."

"The judge comes escorted once a month through this valley by an army patrol out of Fort Stockton. Has ever since a couple rustlers backshot the son of a bitch and left him for dead."

Utter chuckled and dug a fat cigar out from a shirt pocket beneath his dusty frock coat. "Turned out he was only fakin' it though he did end up losin' a shredded kidney. Damn good actor. That had to hurt like the devil's toothache, layin' there in that wash. The soldiers ran those boys down and turned 'em into bobcat vittles pronto."

The marshal bit the end off the cigar and stuck it in his mouth. "The long and short of it is he comes with a patrol nowadays. A good nine, ten soldiers with a sergeant and a licutenant — all gun-handy men. The works."

Prophet unbuckled Mean's latigo strap in frustration, letting the two ends dangle toward the dust. "We gonna be able to hold

116

Blanco till next week?" He tossed a doubt-ful look at the falling-down jailhouse. Even one of the shutters over the lone front window had come loose and was hanging by one rusty nail. "In there?"

"You're just a bounty hunter, Prophet!" Utter stopped lighting the stogie to glare furiously at both Prophet and Louisa. "I'm the law around here. You merely brought Blanco in. I'm the one holdin' him until the circuit judge arrives next week. Do I make myself clear?"

"All right, Marshal." Prophet threw up his hands. "Have it your own damn way."

"Maybe you two oughta clear out right now," Utter said. "I'm startin' to get a little tired of your uppity company."

Prophet had started leading the horse over to the livery barn sitting kitty-corner across the broad street, where Louisa had appar-ently boarded her own pinto with Blanco's and the girl's.

Now Prophet looked back at Utter. He was beginning to get a little hot under the collar himself. The marshal was right — he and Louisa had done their jobs. Now it was up to Utter and his deputy, Rubriz. By rights, Prophet should leave the dirty, most dangerous part of the job to the ungrateful old, wheelchair-bound cuss before him.

"Maybe we *should* light a shuck on out of here," he told Louisa, who now stood leaning against a corner of the porch, her arms folded, looking troubled, uncertain. "We'll take our damn money from this ornery old cuss and head for Albuquerque. I could use a *good* bottle of whiskey for a change, any damn way! You sure as shit can't find such an animal around here!"

"You do that!" yelled Utter.

"We just will, then!" Prophet yelled back, starting once again for the livery barn that sat alone on a big, unkempt lot, with several near-empty peeled log corrals angling off both sides and the rear. Behind it ran the stream between low, grassy banks lined with cottonwoods.

"Lou, hold on," Louisa said, remaining where she was.

"You hold on. I'm gonna stall my horse, get him rested up for ridin' out of here tomorrow." Prophet stopped and looked over his shoulder at his partner. "Say, where's the girl? Inside with the doc?"

Louisa shook her head. "The doc already tended her head. He didn't recognize her. Said he hadn't seen the Tawlin family in over a year, and it had been longer than that since he'd seen Rose. She's walking out yonder, along the creek."

Prophet followed Louisa's gaze to the cottonwoods behind the livery barn. "You let her go out there untended?" he said, incredulous.

"I stabled her horse. How far's she gonna get on foot?"

"How do we know? We don't know nothin' about her."

"You didn't learn anything from the druggist?" Louisa smirked. "Except that he has a pretty swamper?"

Marshal Utter studied the gray coal on his stogie. "Learned she *could* be Rose, *could* have held the horses for Blanco's bunch, and she *could* be a mite on the *wild* side."

"Ah, hell." Again, Prophet continued his tramp toward the livery barn. "She ain't none of our problem, anyways. We're just bounty hunters."

"That's right!" Utter intoned behind him, still as mad as a bobcat tied to a plank. "She *ain't,* and you *are!*"

The bearded gent in the livery barn was sleeping off what, judging by the stench of whiskey in the place as well as whiskey sweat, was one hell of a hangover. So Prophet tended Mean and Ugly himself, rubbing the horse down thoroughly, graining and watering the contrary beast who twice tried to put a new tear in Prophet's multi-patched tunic, and turned him into the corral with the other horses.

Mean and Ugly gave a snort, then ran around the corral to announce himself. When, after pawing the dirt and shaking his head friskily, none of the five livery mounts nor Louisa's and Blanco's horses wanted to fight, he promptly rolled in the dirt, raising whinnies like a demented hyena.

"There you go, you son of a bitch," Prophet said, settling a shoulder against the frame of the door to the holding corral and reaching into his tunic pocket for his makings sack.

"Mr. Prophet?"

The girl's voice made him jerk slightly with a start. He turned.

The girl whom he'd decided to think of as Rose Tawlin until he'd learned of another handle for her was walking toward him from the barn's open double doors. She had a clean, white bandage wrapped around the top of her head. Her tanned elfin face looked almost Indian-dark in contrast.

Prophet troughed a rolling paper between his right index and forefingers as the girl hiked a hip on a nearby oat bin and loosely entwined her hands on her lap.

"You take a walk, did ya?" Prophet asked

her as he dribbled tobacco onto the paper.

"Yeah, but I don't remember anything. Nothing around here looks familiar."

"It'll come back," he said with shallow optimism. "Sooner or later."

"Do me a favor?"

"What's that?"

"Take me out to the Tawlin place?"

Deftly folding the paper closed, he looked at the girl from under his brows, scowling. "What — now?"

"The sheriff said the Tawlin claim is twenty miles away. On fresh horses, we could make it before sundown."

"How 'bout if we ride out there tomorrow? I don't much care for riding an unfamiliar horse, and ole Means needs him a good, long —"

"Please?"

Prophet lowered the half-made quirley and looked at her.

"Do you know what it's like to not know who you are or how you got where you're now standing?" she asked, her voice again brittle. "To not know if you're good or bad, if you come from a home that wants you back or one that doesn't?"

She slid off the bin and walked toward him, holding his gaze with her own, her eyes at once fearful and desperate. "To not know if you belong behind bars or at the end of a hang rope?"

Prophet's own gaze wavered, and he dropped his eyes to the cigarette in his hands.

"If I rode with Blanco's bunch," she said, her voice low and almost menacing, "I'm just as guilty as Blanco for the killing of the people here in Corazon. Including that little boy."

"Back home . . . if it is your home . . . who's to say you'll find out if you rode with Metalious's bunch? They may not know. You mighta been gone a long —"

"I'll find out more than what I've learned here. I'll know if I am who that Blanco creature says I am or if I am really Rose Tawlin. If I'm Rose, then maybe I'll learn from my family about what I was doing in Nugget Town. Maybe I was with my father or my brother."

Her eyes were growing more and more passionate, her voice louder. She grabbed Prophet's right wrist with both her hands, and squeezed. "Maybe we were out hunting or looking for a new claim. Why was I alone when you found me? Maybe they're up there in those hills, injured, and I'd wandered into the town looking for help."

"All right, all right," Prophet said, closing

his left hand over hers as if to comfort the girl.

She was damn near hysterical and he supposed she had every right to be. She wouldn't rest until she found out who and what she was. If he didn't take her out to the Tawlin place, she'd likely sneak off alone.

"Let's give ole Mean an hour's rest. Me, too. I could use a drink and a sandwich. Then I'll saddle him and a fresh mount for you, and I'll meet you on the street."

"I'll help. Something tells me I know how to saddle a horse. I'd like to find out for sure. It's not much, but . . . it's something."

Prophet nodded. "All right. Meet me here in an hour."

An hour later, after Prophet had enjoyed the free lunch that had come with the nickel beers at the Mecca Saloon, they found out that Rose had been right. She knew how to bridle and saddle a horse right down to punching the air out of the stubborn beast's lungs so she could tighten the latigo strap. As she'd said, it wasn't much, but it was something she knew about herself that she hadn't known a few minutes ago. She didn't say anything, but she seemed satisfied.

As the liveryman was still asleep with two empty whiskey bottles standing on the earthen floor beneath his cot, Prophet decided he'd pay the man later. He and Rose led their mounts — hers, a claybank that appeared to have some barb in it — through the corral gate and into the street.

As they rode westward along Brush Street, few people were out, but Louisa wandered out of the mercantile shop near the end of town and on the street's right side. She held a bottle of sarsaparilla in her hand. Her hat hung down her back from the horsehair thong around her neck. Her Winchester was leaning outside the door.

She frowned, puzzled, as she stopped at the top of the loading dock's wide steps.

"We're gonna head on out to the Tawlin place, see what's what and" — Prophet glanced at the girl he hoped was Rose — "who's who."

Louisa glanced west. "It'll be sundown in a few hours."

"We'll just make it," Prophet said. "Wanna come? I see no point in hangin' around a town where bounty hunters are treated like they was trash-mongerin' coyotes."

"I'll take my chances." Louisa slid the top of the brown bottle between her bee-stung lips, glanced skeptically between Rose and Prophet, and took a sip.

She smacked her lips together softly, ran her tongue along the upper one. "Just so you know, I'm not going anywhere till I've watched Blanco hang or at least heard his neck snap. He killed a youngun and, well, you know how I am about that."

"We might just be forkin' trails here, then."

Louisa slid a cool, cryptic glance at Rose waiting behind Prophet. "We've forked them before."

Prophet nodded and gigged the dun forward. Rose booted her own horse up beside him.

"Watch yourselves," Louisa cautioned behind them. "This is wolf country."

10

Sitting on the steps of the mercantile's loading dock, nursing her cherry sarsaparilla, Louisa watched the bouncing backs of Lou and the amnesiac girl until they'd dwindled to dots in the brassy sunlight and the sage and junipers closed behind them. She briefly spied Lou's soiled hat, worn to a faded yellow, and the girl's white bandage glowing in the afternoon sun, before the horses and riders disappeared down the other side of a distant rise and were gone.

Louisa lifted the bottle to her lips once more and drank.

She mentally waved off an annoying twinge of insecurity at Prophet's absence and the touch of jealousy that clung to its heels. She would possess nor be possessed by no one. It was the same for him.

She threw back the last swallow of the sugary liquid that sputtered and popped sweetly in her throat. Drinking the syrupy soda water always reminded her of home, of riding into Sand Creek, Nebraska Territory, once a month with the rest of her family on a supply run — Pa, Ma, the other two girls, and their brother — and of drinking sarsaparilla on the steps of the Sand Creek Mercantile's loading dock while Pa and their older brother hauled the dry goods from the store to their wagon box. Ma would be inside, looking over the yard goods and sewing thread, maybe perusing a Sears & Roebuck catalogue with stars in her eyes.

Louisa and the girls would drink their sodas and keep an eye out for any boys they knew, or talk about the kind of houses they'd have if they lived in town.

Owen. Junie. Opal.

All dead now. Owen had been three years older than Louisa when Handsome Dave Duvall's Red River Gang had ridden hell-for-leather onto their farmstead, hackles raised, guns popping, hooves tearing up Ma's kitchen garden and setting their dog to howling.

Owen had been only half a head shorter than Pa, who'd been just over six feet but who, to Louisa at seventeen, had been a giant of a man. Owen would be a full-grown man now, had he lived. He'd likely have a farm near Pa and Ma's place.

Junie would still be at home, most likely, but Opal would have married Brian Davisson, whom she'd had eyes for since they'd all started school together. They might have even had a child or two by now. Louisa herself had liked the country, but she'd also had aspirations toward a more civilized life, of playing the piano and hosting tea parties in a warm parlor, of maybe having a couple of fine horses in her stable.

No kids of hers would run around barefoot of a summer for lack of rain to make the wheat and corn grow. . . .

Louisa waved that train of thought away, as well.

Thoughts were suddenly like flies buzzing around her head. Or horseflies sure to bite this late in the year, when the cold nights started making them surly and realizing their time was almost up.

She went back into the mercantile, returned the bottle for which she was given back her penny deposit. The mercantile owner ran his gray eyes across her chest and told her to come back real soon. As she turned away from him and walked toward the door she felt his eyes wandering down her narrow back to her hips flaring to her bottom, dreaming of what he could do with a piece of young, supple female flesh like hers if his wife hadn't tied her apron strings so tight around his neck, and he wasn't quite so long in the damn tooth.

She stepped back out onto the dock, letting the screen door squawk shut behind her, blocking the mercantiler's view and running a hand through her gold blond hair before setting her hat on her head. She scooped up her gear — rifle, saddlebags, and war bag — from where she'd left it piled on the floor, and, settling her rifle on her shoulder, looked up and down the street.

Not many people out, just a few milling here and there, a wagon leaving the competing mercantile on the other side of town and heading southeast. There were three saloons on this end of town, beyond the squalid red-light district known as Bayonet Wash, but horses stood bunched to only two of these.

There were two hotels — the French Hotel and Cora's Rooms. Louisa had walked past both, and she not only liked the sound of the French Hotel but had liked the look of the building. Big and solid, with large fancy letters adorning the high false façade.

Cora's Rooms was little more than a narrow, unpainted shack with split cordwood abutting both sides and frilly women's underclothes flopping on the line behind it near a path beaten into the barren ground to a falling-down privy. There was a chicken coop back there, too, and roosters would wake her up too early. And she had nothing to wake up early for now that she was between jobs and was only awaiting the execution of Blanco Metalious.

The killer was all that held her here.

If Utter objected to her staying and waiting for the circuit judge, he could go to the devil. She hadn't run the killer down just so the man's outlaw father and outlaw ranch hands could ride in and spring him so he could go on killing women and young children.

Blanco. Finally a thought that made her feel better.

One that swept away all the heavy, cloying dark thoughts that seemed to haunt her, day and night, even when she didn't realize it. Blanco's drop through the trapdoor, his boots coming to an abrupt halt two feet from the ground, his neck snapping so loudly that crows would light from the false fronts around the gallows.

The boy he'd killed would smile in heaven, where he was surrounded by all the others taken too soon, including Louisa's own sisters and brother, and poor, murdered Ma and Pa, as well.

"One room," Louisa told the man who stood behind the desk in the lobby of the French Hotel — a portly gent sporting a longhorn mustache with waxed and twisted ends and a freshly brushed brown bowler slanted on his head. His fleshy cheeks were florid, his eyes brown and devilish, as they quickly dropped to his open ledger book when Louisa had walked in.

"It's a dollar a night," he grunted. He wore a vest that didn't cover his paunch, and an open shirt fold revealed his deep, dark belly button from which several long brown hairs curled. "Do you have any idea how long you'll be staying, Miss Bonaventure?"

Louisa looked at him. He kept his eyes down. A shy one, but she could read the nasty thoughts in his head. By now, everyone in the county knew that she and Prophet were in town. The bounty tracker on whom the devil held a hefty note, and his blond partner known as the Vengeance Queen. Dangerous, having that knowledge spread so wide. She'd have to keep her guns cleaned and loaded with six full rounds in each cylinder.

"I'll pay through Monday, then one day at

a time after that." Louisa tossed a silver cartwheel onto the ledger book, which the man did not request she sign, and glanced out the clean front windows flanking two tall, potted palms. "Where do they usually build the gallows here in Corazon?"

For the first time, he raised his eyes, creased with surprise, to Louisa's face. Haltingly, he said, "Uh . . . right out in the middle of Brush Street."

"I'd like a room with a good view of the street, then."

The man turned and snagged a key from a ring behind him.

"I'd also like a bath brought up to my room. Not by you. By a female, if you have any around here."

"I'm sorry, Miss Bonaventure," the hotelier said nervously, only able to let his gaze scuttle back and forth across Louisa without focusing. "You'll have to visit Talbot's for a bath. He don't rent rooms, and I don't rent baths."

Louisa considered this primly, scowling at the beady-eyed man with mild disgust. "Well, you and Mr. Talbot have a nice little racket going, don't you?"

The man smiled wanly and kept his eyes somewhere low on Louisa's waist. "He'll launder your clothes for only a nickel extra, and I'll vouch for his workmanship."

"I'm sure you would. Who is he — brother?"

The man's plump, rosy right cheek twitched, and he gave his shoulders a brief hike. "Brother-in-law."

Louisa snorted. "All right. I guess you just made a sale for your brother-in-law."

She snatched her room key off the open register book and reached down for her gear, which she'd dropped against the base of the man's desk when she'd entered.

"I'd be happy to carry those up to your room, Miss Bonaventure."

"No, thank you."

Adjusting the gear on her shoulders — she'd grown accustomed to hefting a good half of her own weight around for long stretches while scouring strange towns for hotels or eateries — she climbed the faded red-carpeted stairs at the back of the lobby. Turning at the first landing, she glanced down the stairs behind her, caught a brief glimpse of the hotelier flushing with chagrin as he jerked his head back behind his desk and out of sight.

"Men . . ." Louisa muttered distastefully.

Her room was in the middle of the hotel's south side, facing the street. When she'd deemed it adequate — really, it was rather well appointed for being this far out in the brushy hills — she gathered up her saddlebags, leaving her rifle and war bag on the bed, and headed back down the stairs.

From the hotelier, she learned where Talbot's bathhouse was located and headed off to the south side of town and a simple brown shack with thick tufts of white wood smoke unfurling from its large, brick chimney.

Talbot was a tall, bearded man with a hawk nose and eyes not unlike those of his brother-in-law. He gave Louisa a towel and ordered his son Junior, a shorter, beardless version of Talbot himself, to fill her tub — his only copper tub, he pointed out — in one of his three rough-hewn bathing rooms that consisted of only the tub itself, a night vase, a wooden bench, a backless chair shoved into a corner as though to get it out of the way, and two railroad spikes driven into a wall for hooks.

There were only three narrow, slotted windows up where the walls met the pitched roof and, unlike many bathhouses she'd visited, the boards of the walls were rammed up close together, with no cracks between them. Surprising. She'd become convinced that most bathhouses were so loosely knocked together as to make it easier for peepers.

Louisa sat on the bench, knees spread, elbows on her thighs, while Junior made several trips with water buckets to fill the tub. When he'd poured the last bucket of hot water into the battered tub that had a little seat built halfway up its narrowing back, Louisa stood.

"Hold on, Junior."

"What?" the young man asked dully, stretching his lips back from a mess of yellow, crooked, tobacco-rimed teeth. Unlike his uncle's, his eyes were brash, insolent. "You paid two bits — three buckets for three bits."

"Yes, but you made no mention of how cold the water would be."

Louisa bent down to drop a hand into the water from which faint steam snakes curled. A scuttling sound rose to her left, and she stayed her hand. Catching movement out the corner of her left eye, she straightened suddenly, palming one of her two pearl-butted Colts that jutted up above her poncho, and wheeled toward the cabin's far left corner.

There was a twitch of a short, cordlike tail.

Louisa's Colt barked once. The rat screamed as it was separated from its tail.

The Colt barked again and the rat turned a somersault beneath the chair. The third shot tore the creature in half and left both bloody pieces fluttering like yellowed paper in a trash-strewn alley.

Smoke wafted, rife with the smell of cordite.

Junior had scuttled well back out of Louisa's way and clamped his hands over his ears, lips stretched back from his teeth as he stared at the quivering rat beneath the chair.

Louisa spun her smoking Colt on her finger, one of her few frivolous indulgences, and dropped it smoothly into its holster. "I hope he wasn't a pet."

Junior looked at her as though he'd just found a bobcat in the room, and slowly lowered his hands from his head. But it was his father who yelled from the front of the bathhouse, "What in *tarnation?*"

Junior echoed the exclamation though from him it was little louder than a hoarse whisper.

"You'd do to keep your bathhouse free of rats, Junior. Men might not mind but most women with half a decent upbringing will. Now go fetch another bucket of water — *hot* water — and I won't demand my money back."

Junior looked at her well-displayed guns and backed out of the room with a constipated expression. He returned with two more steaming buckets. He dumped one into the tub and left the other on the bench beside Louisa's saddlebags.

"Here's an extry bucket of hot water." Junior sidestepped to the door with the empty bucket. "It's on the house."

"Thank you, Junior," Louisa said as the blanket curtain fell over the doorway as Junior's boots thumped off down the hall. "No peeping!"

Louisa quickly undressed. It was Indian summer, and while the front of the bathhouse was warm and humid from the big steam pots, the washroom was cool. Carefully piling her clothes on the bench — she'd turn them over to Junior later for laundering — she grabbed her own soap, a wood-handled brush, and a towel from her war bag, and stepped into the tub.

She lathered the brush with the soap and went to work, scrubbing her face and the back of her neck and then her shoulders, arms, and breasts. When she'd washed her hair, she leaned over the tub to dunk her head in the extra bucket of water, then stood up and washed her legs, privates, and feet. She took her time, enjoying the feel of the brush against her skin that hadn't been cleaned since she and Prophet had left Las Cruces.

When she was done scrubbing her feet, she ran the brush across her perpetually saddle-sore buttocks then spent an equal amount of time on her breasts, rubbing the lavender-scented soap into them, pushing them up high beneath her chin.

Ah, that felt good. All that sweat and grime washing away.

Of course, a good river bath would have been better, because she wouldn't be soaking in her own filth. But this time of year most of the rivers were cold. There was nothing like the feel of a good, hot bath with soap you could work into a heavy lather, really open up and scour the pores. Besides, she'd wash the dirty water off later, with the extra bucket she'd only used for her hair.

She was about to sit back down in the tub when she heard a slight rustling sound.

She followed the faint metallic scratching beneath the chair where the dead rat lay. Louisa frowned, squinting to see better in the shadows. Suddenly, her mouth opened in shock, and her lower jaw dropped. A half second later the small, round mirror that had been sticking up out of the rat hole and reflecting orange light from the slotted windows up near the ceiling dropped back into the notch.

Rage burned like acid through Louisa's veins. Automatically, she reached for her shell belt and two Colts coiled beside the tub. She'd nearly lifted one of the revolvers out of its holster when she stopped. Turning back to the hole, where she could now hear the muffled sounds of heavy breathing, she narrowed one eye devilishly.

"Junior . . ." she muttered.

Just a cow-headed kid. Probably outside the washroom selling peeks at his comely blond client to his dull-witted friends. Blasting them all with her .45s might be a little severe. Besides, they'd probably never seen the likes of Louisa before. Maybe a more appropriate punishment would be to make their little hearts shrivel with insatiable lust.

She'd make them suffer for their voyeuristic sins.

She straightened with the extra bucket in her hands, and poured it over her head. The soap and water sluiced off her willowy frame, and her wet, naked body glistened in the light slanting through the window slots.

Again, she lathered the brush and then, more slowly this time, repeated the scrubbing she'd given herself before. In no time, she heard the *snick-snick* from beneath the

139

chair. She'd turned her back on the hole as she massaged her taut, round buttocks; now she cast a furtive glance over her shoulder.

The mirror was back.

It jerked back and forth as Junior or one of his customers adjusted it from outside. On the other side of the wall near the hole, she heard a boy groan. Then he chuckled.

One of the boys shushed the other and there was a soft wooden thud as one brushed the bathhouse wall. They'd obviously dug a hole beneath the floor and were using the rat hole to snake up a mirror-rigged spyglass. They probably weren't seeing much of Louisa, but it was likely as much as they could handle.

Louisa took her time with the second soaping, sort of dancing around in the bathwater, kicking, splashing, humming, and tossing her wet hair around her shoulders. She spent some extra time caressing her breasts, rolling her nipples between her thumbs and index fingers, groaning and sighing erotically. From outside she heard several more groans and a snicker.

One of the boys smacked another. Someone cursed.

Louisa smiled.

Then she rinsed again, and by the time she'd pulled on clean clothes from her war bag — another wool skirt and a fringed buckskin blouse — the mirror had disappeared from beneath the chair. The show was over.

"I'll have these laundered and delivered to the French Hotel, though what's French about it I have no idea," Louisa told Talbot, the bathhouse proprietor, as she set the bundle atop his plank-board desk.

Talbot, busy feeding wood to the black iron range on top of which two copper kettles boiled, nodded. Louisa plunked her money down beside the clothes and went out. Junior was coming around the corner of the bathhouse. The boy had a loosely rolled cigarette between his crooked, rotten teeth.

He glanced at Louisa devilishly, giving her a lewd up-and-down.

She stepped in front of him suddenly. Some crumpled bills poked up out of the breast pocket of his coveralls. Quickly, she plucked the bills from his pocket.

"Hey!" Junior objected. He reached for the money but missed.

Louisa unfolded the three one-dollar bills that were sticky from chocolate candy and licorice.

"Three whole dollars," Louisa observed. "A dollar a peep?"

Junior's face turned brick red.

"Flattering." Louisa stuffed the bills back in the kid's pocket and strode away.

11

A low growl sounded in the brush on the right side of the trail.

The growl grew shrill until it became a snarl. A creature yipped, and there followed the light thumps of four padded feet, which dwindled gradually as the creature moved away.

"Wait here."

Prophet reined Mean and Ugly to a halt on the trail that he and Rose had been following out from Corazon and swung down from the saddle. He left his double-barreled shotgun hanging from his saddle horn and shucked the Winchester '73 from its boot, then tramped off into the brush, weaving around clumps of buckbrush, sage, and mountain mahogany.

He came to the lip of a shallow but steep-sided dry wash. A cow lay on the wash's gravelly bottom.

A gray coyote had its head buried in the

animal's rear, grinding its back feet into the gravel as it tugged and pulled. It waved its bushy gray tail like a flag.

Suddenly, the coyote jerked its head out of the gaping cavity and looked at Prophet. Its face was a bizarre blood mask. Its yellow-brown eyes were fierce, but they quickly grew wary. The animal must have expected to see a competing member of its own species, and had been ready to scare it off as it had the other.

The smell all around was like that of a filled privy pit. The beast's blood-caked nostrils expanded and contracted. Prophet wrinkled his own nose against the stench and lowered the Winchester, off-cocking the hammer.

A second coyote could be seen weaving off through the brush toward a drab rise of hills capped with gold as the sun nudged the western horizon. The nearest coyote gave an angry moan, then wheeled and slinked up the wash's far side and disappeared into a thick patch of tangled juniper and spindly, leafless shrubs, likely to see what the rifle-wielding stranger would do — remain and dine on the brown-and-black heifer that had likely been dead three or four days, or light a shuck.

"It's all yours, amigo," Prophet said softly,

looking around, then letting his glance slide northeastward where the powdery white ribbon of the main trail curled on up to the log cabin dug into the side of a low, brown bluff about two hundred yards beyond.

A concerned scowl on his face, he walked back to the trail where Rose sat on her claybank. "Coyotes?"

Prophet nodded.

Rose turned her head forward to study the dugout cabin. "Funny there'd be coyotes so close to the ranch yard."

Prophet agreed though he didn't say anything. Keeping the Winchester in his hand, he stepped into the saddle and, feeling uneasy, booted the dun forward.

They followed the trail over several gravelly knolls, spying no more cows either dead or alive though dry gray pies as well as the close-cropped needle grass told Prophet there'd been a herd in here. Where were the rest of them now? This late in the year, Tawlin — if he were any kind of stockman at all — would be keeping them close to home.

And keeping the coyotes away.

As they approached the ranch/mine claim's entrance portal — two peeled logs with another one nailed between them about twenty feet above the trail, with several sets of deer antlers adorning the

crossbar as well as the Circle T brand —
Prophet pulled back on the dun's reins. He
held up his Winchester for Rose to stop as
well.

An Apache arrow jutted from the cross
plank, from the dead center of the Circle T
brand.

Prophet looked toward the cabin and the
shabby stone barn a hundred feet beyond.
Two dilapidated, partially charred corrals
angled off both sides of the stone barn, both
gates drawn wide and tumbleweeds blown
up around them. The ground around both
the barn and the front of the cabin was
scorched black. The cabin's door gaped, the
log frame around it also black though it was
hard to see anything clearly in the quickly
fading light.

"You best wait here," Prophet said and
galloped through the portal.

"No!"

He heard the clomps of the girl's horse
behind him as he charged into the hard-
packed yard and dismounted in front of the
cabin. There was the smell of charred wood,
and more arrows bristled from the door
frame as well as from the gray wooden
frames of the two front windows.

The ground revealed few tracks — dust
and rain had obliterated them. The Apaches

had attacked the Circle T a good while ago, but still Prophet racked a shell into his Winchester's breech as he stepped through the open door.

The fire had gutted the place, so it resembled little more than a burned trash heap. There was a small box range with charred pots on the floor around it. The heavy puncheon table angled down into a mound of gray ash from which part of one leg still stood. Hides hung from two walls in tattered, burned ribbons.

Prophet stood looking around for signs of the dead Tawlin family, holding his Winchester low across his thighs. It was doubtful that anyone was in here. This had happened several weeks ago, but there'd still be the unmistakable odor of rotting flesh if bodies remained.

Running footsteps sounded behind him. He turned as Rose ran up to the door, holding one hand to her bandaged, aching head. "Are they . . . ?"

"I don't think so."

Rose walked slowly into the cabin, looking around. Prophet knew what she was thinking. Had this been her home? Hard to tell now, but maybe something here, the layout of the place, would jog her memory.

Leaving her alone in the cabin, he walked

outside and scoured the other buildings —
there was only the barn and what appeared
to be a small, sun-silvered log bunkhouse.
No bodies in the yard. No blood, either.
Good signs. Maybe the Tawlins had made it
out of here alive, sought sanctuary at a
neighboring ranch or mine claim.

Prophet was looking in one of the windows
of the burned out stone barn when Rose
walked up behind him.

"How long ago, do you think?" she asked.

"I don't know. A month. Maybe a little
longer, or a little less. Those arrows are
pretty sun beat."

He turned to her. Her eyes were stricken
and yet there remained some hope in them.

"They got away, didn't they?" Her eyes
grew stricken again as her thoughts shifted
darkly. "Or were taken . . . ?"

"Doubt it. Coyoteros wouldn't have taken
any prisoners. They'd have no need. The
Comanch — they would have taken the boy,
maybe your mo . . . or the woman who lived
here. This is Apache country, though. Coy-
otero fletching on the arrows. The Comanche rarely stray this far west."

He was walking around the yard now, casting his gaze in all directions. The trail
seemed to end here at the ranchstead. Only
rough hills beyond. He could see the ravine

148

of a creek snaking around behind the place from the southeast and some mine tailings. That must be where Tawlin had his gold claim.

Since the trail ended here, there would be few visitors. That's probably why word of the attack hadn't yet reached Corazon, the closest town. Which probably meant no one had survived it. No point in sharing that bit of reasoning with Rose yet.

Prophet walked toward the bunkhouse on the yard's north edge, hunkered beneath a tall cottonwood and obscured by rocks and brush. It was built of hand-adzed logs and boasted a roof of tightly arranged branches over sod. The door was closed, and there didn't appear to be any of the same scorching like that around the barn and the cabin. Both front windows were shuttered, and a quick walk around the place told Prophet that the building's other three windows were covered, as well.

He wondered why the Apaches hadn't burned it. Maybe they hadn't noticed it sitting off here in the brush.

Returning to the front, he saw that Rose was no longer with him. He looked around, but she was gone. Out investigating on her own. Prophet would leave her to own thoughts and worries — she certainly had her share, for a girl so young.

He tripped the leather latch of the bunkhouse's heavy timbered door and gave the iron handle a pull.

The door opened, giving a bark as it scraped across the threshold and then the packed ground in front of it, the hinges squawking raucously. Stale, pent-up air pushed against the big bounty hunter, who nearly filled the doorway as he stared, ducking his head slightly, into the shadows.

The place hadn't been burned. Left entirely alone, in fact. To the left was the eating area consisting of a small range, a few shelves, stacked tomato crates, and a square pine table. To the right were two sets of bunk beds and one lone cot.

There was a curled, yellow map of western New Mexico on the far wall, above the cot. On that wall as well as on the three others were a dozen sets of deer and elk antlers from which odds and ends of tack and leather leggings hung. A soiled, striped cream shirt drooped from a small spread of elk antlers behind the door, the shirt's cuffs frayed, its collar badly grimed. An empty, soft brown leather holster hung down from behind it.

Prophet stepped inside for a better look around. The place was neat, tin plates, cups, and silverware stacked in their respective tomato crates. A pyramid of airtight tins was on the stove's warming rack. The table was scrubbed, the cots and bunks carefully made, fluffed pillows propped at their ends, waiting. There was a thin coating of soot and dust over everything, but something told Prophet that the place had seen visitors since the Indian attack.

He set his rifle across the table, doffed his hat, and ran his hands wearily through his hair. It had been a long day and he knew his thinking would be less crowded tomorrow, but the question of where the Tawlin family had gone gnawed at him.

The gnawing was interrupted by a shrill scream.

Prophet jerked his head up, heart thudding, and stared through the darkening doorway and into the sandy light of the yard beyond.

"No!" Rose cried. "Oh, *nooooo!*"

Prophet clamped his hat back down on his head and grabbed his rifle. *Apaches!* He ran out the open bunkhouse door and followed Rose's continuing anguished cries — more sad than terrified — out around the main house, over a knoll, and across a wash that angled off away from the creek.

There in a hollow he found Rose on her

knees beside three graves sprouting crude wooden crosses. Rocks mounded the graves. On a slightly higher knoll beyond the graves was a large plank into which had been carved: PA, MA, BROTHER JASON. KILT BY INJUNS JULY 28, 1878.

Rose turned her face toward Prophet. The dying light caught her eyes and shone gold in her tears. "They're dead!"

Prophet stared, his heartbeat gradually slowing. He was as much surprised as he was heartsick for the girl, realizing what this meant to her.

"Now I'll never know," she said, pounding her fists against her thigh and curling her upper lip in anger.

Prophet didn't know what to say. His tongue lay heavy in his mouth, his rifle a lead weight in his hands.

Finally, he walked over to her, dropped to a knee beside her, slid his right arm around her shoulders, holding her closely against him. Sobs racked her.

"I must have survived it somehow. Or I wasn't here, found 'em later. And then I buried 'em."

She was only giving the words to Prophet's thoughts. It was the best explanation for who'd buried the Tawlins. It wasn't solid proof that the girl beside him was the daughter, Rose, who'd buried her family, but it certainly pointed in her direction.

Who else could she be? Utter thought she was Rose. Rose had lived here. Rose's family had been killed by Apaches, and a surviving family member had buried them.

But neither Prophet nor, most of all, the girl herself, would ever be satisfied until they were sure. Until they'd been given solid proof. Or until she'd gotten her memory back. Barring that, they needed a close neighbor, someone who'd seen Rose recently and recognized her without a doubt. Then she'd have her identity. Or at least she'd know her name and where she was from.

But what had she been doing in Nugget Town? That would still take some investigating. . . .

"My parents are dead," she said, running the heel of her hand across her nose and sniffing. "And I don't even feel sad. Just frustrated that they're not alive to tell me who I am."

"Easy, girl." Prophet gave her another affectionate squeeze. "Let's get you back to the bunkhouse. Gonna be dark as the inside of a glove out here soon."

"You know what I do feel?" she said when he'd gotten her to her feet.

She was no longer sobbing but only standing there, staring down at the graves dully, in shock, completely overcome by the situation in which she found herself.

"I feel alone." She shook her head slowly. "No memories, no name, not even any real sadness at finding my family dead. Just as alone as each one of those rocks piled on their graves."

Prophet squeezed her again and gently turned her. They started back toward the ranch yard, arm in arm, but as they started up a rise she pushed away from him and walked off several feet to his side.

She was silent, but her angst was almost palpable. When they got back to the yard, Prophet took the reins of his dun and began leading the horse to the corral off the barn's north wall.

"Why don't you go inside the bunkhouse? Start a fire in the stove. I'll tend to the horses."

The sun was almost down, silhouetting the western peaks in front of it. The barnyard was all dark purple shadows trimmed in shards of glassy salmon light.

"No, I'll help," she said with dull insistence and began leading her claybank along behind him.

Prophet, watching furtively, saw that she

unsaddled her horse in the same automatic manner as she'd saddled it, not having to give much thought to her actions. When she had the tack hanging over the corral, she carefully rubbed the mount down with a gunnysack, starting at the neck and withers and with purposeful, confident movements, worked her way back to the hips and rear cannons. She checked each hoof when she'd finished, plucking a pebble from the clay's right rear frog and tossing it over the back of the corral fence.

She'd obviously thrown stones before, as well as having tended horses. She had a smooth, boyish delivery.

Prophet had brought enough feed for both horses for one night, and when they'd fed each a half a bucket of parched corn, they headed into the bunkhouse where Prophet built a fire and filled his coffeepot with water from his canteen. Rose sat at the table, watching him though she appeared to have something on her mind.

When Prophet had set the coffeepot on the range, then opened the stove's door to add another stick of split mesquite to the fledgling fire, she folded her hands on the table and looked at him seriously, maybe a little challengingly. "I have a holster. I must have had a gun to go in it."

155

Prophet closed the stove door and straightened with a grunt, feeling the day's weariness deep in his knees. He went over to where his saddlebags were draped over a chair and opened one of the flaps. He pulled out the Colt Army revolver he'd found near her unconscious body, hefted it a couple of times in his hand, a pensive cast to his own gaze. He flipped the heavy gun, a .44, in the air, caught it by the barrel, and held it out to her.

"This what you're talking about?"

She took the gun, looked at it as though trying to nudge the cobwebs away from the secluded canyon of her hidden past. She gripped the gun in her right hand, hefting it some more, pursing her lips and frowning.

"Here." Prophet tossed a small leather pouch onto the table in front of her. "That was stuck behind your belt."

She frowned up at him for a moment, then set the gun on the table, opened the small flap on the pouch, and dumped onto the table a handful of paper cartridges, percussion caps, and nipples.

"Had a gun like that when I was in the war. Anyone who hadn't used a gun like that before would have a devil of a time loadin' it."

Prophet stood at the side of the table, his

hands resting on a chair back, as he watched in amazement as the girl picked up the gun and peered down its barrel as though to make sure there were no obstructions. Then she went to work as automatically and as purposefully as she had when she'd tended the claybank, biting the ends off six paper cartridges and smoothly loading them into the pistol's six cylinders. She drove the .44-caliber balls into place with the loading lever and crimped percussion caps on the nipples.

She set the loaded gun on the table and, resting her chin on the heel of her right hand, looked from Prophet to the pistol and back again. She appeared as surprised as he.

"I didn't even have to think about it. I just let my hands do what they wanted."

Prophet gave her a wry look, picked up the gun, and slipped the cylinder free of the barrel. He set the gun on the table and pocketed the cylinder. Rose continued to sit with her head in her hands, thoughtfully tapping the fingers of her other hand on the table.

The coffeepot hissed and spat, and Prophet went over and dropped a handful of ground beans into it. When it had boiled a minute, he poured in some cool water from his canteen to settle the grounds, then took the pot over to the table where he'd set out two cups.

"You drink coffee?"

"I reckon we'll find out."

Prophet tipped the pot over the cup on the table in front of Rose.

There was a dull, metallic thud. The coffeepot was flung out of Prophet's hands to smash the door of the range with a loud bang that partly covered Rose's shriek and the distant crack of a rifle.

12

Prophet had seen the gun flash out the cabin's open door. Now, ears ringing, his hand aching from the sudden tearing of the pot from his grasp, he looked down at Rose. She sat back in her chair, eyes wide in shock, not quite realizing that they'd been bushwhacked.

Prophet lunged forward and threw himself into the girl. They hit the floor with a loud thud, Prophet cushioning her fall with his own bulk and then rolling the girl beyond the open front doorway and into the bunk-house's sleeping quarters. He gave her a shove toward one of the bunks.

He and Rose had opened the other three windows to air the place out; now as two more rifles cracked outside the cabin, bullets screamed around inside, one apparently flying out an opposite window while the other slammed loudly into a kitchen wall, knocking last year's calendar off its nail.

Rose sat back against a bunk, eyes wide. "Holy shit!"

Prophet bolted off his heels, grabbed his Winchester off the table, and racked a shell into the chamber.

As three more shots hammered into the walls, another into the table, spraying splinters against the kindling crate, Prophet ran at a crouch to the front window left of the door. He rammed his right shoulder against the wall, holding back behind the frame as the shooter in the front yard triggered another round, which whistled six inches past the end of Prophet's nose and buried itself in an open shutter with a loud *thwack!* that made the entire room jump.

Rose clapped her hands over her ears and hissed.

Prophet snaked the gun out the window and fired three rounds quickly at where he'd last seen the front shooter's rifle flash. Through his own wafting powder smoke, he saw two bulky shadows moving around out there, between the corral and the house, but he couldn't tell if he'd hit anything.

A bullet fired from the rear of the cabin screamed through one of the two back windows and thudded into the wall above his head.

"Jesus!" Rose screamed and bolted to her feet.

"Stay down!" Prophet yelled.

Ignoring the order, the girl ran over to the first shutter, slammed it closed, and latched it. She ran to the next one and did the same. To give her a modicum of protection, Prophet fired out his own window and then out the one on the cabin's south end — hammering blasts that made the cabin leap and jounce beneath his boots, his empty shell casings clattering to the floor and rolling.

Two more bullets screeched through the bunkhouse, and Rose slid down the wall near the last shutter she'd closed, clapping her hands once more to her ears. "Who are they?"

"I don't know." Prophet fired three more quick rounds out the window left of the door and felt a twinge of satisfaction when he heard a distant, muffled groan. "Not Apaches."

"Apaches don't fight at night," Rose said. "Somehow, I remember that."

"Some do, some don't." Prophet quickly closed the shutter over the window he'd been shooting through, then ran past the open doorway. "But these are white men. Non-Injuns, anyway. I can tell by the way

161

they shoot." He fired two shots out the door, then kicked the door closed.

"How's that?"

"They're careless. Injuns take their time. They'd wait till we went outside to check the stock. Or they'd run the stock off to draw us out of the cabin."

Rose buried her head between her knees as more lead whined through the cabin and splinters sprayed across the table and floor. One slug clattered off an iron skillet hanging from a ceiling joist.

Prophet sank down against the front wall, quickly thumbing fresh .44 cartridges from his shell belt. "These fellas are right angry. All this quick shootin' after dark . . ."

"What do you suppose they're mad about?"

There was a momentary lull in the shooting.

"I don't know." Prophet was thumbing cartridges into his Winchester's breech. He turned his head toward one of the two open windows — the one on the cabin's far end. "What the hell you fellas so sore about? If we crossed you, we shore didn't mean it!"

"What's that?" a man yelled from the front.

Prophet turned to yell out the front window right of the door. "I said we didn't

162

mean to rub your fur in the wrong direction! Must be a misunderstandin' here! Maybe we oughta talk about it!"

"Talk about this, you claim-jumpin' son of a bitch!" shouted a man from the cabin's south end.

Two bullets hammered the shutter over the south window.

"Claim jumpers?" Prophet said to himself.

Still hunkered low against the east wall, arms wrapped around her knees, Rose looked at him curiously.

"They must have taken advantage of the Apache attack to jump Tawlin's claim."

One of the men out front laughed. The laughter was drowned by a barrage of gunfire from the cabin's three sides. Two in front. One on both the south and west side.

Prophet dropped low beside the front window, thinking it over while more slugs hammered the shutters and walls. No telling how much ammo the claim jumpers had. By the way they were going through it, they were either cow stupid or they had enough to throw away.

On the other hand, Prophet had only half a cartridge belt's worth, plus a single box in his saddlebags. Not enough to hold these lobos off for long.

He probably wouldn't have a chance to

cap even half his own arsenal before the claim jumpers moved up on the cabin and tried to burn him and Rose out. That could easily be done, as the pole-and-thatch roof would catch the smallest spark and go up virtually like dynamite.

And, judging from the angry gun blasts that were causing dirt to sift from the rafters and which had Rose clamping her ears shut again, head between her knees, these claim jumpers wouldn't stop shooting long enough to listen to reason. Being greedy privy snipes themselves, they wouldn't even consider the idea that Prophet and Rose might be here on a legitimate mission.

Prophet had to make a move.

Quickly, wincing as two slugs screamed off the lip of the windowsill, Prophet reached up and rammed the shutter closed with his rifle barrel. Just as quickly, he dropped the steel hook over its rusty nail, latching it.

"You keep down and don't lift your head till I tell you it's all clear," he told Rose, crawling across the width of the kitchen to the back window just right of the girl.

"What're you going to do?" she yelled above the din.

"I'm gonna go outside."

"What?"

"Just do as I tell you."

"At least give me my gun so I can protect myself. You're liable to get greased out there!"

Prophet looked at her, his brows ridged. She had a point. He straightened just enough to grab the pistol off the table. When he'd slipped the cylinder back into place and made sure that all the nipples were still capped, he handed her the weapon butt first.

"Thanks," Rose said dryly.

"All right." Prophet reached up to unlatch the window in the kitchen's rear wall. "Just don't shoot *me* with the damn thing."

"Do I have cause? I wouldn't remember."

Prophet gave a rusty chuff and slid the shutter back against the wall with his rifle barrel and lifted his head above the sill just far enough to see out into the stygian night. There was a rifle flash back there, but the slug hammered the shutter to his right.

He waited a few seconds, and when the shooter behind the cabin continued firing at the other shutter, apparently not having seen this one open up, Prophet rose to his feet and scrambled through the window, first one leg and then the other but moving so quickly that he got his spur caught on the sill and hit the ground on the back of his head.

Stars wheeled in his vision, and his neck ached.

Suddenly the rifleman firing from about thirty yards out sent a slug drilling the cabin wall over Prophet's head. He must have seen the bounty hunter drop out of the window. Trying to ignore the bite of pain in his neck and the duller throb in the back of his head, Prophet gained a knee quickly and slammed his rifle butt to his shoulder. The shooter's rifle blossomed. The slug slammed into the cabin left of Prophet, who squeezed his own Winchester's trigger.

A yowl. The thud of a dropped rifle.

Prophet quickly ejected the spent shell casing and seated fresh in the Winchester's chamber as he took off running toward where he'd last seen the shooter's rifle flash. By starlight he avoided rocks and low junipers and cedars, and found the claim jumper down on his back and holding one knee that glistened brightly. He groaned and cursed, and as Prophet ran up he released his knee and reached for a sidearm.

Prophet stopped and fired twice from the hip, his first shot puffing dust just above the claim jumper's head. The other snapped the man's head back against the ground, and all his limbs fell slack at once.

Prophet froze, listening. There was one more rifle report from the ranch yard, then silence. The man beyond the cabin's south end had been yelling, and now Prophet realized the man had been yelling for the others to stop shooting.

He could sense the other three claim jumpers' confusion. There hadn't been any shots fired from the cabin in the past few minutes. The man south of the cabin had probably heard the dead man's yelp when Prophet had drilled his knee.

"Channing?" someone yelled. The voice was clear in the sudden silence after the fusillade. He was somewhere in the brush south of the cabin.

Prophet dropped to a knee, looking around and caressing his Winchester's hammer with his thumb.

"Hey, Boyle!" the man south of the cabin yelled. "I think the claim-jumpin' son of a bitch drilled Channing. I think he's out there. Seen somethin' move out from the back of the cabin."

"You sure?" yelled a man from the front yard.

A tendril of an idea wriggled in Prophet's brain. He cupped a gloved hand over his mouth to muffle and disguise his voice. "It's Channing! I'm hit!"

Silence.

A shred of a breeze touched the limbs of a near cedar, rustling them gently.

"Channing?" came the faintly skeptical call south of the cabin. "That you?"

"I'm hit!" Prophet shouted into his cupped hand, adding a pinched groan. "But I got the son of a bitch!"

Either they'd buy it or they wouldn't. He didn't have much to lose. He was outnumbered, he had the girl to think about, and it was only a matter of time before they either blasted or burned her out of the bunkhouse.

Boyle yelled, "He dead?"

"Yep. Ah, damn — I'm hit bad!" he added, pinching his voice down even tighter.

"Karl, check it out," Boyle ordered. "We'll meet you over there."

He'd let it go at that. Let the others come around and see what was happening. . . .

Scrambling around behind a cedar just beyond Channing, he dropped to a knee and waited, slowly, absently slipping cartridges through his Winchester's loading gate, then freeing the keeper thong from over his Colt's hammer.

He thought about Rose. Did she realize he was trying a ruse? If not, she might try and slip out of the cabin.

Prophet pricked his ears, listening. In the

distance, coyotes yipped and yammered. Faintly, footsteps sounded. They grew gradually louder south of the bunkhouse. Prophet could hear Karl's strained breaths, heard him spit as he continued walking in Prophet's direction.

Nearby, a twig snapped. Prophet stayed low, trying to see the newcomer through the cedar, but the branches were too thick.

Karl's voice sounded clear and crisp, only a few feet away. "Channing?"

Prophet bolted out from behind the cedar, bringing his Winchester up tight against his shoulder. "Nah, Channing done bought one from the claim jumper."

Prophet thought the man might freeze when he saw the bounty hunter's rifle bearing down on him. He did the opposite, raising his own rifle quickly.

Prophet's rifle leaped and roared, its flash in the dark night for a quarter second casting an eerie red glow over the back-flat body of Channing and over the patch-bearded Karl, who jerked as though he'd been punched in the chest. Karl's own rifle thundered, blowing up dirt and gravel near his boots, and then Karl twisted around, staggering as he tried to run, tripped over his own feet, and fell in a heap.

Knowing his own rifle shot had betrayed

his position, Prophet lurched to his right. A gun flashed from the direction of the cabin, and the shooter's loud curse reached the bounty hunter with the rifle's resonating bark.

Prophet was momentarily blinded by the bright flash, but he fired three quick rounds from his hip and heard the heavy thud of a body falling against the bunkhouse.

"Oh," the man said, wheezing. "Oh, for . . . chrissakes . . ."

The metallic clatter of a rifle hitting the ground. The softer ching of a spur rowel being dragged across gravel. A man's hoarse, anguished sob.

"You kilt me, you son of a bitch!"

Prophet racked a fresh shell into his Winchester's breech, then stepped back to the left, knowing there was another bush-whacker out here somewhere. He jerked the rifle in his hands with a start when he heard the loud wooden thud of a boot heel against a solid wooden door.

The fourth man was busting into the cabin!

Prophet bolted forward, shouting, "Rose!"

He hadn't taken three steps before he heard the muffled pop of a pistol. He kept running as two more pops sounded from inside the bunkhouse. There was a fourth from the front yard. Prophet ran around the cabin's front corner and stopped.

A tall man stood about ten feet in front of the bunkhouse's open front door. Rose's slender, shadowy figure stood just outside the door, starlight flashing off the gun in her outstretched right hand as well as off the thick powder smoke wafting around her head.

The tall man was teetering back on his heels. He held both arms down by his sides and slightly out from his hips as though to help him maintain his balance. In his own right hand he held a rifle, the barrel aimed at the ground. His hat lay on the ground behind him.

He staggered backward — a quick, heavy step, making his spurs ring. He stepped on his hat, flattening the crown.

Haltingly, in a deep voice, he said, "A girl?"

"What's that?" Rose said.

"A girl done killed me?"

Rose thumbed the revolver's hammer back with a loud, ratcheting click.

"You got that right," she said tonelessly and pulled the trigger.

13

Louisa took a swig from her root beer soda pop, set the bottle on the table, then plucked a .45 cartridge off the neckerchief she'd spread on the table before her, beside her castaway supper plate, and slipped the cartridge into the wheel of her pearl-gripped Colt.

She spun the cylinder and, holding the gun up to her right ear, enjoyed the smooth, heavy clicking sounds of the recently cleaned and oiled weapon.

"Good Lord, young lady! What in tarnation do you intend to do with that thing?"

Louisa looked up to see the chubby woman who ran the Bear Paw Cafe staring down at her, one pink fist planted on the woman's broad, apron-clad hip.

"Whatever I have to do, Mrs. Haggelthorpe." Louisa set the pistol on the table and picked up its twin. "Whatever I *have* to do."

She gave the cylinder of that freshly cleaned and loaded revolver a spin. Her hazel eyes acquired a slightly dreamy look as she enjoyed the fluid, snakelike hiss. Her guns had never misfired on her, and as long as she kept them clean and running as smooth as Swiss watches, they never would.

She'd seen for herself what happened to those who did not conscientiously tend the instruments of their trades. They were moldering in shallow graves with Louisa's own lead in them.

Mrs. Haggelthorpe gave a disapproving chuff. "Why don't you get shed of that crazy bounty-hunting profession? Not to mention that Prophet devil and his sawed-off shotgun. Him and that consarned trade are gonna get you killed, you pretty young thing!"

Louisa looked up curiously at the round-faced woman.

"Yeah, I know Lou Prophet," Mrs. Haggelthorpe said. "Back before I married Harry, I, too, was in a less-than-respectable profession. Worked the cow towns for a time. Hays and Dodge City and the like. Omaha and Council Bluffs. Ran into that big crooked-nosed bounty man a time or two — the old sinner. Oh, we never did any business, but I know him to see him."

She shook her head sadly. "Death dealer, that's what he is. And everyone knows he sold his soul to the Devil after the war."

"I prefer to see Lou, as well as myself," Louisa said, "as justice dealers."

"Call it what you want. It all means kickin' men out with cold shovels. And an early death for yourself, Miss Louisa. I tell you what — I could use an extra girl around here. Twenty-five cents a day plus tips. With a figure like yours, you'll be shovelin' it from a buckboard wagon into the bank vault!"

Louisa plucked a silver dollar from a pocket of her serape, and flipped it into the air. Mrs. Haggelthorpe gasped with surprise when she saw the coin and reached out to grab it against her bosom with her pink, fleshy fist.

"Obliged for the offer," Louisa said, rising and holstering her six-shooters. "But I reckon I've been summoned by a higher purpose."

"You'll be sorry, young lady."

Louisa grabbed her neckerchief off the table and, knotting it around her neck, headed out the small, nearly deserted cafe's front door and onto the narrow porch beyond. A slight, stooped male figure was angling toward the cafe from the other side of the street, a badge flashing on the man's denim jacket. A cigarette smoldered beneath the battered Stetson sitting crooked on Deputy Ivano Rubriz's gray head. The man's gray mustache fairly glowed in the starlit darkness.

As the man approached the porch, he looked up to see Louisa and stopped, removing the cigarette from his lips, holding it between his left index and forefinger. In his other hand was a Spencer repeating rifle. On his hip he wore an old Schofield revolver.

"Who's watching the prisoner?" Louisa asked him.

Rubriz studied Louisa for a moment, flicking ashes from his cornhusk quirley. "Marshal Utter. Who else, senorita?"

"The man's confined to a wheelchair."

"*Si.* But he's hell with a double-bore!"

Rubriz chuckled, then mounted the steps and walked past Louisa as he stuck his head through the café door. He did not go inside the eaterie but only inquired, "Everything all right in here this evening, Senora Haggelthorpe?"

"As good as can be expected, Ivano," Mrs. Haggelthorpe called above the clatter of dishes. "Coffee?"

"Later. *Buenas noches,* senora."

"You have a good one, too, Ivano. See ya later!"

Louisa stood in the side street the cafe was on, staring toward Brush Street and the marshal's office and jailhouse, where a dull yellow light shone in both front windows. Rubriz walked down the porch steps to stand beside her, puffing his quirley with one hand while holding his rifle with the other.

"Do not worry, senorita. Even without the use of his legs, Marshal Utter is twice the man of most. He will not allow your prisoner to escape."

"Are you saying you don't think I oughta wander over and offer my prisoner-watching services?"

Rubriz puffed the quirley, his shoulders jerking slightly though his chuckles were silent. He turned and moved off along the street with his limping stride, his boot scuffs dwindling gradually in the quiet night.

Louisa decided to head on over to the hotel. She likely wouldn't sleep. Why was it she had so much trouble sleeping when Prophet wasn't around? For some reason, his absence left a vacuum inside her. Not quite a vacuum, but an emptiness populated only by the occasional, faint but persistent cries of her dying family.

■ ■ ■ ■

"Hey, Utter," Blanco said. "How 'bout you get us a couple whores in here? I'll buy."

Chuckling, Marshal Utter reached into the wood box for a stick of pinyon, and, with his free hand, wheeled himself over to the stove, the hot door of which he opened with a leather swatch, then stuffed the firewood inside.

"Blanco, you done got your rocks off for the last time. No more tail for you, my friend. Unless there's tail in hell, and I doubt ole Lucifer offers such accommodations as that."

"You're the one goin' to a fuckless hell." Blanco stared through the bars of his cage in the jailhouse wall's right rear corner. He took a drag off his cigarette and blew a smoke ring, narrowing his gray eyes with evil glee. "Me, I'll be back in town here by Saturday night, visiting the girls at Miss Flora's Corazon House, or them purty *putas* on Bayonet Wash."

"You keep dreamin', Blanco," Utter said, rolling his wheelchair up to his desk, off of which he grabbed his double-bore barn blaster. "That's what you're good at."

Utter breeched the gun, made sure there

was a wad in each barrel, then snapped it back together with a loud click that echoed off the wainscoted, green-painted walls of the wood-frame building.

"If you get me a whore for tonight, give us fifteen minutes alone to do what comes natural, Marshal" — Blanco blew another smoke ring — "I'll have my pa go easy on ya. Maybe just take the wheels of your chair, leave you howlin' like a mad lobo out on Brush Street."

Wheeling himself toward the front door, his shotgun laid across his skinny, useless thighs, Utter glared over his shoulder at the outlaw.

"Hey," Blanco said, "it's better than lettin' him hang ya from your own porch roof. You and that greasy bean eater, Rubriz. Side by side for all eternity."

Another smoke ring came sailing out between the bars. Blanco lowered his head slightly to stare through the ever-widening and slowly dissipating smoke circle at Marshal Utter, who ground his dentures and dimpled his jaws with fury.

"Like I said, Blanco." Utter threw open the front door. "You just keep dreamin'."

"Fetch me a whore, you crippled old bastard!" Blanco shouted as Utter wheeled himself over the threshold and onto the jailhouse's dark front porch.

Utter threw his arm back into the office, loosing his loud, mocking guffaws at Blanco glaring at him through the cell's bars, and pulled the office door closed behind him. As he rolled his wheelchair out to the front of the porch, he could hear Blanco cursing him.

Blanco continued to curse him until the outlaw was nearly hoarse, and then the tirade died and there was only the sounds of the distant coyotes, the crickets, an occasional breeze shepherding a tumbleweed across Brush Street, and the quiet, midweek strains of a mariachi band emanating from the south. The charros would be sipping tequila and bacanora to the strains of the fiddle and mandolin while they awaited their turns with Senorita Loretta upstairs, or with the new girl that Hector Domingo claimed to have brought in from New Orleans.

She was a mulatto, some said. Utter couldn't attest to that, for he hadn't yet seen the girl. Hector kept his girls close to his smoky little adobe-brick cantina on the bank of Bayonet Wash so they couldn't be lured away by some gringo cowboy who'd suddenly acquired a sizable stake for himself after an all-night stud game. That had happened to Hector before, and the girl had been found, stumbling around in the foot-hills of the No-Waters, clothes in tatters, dying of thirst and starvation.

And she hadn't been worth a dime after that.

Utter gave a rueful chuff at his bored mus-ings. Sometimes, he thought that he and Ivano should have continued to ride the op-posite side of the law, steered clear of towns like Corazon, swung wide of so-called civilization. But for some reason — no, he knew the reason: old age and fear — he and Rubriz had decided, well over a decade ago, to try to acquire a little respectability before they saddled a cloud and rode to the great robbers' roost in the sky. Gun work had been all they'd known, though Utter had once, a long, long time ago, worked as a packer for the army, so they'd sort of naturally drifted into the badge-toting busi-ness, hesitating only briefly when Corazon's town council had offered them the local lawdogging jobs.

They'd been damn good at it, too. Before Rubriz had gotten old and arthritic and Ut-ter had gotten himself backshot by rustlers. He'd outstayed his abilities; he should have heard those long-loopers sneaking up be-hind him, but his hearing had gone the way

180

of his eyesight and his pecker.

He wasn't worth a damn anymore. The trouble was neither he nor Ivano had built a stake to retire on. So they either continued in their chosen professions or took to milling around the saloons with their hands out, maybe living with the whores in their falling-down cribs on Bayonet Wash. Or in the dry wash itself, where Utter had stumbled upon more than one useless old-timer who'd gone there to drink himself into eternity.

Used up, he might be . . .

Utter scowled out into the night and caressed his old Greener's hammers with his thumb.

. . . But he'd be damned on a tall horse if he'd let "Man-Killin' " Sam Metalious break his son out of Utter's jail. He had a history with that wild-eyed old lobo — it was likely Metalious's riders who'd shot Utter, though he had no solid proof of that. He wouldn't let the man get the best of him again. His legs might be as useless as Chinese noodles, but he still had his Greener, and he'd like nothing better than to use it to blast "Man-Killin' " Sam and his son into the next world.

Hoof clomps jerked Utter from his reverie, and he looked to his right where four riders cantered into town from the northwest.

Utter tightened his hand around the neck of his shotgun and leaned forward in his chair a little to get a better look at the newcomers. They passed a saloon on the other side of the street, whose reflector oil lamps dimly illuminated their faces — four riders off Burl Farmington's ranch only a couple miles from town. Harmless thirty-a-month-and-found punchers in billowy neckerchiefs, undershot boots, battered hats, and fringed chaps.

They'd get pie-eyed a few times a year in Corazon, might even break a window or each other's jaws, but they were harmless enough and brought good business to the Tumbleweed, the favorite watering hole of area drovers at the far south end of Brush Street.

None of them looked at Utter as they passed the jailhouse. They were a quiet, bashful lot, like most punchers, and when they'd disappeared around the dogleg in Brush Street a couple blocks south, Utter sat back in his chair and blew a heavy sigh.

He jerked his gaze back south. The four Farmington riders had disappeared, but three more riders appeared, trotting out of the dogleg and coming on toward the jail-house. They rode straight-backed in their saddles, and though Utter couldn't see their faces in the darkness, he could tell that their hat brims were aimed in his direction.

His heart quickened, and he wrapped both hands around the Greener in his lap. Metalious's men? Awfully soon. Utter had expected Sam to make him and Rubriz sweat awhile. He'd also expected that when the time came for Sam to send men for Blanco, old "Man-Killin'" Sam would be leading the pack himself.

That they were Metalious's men was obvious, however, when Utter saw the Metalious Triple 6 brands blazed into the withers of the three horses that were checked down in front of the jailhouse and turned toward the porch atop which Utter sat his rickety old chair. Utter frowned, befuddled, wary, and shifted his gaze around to see if others would soon join this first three. Maybe Sam himself would come storming in from the north, eyes afire.

"Evenin', Marshal," said the tall, lanky man who sat in the middle of the three-man pack and whom Utter knew to be Dwight Beaudry — Metalious's *segundo*. He had no proof, but a sixth or seventh sense had told him that it was Beaudry's bullets lying snug as ticks on a dog up close to Utter's spine.

Raw fury blazed in the marshal.

"Mornin', Dwight." Snarling, Utter raised his Greener, making his chair creak beneath his considerable girth. "You come to get your ugly fuckin' head blowed off, did you?"

14

"Take it easy with that thing, Utter," Dwight Beaudry warned, glowering out from beneath the broad, flat brim of his brown Stetson. "Less'n you want me to take it away from you and trigger it up your fat, old, crippled ass."

The man sitting a dapple gray to Beaudry's left smiled. The man sitting a grulla to Beaudry's right kept his hard, chocolate-dark eyes on Utter, maintaining a firm rein on his mount that had suddenly started chewing its bit. Utter knew neither of these two, only Beaudry.

Gunslicks came and went from "Man-Killin' " Sam Metalious's so-called ranch.

With a loud, ratcheting click, Utter rocked back his barn blaster's left hammer, then its right. "Why don't you just climb down off that pinto and try it, Dwight!"

"Don't talk that way to me, Utter." Beaudry's jaws were set, his lips forming a

185

straight slash beneath his thick dragoon mustache. "Your old popper there means nothin' to me. I could drill you right now before you even got them barrels raised."

Behind the three Metalious riders, gravel crunched under a stealthy foot. At nearly the same time, a rifle was cocked, the rasp of the lever action echoing suddenly and loudly around that end of Brush Street.

Ivano Rubriz stepped into the light from the shadows on the street's other side. The drab illumination of the jailhouse lights as well as the near saloon's oil lamps slid across his leathery cheeks and danced in his trimmed gray mustache, casting deep shadows against the lee side of his long, straight nose.

Rubriz stood there, not saying anything, resting the rifle barrel negligently across his right forearm, his eroded, nut-brown face as expressionless as limestone.

Utter felt his cheeks roll up slightly in a satisfied half smile. He'd figured Rubriz would note the riders. The man was old, but his senses were still as keen as those of an old brush wolf that had long outrun its enemies and was still, for the time being, staying one step ahead of the crows.

Beaudry and the others glanced over their shoulders at the old mestizo, their faces

186

tightening with chagrin.

"Ain't much fun getting flanked, is it, Beaudry?" Utter said. "At least he didn't shoot you in the back. Not yet."

Beaudry stared long and hard at Utter over his pinto's twitching ears. "We come to talk civil-like, Marshal. We come to get Blanco out of jail real peaceable. You know we could do it the hard way. Sam don't see no point in that."

Utter's grim smiled faded. He felt another surge of hot fury work its way up from his tailbone to the back of his neck.

Metalious had so little respect for his and Rubriz's abilities that he hadn't even come himself to spring his worthless, murdering son. He's sent his number one and a couple of lackeys who'd likely honed their shooting skills in the Nations or out on the Llano Estacado. Metalious thought Utter would scare or, worse, listen to Metalious's own brand of twisted reason. That Utter would see the futility in holding the killer against a certain insurmountable onslaught and, ignoring the badge pinned to his vest as well as his own self-respect, toss Beaudry the keys.

He'd sit back in his chair and watch Blanco walk.

Utter swallowed the hot, tight knot in his

throat. He didn't know which was worse — having only three men sent to talk him out of his prisoner, or having all dozen or so of Metalious's riders gallop in with guns popping like firecrackers on Cinco de Mayo.

Utter spat to one side. "You go on back to the Triple 6 and tell your boss that his son's goin' in front of the judge. He *deserves* to go in front of the judge. And then he deserves to hang. His boys killed innocent citizens here in Corazon, including a little boy." He waved the shotgun menacingly. "Go on and tell him that, and stop wastin' my time with this nonsense about turnin' a cold-blooded killer free on the world. I ain't got the use of my legs no more, but I'm still the law, by god. And as long as me and Ivano's the law here in Corazon, no killers'll be walkin' free from our jail."

"Ah, shit." Beaudry shook his head and cast dark glances to the men on either side of him.

"What do you want to do, Boss?" asked the man to his left.

Beaudry glanced over his shoulder at Rubriz. The old deputy stood as before, holding his Spencer carbine across his forearm, bowed legs and mule-eared boots spread a little more than shoulder-width apart.

Beaudry looked at Utter but addressed

his men coldly, with obvious threat to the two aging lawmen. "I reckon we go on back to the Triple 6 and tell Mr. Metalious these two old fossils just will not listen to reason."

Beaudry's horse jerked its head up, trying to toss its bit. Its rider checked it down angrily and, keeping his dark gaze on Utter, swung the mount around and booted it back hard in the direction from which he'd come. The other two riders followed suit, both glancing with black menace at the two lawmen watching them go.

The three galloped back around the dogleg and out of sight, the thuds of their horses quickly being replaced by the strains of a banjo and a woman singing softly in Spanish while, on the east side of town, a dog barked and a baby cried.

Utter turned his own bleak gaze on Rubriz, who stepped forward, cradling his rifle in his arms.

"You finish your rounds?" Utter asked his deputy.

"*Si.* The first one. Maybe I better walk around some more, uh? They might swing back."

"Yeah, I reckon. You want a cup of coffee first?"

Rubriz shook his head and turned eastward. "Senora Haggelthorpe has provided two cups already. And Senora Evelyn will offer another." He looked sidelong at Utter and gave a little stress-relieving grin. "She puts molasses in it."

Utter looked off up the street once more, where the dust of the three riders was still sifting like a thin, tan curtain in the darkness. "Yeah, you go have your coffee with Senora Evelyn. But you watch your back out there. I don't trust that Beaudry as far as I could throw him uphill in a stiff Texas wind."

"*Si, si.* If they come around from the north, signal me with a pistol shot. I will come running."

"Ah, shit, Ivano," Utter laughed overloud, "you haven't run a lick in thirty years, and that was when that Don Lopez-Vargas from Monterrey caught you with his daughter's fancy festival basque pulled up to her chin. Ha! Remember that?"

"How could I not remember?" Rubriz said, showing his large, yellow teeth beneath his mustache. "I left a good Allen and Wheelock rifle behind when I ran."

The two laughed for a time, and then Rubriz drifted off up Brush Street, his thin, bandy-legged figure dwindling almost silently in the lantern-slanted shadows. He did not wear spurs when making his night rounds. Utter wheeled himself back into the office for a cup of coffee.

Blanco was grinning at him through the bars of his cell door. "Don't worry, Utter. They'll be back. With my pa, most likely. And he ain't gonna like to be called off the ranch on a fool errand like this."

"*Fool's* errand," Utter chuckled as he splashed coffee into his chipped stone mug. "I'll say it is at that."

"That's real funny, Sheriff," Blanco said, sagging down onto the edge of his cot. "You go ahead and have you a last good laugh."

Utter chuckled again, then, sitting near the stove with his shotgun across his legs, facing his desk, he blew ripples on the surface of the piping hot brew and sipped. In the distance, a rifle cracked. Utter tipped the coffee mug up with a start, burning his lips, then jerked it back down, grimacing, his pulse quickening.

Two more shots fired quickly, angrily.

Blanco's cot squawked as he rose and came back to the cell door, squeezing two bars in his fists, his gray-yellow eyes alive with mockery in his wax-pale face. "What the hell you suppose that's all about, Sheriff?"

The outlaw fingered the whiskers that

hung like cream threads from his pointed chin.

"Don't know."

Utter leaned far to his right to set his cup down on the edge of his desk, then wheeled himself around toward the door, which he'd left open a foot so he could open it all the easier when he returned to the porch, which he did now in a hurry, leaving the door open behind him.

He'd just gotten his big back wheels over the door jam when a scream rose over the dark town. A man's scream. A scream of bald terror and fury.

There it came again, pinched at the end, as though the man were struggling for his life.

The rifle barked again, louder now that Utter was outside. It came from a few blocks to the south and west, likely near Bayonet Wash, which had been where Ivano had been heading when Utter had last seen him.

A man laughed. It was a victorious howl, like those you could hear on Friday nights after the cowhands had been paid or during a rodeo and one of the punchers was riding that big seed bull of Denny Lomax's into a hefty payoff.

A horse whinnied and there was the loud

scuff of shod hooves before another laugh and then, seconds later, a groan.

Utter's heart raced. Leaving his shotgun across his legs, he grabbed the rope that hung down the post on the right side of the steps and used it to ease himself and his chair down the ramp to the street.

"Ivano?" he called, hearing the brittle fear in his own voice.

Working hard and panting with the effort, he wheeled himself through the ground dirt and dung of Brush Street, heading south down the middle of the rutted drag. By the time he'd gone two blocks and was heading around the dogleg, he was out of breath and his arms were on fire.

He cursed Beaudry and the bullets in his back that could not be removed without killing him, and ground his teeth and kept going.

Five minutes later, he'd wheeled himself down the Bayonet Wash trail and put a couple of hog pens behind him and saw the flares burning from their wooden brackets at the front of two adobe-brick cantinas that were suddenly eerily quiet even for a weeknight. The big cottonwood flanking the two Mexican watering holes churned in the night breeze, the bending branches jostling their leaves amongst the high, white stars.

A groaning, rasping sound came from the shadows on the street's left side where several whores' cribs hunched in the ironwood and yucca. Utter, continuing to wheel himself along the track, had just made out an elongated figure in the shadows of one of the cribs when someone appeared from the darkness ahead of him, running toward him.

The woman's loose, black wrap flapped like bats' wings and her black-and-red silk skirts billowed about her legs, jewelry flashing in the starlight, long, black hair bouncing about her shoulders.

"Ivano!" Senora Evelyn screamed, her sandals slapping her feet as she angled toward the crib from which Utter had seen the figure. Her voice warbled and cracked as she screamed again, "Oh, Ivano! What did they *do* to you?"

Utter increased his speed though his arms felt like lead. His heart pounded in his temples as the woman dropped to her knees in the shadows before the crib and gave a heart-twisting shriek of horror mixed with sorrow. *"Ivano!"*

"Oh, Christ," Utter heard himself say as he stopped the wheelchair near the woman. "Oh, goddamn them to holy hell!"

He tried to push himself up in his chair,

to make his legs work in spite of the bullets that had mostly paralyzed him. Finally, when he was on the verge of fainting, he let his bulk sag back down in the rawhide seat. Breathing hard, his heart hammering in his tight chest, he stared up in horror at Ivano Rubriz, who was still twitching, lips stretched back from his teeth, as he hung from the stout beam protruding from the side of the crib and from the end of which dangled an unlit lantern.

Ivano's neck hung at a grisly angle, pushed askew by the heavy hangman's knot that bulged above his left shoulder. His eyes were open, dimly reflecting the light from the cantinas across the street. Blood glistened from his upper right chest and his lower left side. Only his right foot twitched now as he turned gently toward the crib, as though embarrassed by his predicament and no longer able to bear the gaze of his old friend and partner.

As Senora Evelyn sobbed on her knees near Ivano's dusty boots, her head down, hands on her thighs, Utter jerked his head toward the cantinas that sat side by side beneath the sprawling, gently churning cottonwood. Several dark figures stood there in the silent shadows, smoking.

"For chrissakes, a couple of you get over

here and cut him down!"

The figures continued to smoke in the shadows. Two turned slowly and, coals of their cigarettes or cigars glowing dully, strode through the cantina's arched doorway from which no music issued as it had a short while before. Only silence. One lone, short figure, partially hidden by a stout arch support, remained leaning against the cantina's front wall, a sombrero tipped lower over his eyes.

Utter cursed again. He saw where Beaudry had tied off the end of the hang rope to the bottom of a post that held up the straw roof of the crib's porch. He wheeled himself past Senora Evelyn's slumped, quaking figure, and stopped beside the post, grunting as he shoved a hand into a pants pocket for his folding knife.

Hoof thuds and victorious whoops rose from the direction of the marshal's office. Utter, who'd just fished the knife from his pocket, turned his exasperated stare toward Brush Street.

"Those bastards," he muttered as the yowls and celebratory shouts continued to rise in the quiet night over which the stars glowed and winked like jewels at the bottom of a vast, inverted bowl.

"Here." Utter tossed the knife in the dirt

near Senora Evelyn's knees. "Cut him down."

Ivano was dead. There was no helping his deputy, his friend, now. The bullet wounds alone would have killed him. Maybe Utter could pump some double-ought buck into Beaudry before he and his men rode out of town with Blanco.

Utter wheeled himself back in the direction from which he'd come. He'd thought he'd expended the last of his energy, but from somewhere he summoned enough to get him back to the corner of Brush Street in time to see three figures step away from three horses in the street fronting the marshal's office. Beaudry and his two hands moved negligently up the jail office steps, laughing, spurs ringing loudly.

"You think so, do you, you son of a raging syphilitic whore?" Utter growled as he continued wheeling himself toward the office from which laughter continued to issue.

The jail office door clicked, the hinges squawked. A wedge of yellow light spilled onto the front porch.

The three shadowy figures stopped in the wedge of light, all three jerking their hands to their holstered revolvers, startled.

Sharp light flashed inside the jailhouse, and the reports of the hastily fired pistol reached Utter's ears about a sixth of a second after he saw each of the three flashes. Beaudry and the other two men screamed as the slugs fired from inside the jailhouse punched them back off the porch, down the steps, and into the street where they fell in heaps, frightening their three ground-tied mounts.

Utter wheeled himself at an angle across Brush Street, blowing out his cheeks as his breath rasped in an out of his old, ragged lungs. Sweat streaked his pocked, fleshy cheeks. Before him, Beaudry lay belly down in the dirt, bending one leg in agony as he groaned. Blood darkened the dirt beneath the Triple 6 *segundo*'s chest and belly.

"Goddamn crazy bitch!" Blanco Metalious shouted from inside the jailhouse, spitting as though relieving himself of a gag.

Utter stopped his wheelchair as Beaudry gave his last grunt and died. The marshal looked toward the jailhouse door. A blond-headed silhouette moved through the doorway and down the steps, taking long, measured strides. A wool skirt swished about long, supple legs.

Louisa Bonaventure stopped at the bottom of the porch steps, the pearl butts of her twin Colts glowing in their cross-draw holsters on her hips. She kicked one of the men over on his back, and the light from the jailhouse's open door caught the blood issuing from the quarter-sized hole in his forehead.

"No offense, Marshal." Louisa lifted her hand to adjust the angle of her hat on her head. "I thought you could use some help, that's all."

She turned and walked away in the darkness.

15

Prophet had finished dragging his latest set of dead owlhoots off into the scrub and was vaguely awaiting the inevitable carrion eaters when boots crunched outside the bunkhouse's open door.

"Rose," the girl announced herself softly.

Standing at the table, Prophet was closing the flap on one of his saddlebag pouches. The girl stood in the open doorway, looking gaunt. She'd started to help him drag the bodies away but then, gagging, she'd stumbled off in the brush.

He'd heard her out there, violently retching.

"You don't look so good. I'll get some more coffee goin', soon as we get settled in."

"We're not staying here?"

Prophet shook his head. "Best not. Never know what the shootin' will attract, and I reckon we could both do with a good night's sleep. I spied a low ridge over yonder. Probably be good cover there. Don't look like rain or nothin'."

The girl sniffed as she ambled into the shack and placed a hand over her belly. "Sorry about that."

"It's all right." Prophet hefted his saddlebags over a shoulder. "I was getting worried, seein' how easy it was for you to shoot that claim-jumpin' scalawag. Not that he didn't deserve it. But I reckon it wasn't so easy, after all."

"Maybe it means I've never done it before." Standing near where she'd piled her gear on a top bunk, she placed a hand on the cap-and-ball hogleg riding in the holster on her right hip. "But it don't mean I didn't ride with Blanco's bunch."

"Ah, hell, you ain't a bad sort, Rose. I can tell." Prophet walked over and wrapped an arm around her shoulders, pulled her toward him gently. "You had you a good reason for being in Nugget Town. And most likely you got a good reason for carryin' that old horse pistol and bein' right handy with it. Look at Louisa. That girl's pure hell with the fires out, but if she knows a man's bad, she'll kill him as like to bid him howdy-do."

Rose smiled up at him. Some of the color was beginning to return to her cheeks.

201

"Thanks, Lou. I reckon I'd know if I was bad, wouldn't I? I'd feel bad, rotten inside. And I don't." She grabbed her saddlebags and bedroll from off the bunk. "I wonder if I'll ever know for sure."

"I've heard say," Prophet said, as he ducked on out of the bunkhouse, "that folks who lose their memory on account of a blow to the head can often get it back with another blow. Maybe you just need to knock your head on somethin'."

"No, thanks," Rose said with wry chuff, walking along behind him as they headed for the corral. "The way my luck's been goin', I'm liable to forget everything I remember after wakin' up and seein' you and Louisa in Nugget Town."

"Like as not."

Spying its rider heading toward him, Mean and Ugly gave an excited snort, then nipped the claybank's ass as it ran over to the corral gate. "All right — stand back, you owly son of a bitch."

Prophet lifted the latching wire over the front corral post and opened the gate just far enough for him and Rose to enter. Mean and Ugly ran up to Prophet, stomping and flicking his ears playfully and bobbing his head as though he were about to take a nip out of Prophet's hide, as the horse was wont to do for no better reason than he was simply mischievous and contrary.

"Why do you put up with that horse, Lou?" Rose said, grabbing her saddle blanket off the top corral post. "Seems I heard somewhere that a horse is no good if you can't turn your back on him."

"Well, some would say the same about me, Rose," Prophet said as he threw his saddle over Mean's back, then jerked his arm up just in time to avoid a painful nip. *"Ornery goddamn cuss!"*

When they had both horses saddled, they rode about two hundred yards back along the trail they'd taken out from Corazon, then swung right of the trail and into the scrub. The shelf Prophet had spied was a dark hump in the starlit night.

The slow plodding thuds of the horses, the jangle of bridle chains, and the creak of leather sounded crisp and clear in the heavy silence. Occasionally, a breeze would slide over the ground and rustle the brush through which Prophet and Rose wove their horses, but mostly the air was as still as that in a well.

Prophet was glad when he heard the soft, tinny rattle of water as he approached the ridge, which was a shelving volcanic dike with black lava-flow boulders strewn about

203

its base. The wall of the dike was composed of layered sandstone and porous, chocolate-colored lava, and there were several deep eroded notches into which Prophet and Rose could seek cover if a storm came up, which, judging by the clear sky, didn't look likely. But the White Mountains rolled up in the west, and near mountains you could never tell what the weather was going to do.

They stripped the tack from their horses and hobbled both mounts near the runout spring that meandered along the side of the shelf before dropping into a ravine and sending up faint splashing sounds. There was plenty of bunchgrass graze, and the water was cold and sweet, probably bubbling up from deep inside a volcanic vent.

Prophet built a fire and brewed coffee in a tin sauce pan. Rose, who'd laid out her bedroll on the other side of the fire, with the shelf behind her, declined a cup of the hot brew. She also declined the salt pork that Prophet roasted on two sticks over the fire, and his stale baking powder biscuits.

"No offense," Rose said, reclining on her bedroll and resting her head on the wooly underside of her saddle. "Just not very hungry tonight. I reckon water'll do me."

"It's been a long day," Prophet said. "You gotta eat somethin'. The biscuits been in my possible bag awhile, I admit, but I bought the salt pork fresh in Corazon."

"Like I said . . ." Rose kicked one of her boots off. "No offense."

Prophet shrugged. He bit into a hunk of salt pork and chewed hungrily, sitting Indian style beside the fire, one of the roasting sticks resting against his thigh where two biscuits were perched.

"Lou?" Rose stopped. "Is it all right if I call you Lou?"

"I take to 'mister' about as well as a dog takes to a snoot full of porcupine quills. What's on your mind?"

She rolled onto her side to face him, and rested her cheek on the heel of her hand. "What's that Louisa said about you and the Devil?"

"Oh, that." Prophet chewed, then swallowed a mouthful. "I done sold my soul to Ole Scratch, as we Southern folk call that green-fanged, fork-tailed demon, just after the war." He ripped off another chunk of salt pork and spoke as he chewed. "You see, I never expected to make it. Vicksburg, Antietam, Chickamauga — I seen it all, and lost every one of my kin who went along with me when we threw in with Jeff Davis to help turn back Lincoln's forces of Northern aggression. Ugly things happened. And

I mean *ugly*. Don't wanna go into it."

Prophet swallowed another mouthful and, holding the half-eaten chunk of pork down beneath his chin, he stared into the small ring of rocks containing the leaping flames. "Suffice it to say that when Lee finally surrendered to Grant, and none too soon as far as I was concerned, and I headed home to find out I no longer had a home to go home to — the farm burned, Ma and Pap livin' with relatives and nearly starvin' to death — I headed west. And along the way I indeed sold my soul, what I had of one to begin with, to Ole Scratch."

"For what?"

"All the good times one man can possibly have on this side of the sod . . . in return for my coal-shoveling abilities down below when it comes time for me to make that long walk through those glowin', smokin' gates."

Rose sat up, looking shocked. "You're gonna shovel coal for the Devil?"

Prophet tore another chunk of meat off the bone. "I had lots of practice back home of a Blue Mountain winter. We burned lots of coal! He can't wait to get me."

Rose stared across the fire at the big bounty hunter hungrily eating the side of pork and wiping his greasy hands on his trousers. "How's he holdin' up his end of the bargain?"

Prophet shrugged. "Fair to middlin'. He's been puttin' plenty of badmen in my path, but I just wish he'd put a little higher bounty on their heads. On my downtime I do like to have fun, but fun don't come cheap. And the more you have, the more you want."

Rose lay back down on her soogan and crossed her arms behind her head, staring up at the stars. Firelight flickered across her heart-shaped face. She was silent for a time, but then she said softly, pensively, "Is Louisa part of what you got from Ole Scratch?"

Prophet had just tossed his pork bone into the brush. Now he turned to Rose and gained a thoughtful, wistful expression of his own. "Didn't she tell you? Why, Louisa's the Devil's mistress her ownself." Prophet sagged back on one elbow and dunked the biscuit in his coffee. "Yes, ma'am — I ride with the Devil's mistress. Some might call her the Vengeance Queen. I reckon Scratch sent her to keep me honest and bedevil me more than a little."

He chuckled at the thought of that, then bit off the soggy end of the biscuit. "And she does do that. She purely does!"

When he'd eaten his biscuit, he put away

the leftover food for the next day's breakfast, then walked into the brush to evacuate his bladder and check on the horses. He came back to the fire, threw a couple of small branches on the waning flames, then kicked out of his boots and curled up in his soogan. Rose lay as she'd been lying before, head resting in the cradle of her crossed hands. The fire was shunting too many shadows for Prophet to tell for sure, but he though her eyes were open, staring at the stars.

"Good night, Miss Rose."

He flipped his saddle over with a sigh, lay back against it, and tipped his hat over his eyes.

"Lou?"

He tipped his hat up. Rose was sitting up, looking at him expectantly, almost worriedly.

"Mind if I lay over there with you?"

Prophet blinked. Then he chuckled. "I don't 'spect I'd ever say no to a purty gal who wanted to share my side of any fire."

Rose got up, brought her blankets over to his side of the fire, and dropped them down beside him. She retrieved her saddle and saddlebags and arranged those too beside Prophet. He tugged his hat brim back down over his eyes but he could hear her removing her cartridge belt, then kicking out of her boots. There was more rustling, as though she were removing more clothes than was sensible on what was sure to be a chilly night, but Prophet kept his eyes closed, giving the girl a little privacy.

"Lou?"

Prophet opened his eyes. She was crouched over him, her face only inches from his. Her shoulders were bare. Not only her shoulders.

As he ran his eyes farther down her torso, he saw that she'd removed her blouse. Her breasts sloped toward him, partly concealed by the shadows between them, her nipples gently caressing his buckskin tunic as she breathed.

He could smell her — salty and horsey with a distinct feminine scent all her own. Strands of her hair curled down the sides of her round breasts. She ran her tongue lightly across her upper lip, staring at him as though trying to read him from a great distance.

Suddenly, she pressed her lips to his, kissing him hungrily.

Prophet was so taken aback that he vaguely wondered if he hadn't drifted off to sleep and was dreaming. She placed her hands on his face and mashed her lips even harder against his, groaning softly. Her fingernails made a light rasping sound as they gently raked his beard stubble. He placed his hands on her shoulders, and when he finally managed to steel himself against his own automatic desires, he pushed her back away from him and stared up at her, tongue-tied.

She stared down at him, wet lips slightly parted. She was breathing harder than before. Her eyes quickly acquired a troubled cast.

"Cripes!"

She straightened her back and slowly crossed her arms over her breasts. Even in the deep shadows, with the fire behind her, he saw the blood rise in her cheeks. "I reckon I have even more to learn about myself than I thought, don't I?"

She gave her back to him, her fragile spine curving down into the waistband of her denims, and drew her blouse back on. Prophet felt a constriction in his throat and chest, and his heart was shuddering.

"It's all right," he said at last, trying to quell her embarrassment as well as his own. "You're just feelin' lonely's all."

She buttoned her blouse and sat staring into the fire, saying nothing.

Prophet turned onto his other side away

from her, crossed his arms on his chest, and closed his eyes. A while later, he heard her lie down beside him, only two or three feet away.

It was a long damn time before sleep overtook him.

16

Prophet woke during the night to the coyotes yipping and mewling in the direction of the ranch, where they'd likely discovered the bodies of the four claim jumpers. He chuckled, pulling his hat brim low once more and smacking his lips wearily. "Cleanup time."

He closed his eyes but then lifted his head once more and turned to his right. Rose lay curled beside him, her forehead brushing his shoulder, her mouth open as she slept. Her blanket had come down a ways, and Prophet reached over now to pull it back up to her chin. Her lips moved, as though she were trying to speak, but then they stopped moving and she gave a ragged sigh, snuggling down deep against the wooly underside of her saddle.

He was up at the first flush of dawn, loudly cracking branches over his knees. Rose was dead asleep, almost entirely covered by her blankets, only her stocking feet protruding from the bottom. It took the third mesquite branch loudly snapped under Prophet's boot heel to get her up groaning, smacking her lips, and wiping her hair away from her face before she pulled her boots on, wrapped her gun and shell belt around her waist, and stumbled off into the brush to tend nature.

Over breakfast, which she only picked at, neither said a word about what had happened between them the night before. They broke camp as soon as they'd each scrubbed their plates and coffee cups at the runout spring and were on the trail a few minutes later.

"Look there," Rose said as they topped a rise two hours later to see Corazon spreading out in the brushy, adobe-colored bowl beneath them.

"Look where?"

Rose pointed to a low, rocky rise north of the town. There were three spindly cottonwoods near the crest of the hill, lined up as though they'd been planted there though they were too old to have been anything but wind- or bird-dropped. Spread out across the hill below the trees were a couple dozen crude wooden crosses with a few cement or rough board slabs thrown in to give the

213

place some semblance of civility. There was even what appeared an iron-pipe rail enclosing a couple of the larger cement slabs, with a splash of color inside bespeaking flowers.

Near the trees, ten or so mourners stood near a freshly mounded grave. Most were dressed in black, but a couple of the women were dressed more colorfully, even gaudily, with what appeared to be feathers in their hair. Whores, most likely.

"Must be the boneyard up yonder."

Prophet felt a twinge of unease. Corazon was home to nearly five hundred inhabitants, some sick, some old, and one of them could have given up the ghost in ways most natural. Still, a little worm of concern was twitching its tail in his belly.

"Let's go," he said and booted Mean and Ugly on down the hill and along the powdery, two-track trail and into the town.

He darkly noted that the street appeared unusually quiet for midday and that there were none of the usual displays — barrels of ax handles and tables heaped with bolt goods and such — arranged on the boardwalks fronting their respective businesses. Even the Mecca Saloon on the town's north edge was quiet, with only one rangy black gelding with a beat-up saddle tied to its hitchrack, a yellow cur sniffing the weeds in the gap between the saloon and a crumbling adobe shack beside it.

The jailhouse swung up on Prophet and Rose's left. What he immediately noted about the tumbledown place, burning in the high-desert sun, was the funeral wreath of black voile and artificial red and blue flowers nailed to the drab front door. The worm of dread in his belly turned over, and then calmed a little when he saw the slender figure in the chair beside the door, nearly concealed in the midday shadows under the porch's brush roof.

Louisa's blond hair falling down from her felt stockmen's hat was unmistakable. She sat in a hide-bottom chair, leaning back with one foot propped on the rail in front of her, the hem of her camisole showing beneath her skirt. She'd polished her men's brown boots, even shined her spurs. She held an open, dark brown bottle of sarsaparilla in her hand, propped on her thigh.

"Any luck?" she said.

Mean blew and tromped over to the stock tank on the other side of the hitchrack. Prophet glanced at Rose, who shook her head.

He looked through the gap between the jailhouse and the harness shop to its right, toward the cemetery where the mourners were now spreading out along the slope and heading back to town, flanked by a priest in flowing black robes and a black cap. They were singing "Bringing in the Sheaves" as they walked, a large woman in a black mourning outfit keeping her head down as she clutched a crucifix in both her hands. A tall, hatless, gray-haired man was pushing the bulky, chair-bound figure of Max Utter down the hill, getting caught up frequently on rocks and grave markers.

The tall man was singing with the others, his jaws moving, but Utter just looked silent and grim.

"Rubriz," Louisa explained. "Last night. Triple 6 men."

Just then, Blanco's muffled voice rose from inside the jailhouse, joining along with the hymn though lagging several notes behind the singers on the hill. His voice owned a mocking, jeering pitch. Louisa ignored it.

"They shot him," Louisa said. "Then they hanged him."

"They get away?"

Louisa regarded him without expression. "What do you think?"

She lifted her chin slightly, and Prophet turned to regard Lester Hedges's undertaking and knife-sharpening establishment, housed in a two-story shed, on the other side of the street.

The shed had two large, barnlike front doors. One of the doors was closed, and three open coffins were propped against it. Prophet could see that a dead man lay in each coffin, each one with his hands clasped over his chest.

Prophet jerked Mean's head up from the water trough and rode over. The dead men had been dressed nicely for burial, though the clothes were obviously hand-me-downs that the undertaker had taken off previous clients. Their hair and mustaches were neatly combed.

Flies buzzed around the ragged bullet hole in one cadaver's waxy blue forehead.

Prophet rode back up to the jailhouse, before which Rose sat staring toward the dead men fronting the undertaker's. Louisa sat as before, sipping her sarsaparilla. Blanco had ratcheted his rendition of the funeral hymn up a couple of octaves, though the dispersing mourners had broken the song off completely. Prophet could tell by the pitch of the man's voice that he was lying down, probably lounging on his cot with his feet kicked up on the wall.

Feeling very satisfied with himself.

"Only three rode in for that yellow dog?"

217

Prophet asked Louisa.

"They asked Utter very politely to let him go, and when Utter declined, they rode Rubriz down and hanged him over yonder. Utter went over to help Rubriz. This was all after dark, but I'd been keeping my eye on the street from my hotel window and got over here before the three about-to-be-dead men rode back to spring Blanco from what they figured would be an unguarded lockbox."

Prophet jerked a thumb over his shoulder. "Was that Dwight Beaudry?"

"It was."

"Shit, haven't seen him for years. A gun thrower from Alabama. Fought with him during the Little Misunderstandin'. One of the few I knew who didn't want the war to be over. Never wanted *any* war to be over." Prophet had turned to look back at the mustached dead man on whom no wounds were visible. "Heard he went up to Wyoming with the Texas herds and started a couple of range wars just for kicks and giggles."

"Well, he's dead now." It was the first sentence that Rose had uttered since they'd ridden into town.

Prophet looked at her. The girl didn't look well. But who would look well, not knowing who they were? Not remembering a thing beyond two days ago.

"Why don't you go on over to the hotel there, get yourself a room and a hot meal."

"I don't have any money," she said boldly, shaking her hair from her eyes.

Prophet reached into his pants pocket, but Rose threw up a hand. "No. I don't take handouts. At least, I don't think I do. I'll work for my keep. Saw a sign in their window yesterday." With that, Rose turned her horse around and heeled it hard for the French Hotel two doors down from the jailhouse, back the way she and Prophet had come.

Prophet watched her go, then turned to Louisa, who eyed him curiously.

"Just graves out at the Tawlin place. Apache attack."

"No marker for Rose?"

"None."

Louisa sighed, knowing they were little closer to discovering the girl's true identity than they were before Prophet and Rose had ridden out to the Tawlins'. Prophet swung down from the saddle and unbuckled Mean's belly strap. As he slipped the bit from the horse's mount but kept him away from the water tank till he cooled, a wooden rattling rose from the gap between the jailhouse and the building beside it.

Shortly, Max Utter appeared at the mouth of the gap, a tall, gray-haired gent pushing his chair. The tall man stopped and looked sharply at Prophet, narrowing a wary eye.

"It's all right, Henry. Bounty hunter." Utter spat the words out distastefully. He shifted his gaze between Prophet and Louisa, who still sat in the chair atop the porch. "I suppose she told you all about it. Got your chest all puffed out?"

"Sorry about Rubriz," Prophet said. "He was a good man."

"He was a damn fool, lettin' himself get caught out like that." Utter ground his jaws, his brown eyes angry but also bereaved. "I had the undertaker set the bodies out in plain view for Metalious. He'll likely be sendin' more men."

"Might be sendin' 'em now."

Prophet had shifted his gaze east along Brush Street, where riders had appeared, coming around the dogleg and flanking a buckboard wagon that was bouncing through the wheel ruts of the deserted trail. There were a dozen or so men riding about thirty yards behind the wagon.

"Miss Bonaventure, I'd be obliged if you tossed me my barn blaster," Utter said, caressing the two pistols holstered to his wheelchair arms and keeping his eyes on the oncoming wagon and riders.

Louisa rose from her chair, strode into the jailhouse where Prophet could hear Blanco speaking to her though he couldn't make out the words above the thunder of the wagon's wheels and the thudding hooves. Louisa said nothing. She came out of the jailhouse and tossed the gut shredder over the rail at the end of the porch.

Utter caught it and breeched it to peer into its barrels. The tall, gray-haired gent remained behind Utter, hands on the chair back, as if using the marshal to shield him from the badmen.

"Henry," Utter said. "You best run along, lessen you wanna pin Ivano's badge on your suit coat."

The mayor looked relieved. He released the handles of Utter's chair as he stared toward the oncoming riders. "Yes . . . uh, yes . . . I reckon I better go find Alma. Make sure she's off the street."

He turned and long strode back the way he and Utter had come. Meanwhile, Prophet slid his Winchester from his saddle boot, loudly racked a shell in the chamber, and slapped Mean and Ugly's rear. "Make yourself scarce, jackass!"

The dun gave an angry whinny and galloped north along the street, fiddle-footed and glancing behind him to see what his rider was up to.

When Prophet turned back east, the burly man driving the wagon was hauling back on the reins of the two horses hitched to the singletree. *"Whooo-aaaaawwww!"* he bellowed as the horses stopped on the other side of the street, in front of the three boxed-up cadavers.

He wore a long, ratty alpaca coat, a long-barreled pistol holstered on his right thigh. The coat was open, and his huge belly bulged out between its ratty, dusty, seed-flecked flaps.

The man's hair was dark and shaggy, with streaks of gray in it. Gray streaked his thick mustache and chin whiskers, too. His eyes, set deep in sun-cured sockets, were small and belligerent, his short red lips arrogant and cruel.

When he had the wagon stopped and the dozen riders had halted their horses in the middle of the street thirty yards behind him, he sat there on the wagon's seat, looking dully toward Prophet, Utter, and Louisa, who stood atop the porch steps, her poncho lifted above her pearl-gripped Colts.

Tan dust rose up and around the big man in the wagon and the riders behind him, obscuring them all. Even through the dust, however, it was plain to see that each of the newcomers was armed for bear.

Prophet spread his feet, planted his rifle butt on his right hip, and waited for hell to pop. Only it didn't pop. Not there, anyway. Not yet.

The big man in the wagon yelled defiantly, "I bury my own dead on Triple 6 ground!"

He climbed down off the wagon, huffing and puffing with the effort, and walked over to the dead body of Dwight Beaudry. One of the men from the rough-hewn group behind him — as sweaty, as dirty, and as mismatched a bunch of cold-steel artists as Prophet had ever seen — yelled, "You want help, Mr. Metalious?"

"Stay there!" the big man snarled.

He reached into Beaudry's coffin, grabbed Beaudry's stiffening right arm, and crouched as he hefted the body over his shoulder. With a grunt, he turned to the back of the wagon — the end gate was already down — and tossed the body inside like it was a chunk of heavy lumber.

Beaudry hit the wagon bed with a hollow thud.

Blanco's muffled voice emanated from the open jailhouse door: "Pa? That you out there?"

Metalious glanced at the jailhouse, and

his face crumpled with anger. "Shut up!"

Metalious walked over to the man whom Louisa had drilled through the forehead and tossed him into the wagon with Beaudry.

"Come on, Pa," Blanco urged from inside the jailhouse. "Drop them tinhorns and git me outta here!"

Matalious swung his heavy, whiskered chin toward the jailhouse like a steel wedge. "I told you to shut up, Blanco. I'll get you out when I'm good and ready!"

A minute later, all three dead men lay in a tangled heap in the back of the buckboard. Metalious dusted himself off then walked over to the side of the wagon, hitched his canvas trousers up his broad thighs, and climbed back up into the driver's box. He grabbed the reins from the brake handle, released the break, and whipped the team around until the wagon sat in front of the jailhouse, pointed in the direction he'd come from.

The outlaw rancher looked at Prophet, Utter, and Louisa, his tongue thoughtfully probing a back tooth.

"Whose work is this?" Metalious canted his head toward the dead men behind him.

Louisa said, "Mine."

Metalious stitched his grizzled brows together, sizing her up. He narrowed one eye at Prophet, the other at Utter. Then he returned his attention to Louisa, giving her the cool up-and-down, noting the pearl-gripped pistols on her hips and the cool way she stood atop the porch steps, seeming to not only be waiting for something to happen but yearning for it.

Finally, Metalious said, "You'll die screamin', little girl."

He shook the reins over the horses' backs, and as the wagon lurched forward, the wedge of gun-heavy riders parted like the Red Sea to let him pass. When he had, they swung their horses around and spurred them into lopes, the entire group fading around the dogleg in Brush Street, though Metalious's yells at his horses and the rattle of the wagon and the thunderlike rataplan of his riders dwindled slowly.

Silence fell with the sifting dust. Louisa was staring after the group.

Mildly, she said, "When hell freezes over and the Devil has icicles in his beard."

17

The hostler of the Acme Livery Stables was a tall, bald, cantankerous, one-eyed gent named E. E. Spalding. When Prophet had brought his and Rose's horses down the barn's main alley, Spalding had come out of his back-room office smelling like stale sweat and fresh liquor.

When Prophet had stripped his tack off Mean and Ugly's back, he paid the man in advance for three days' stabling. "Give him plenty of oats in the morning, just hay at night. Give him his fill. He don't look like much, but he's bright enough to know when he's had enough. Curry him every morning but don't turn your back on him or he'll take a chunk out of your shoulder."

"Look at him," Spalding said as Prophet led the snorting, angrily high-stepping line-back dun into a stall. "He looks pure snake-venom mean."

"Oh, he's a peck meaner than that."

"Why do you keep such a beast?"

"He's damn good ridin'. Never did know a horse with Mean's bottom. Besides, you want a horse with spirit less'n you're an old widow lady just lookin' for a nag to hitch to your hack of a Sunday morn."

"Spirit, yes," drawled Spalding, standing away from the stable as Prophet quickly closed and latched the door on the lineback dun that stomped and snorted angrily, incensed at the sudden confinement in spite of the barn's rich feed smells. "But that there's a snake in horsehide. You can see it in his eyes."

"Like I said, don't turn your back on him." Prophet set his saddle on a stall partition and draped his saddlebags over a shoulder. "And I'd go easy on the coffin varnish, too. Tanglefoot'll make you careless, and he'll take a bite out of you, for sure. You don't smoke in your barn, do you, Spalding?"

Spalding glared at the bounty hunter through his one eye, indignant.

"Day drinkers sometimes get careless," Prophet explained. "And I want my horse taken good care of. For what you charge, he oughta have him a stall twice that size, and thrice-a-day groomings as well as a bath now and then."

"You sure got some gall, mister!"

Prophet started for the door with his rifle and saddlebags.

"Why don't you just come on back and tend him yourself if he's so damn much trouble and you're so damn proud?"

"You can handle him."

"If he tears my clothes, you'll be payin' extra!"

Prophet threw up an arm in farewell and stepped out the open barn doors and into the dusty side street that intersected Brush Street one block east. He went over and draped his gear over the splintery rails of the barn's holding corral, poked his hat back off his forehead, and dug his makings sack from his shirt pocket.

Slowly building a smoke, he looked around at the shabby side street lined with old adobe shacks and stock pens, with an ancient Spanish-style church off where the street became a trail meandering away into the juniper- and cedar-stippled hills. The church was grown up with weeds, and it looked abandoned, but it would be a good place for desperadoes to hole up while they were awaiting a chance, say, to break their boss's son out of jail.

Prophet twisted the quirley closed and licked it. He'd check the church later. He

228

was about to fire a match on his shell belt but stopped. Two coyotes ran, one after the other, over a low hill just beyond the church. The first one was glancing over its shoulder as it disappeared down the hill's other side.

Spooked by something.

Prophet stuffed the match and quirley into his shirt pocket.

He picked up his Winchester from where he'd leaned it against a corral post and racked a shell in the chamber. Setting the hammer to half cock, he rested the rifle's barrel on his shoulder and began strolling down the middle of the shabby side street that burned under a high, penny-colored sun. Most of the shacks looked abandoned, though a thick-set Mexican woman with long, blue-gray hair was hanging colorful, wet clothes on a line behind one cracked adobe hovel, a bantam rooster pecking the ground at her leather sandals and clucking.

Prophet walked up close to the church and peered over a half-ruined wall. Inside was only rubble and a few remaining benches with plenty of twisted, grainy coyote dung amongst tumbleweeds and buckbrush growing up through cracks in the fieldstone floor. He continued into the country beyond the church, roughly following the coyotes' course. When he'd crossed the same knoll they'd crossed a few minutes ago, distant horse thuds rose on his left.

He turned quickly, lifting his rifle from his shoulder. A horse and rider were galloping over the crest of another knoll a hundred yards away — merely a blur of movement so quick that Prophet could make out no distinguishing characteristics aside from the horse's dapple-gray hindquarters and the man's dark green hat. Gray-brown hair gathered into a ponytail bounced down his back. Dust rose from the other side of the hill, dwindling quickly.

Prophet walked that way over several hills between him and the one over which the rider had disappeared. He came to a sandy, shallow wash bottom and stopped. Two cigarette butts lay in the eroded sand, one half smoked, the other smoked to a nub. Prophet crouched and picked up each butt in turn.

Still warm.

Behind him there was the scratch of a branch on cloth, and he wheeled, automatically rocking the Winchester's hammer back before squeezing the trigger.

The Winchester hiccupped loudly.

The man who'd just stepped out from a hackberry snag shielding a slight notch in the wash gave a grunt and jerked straight backward, triggering his own rifle into the air. The man tried to set his feet and swing the Winchester down once more, but Prophet cocked and fired two more rounds from his hip.

The would-be backshooter jerked back and sideways. He tripped over a rock and piled up at the base of the wash's curving northwestern bank where he lay moaning softly and grinding one spurred boot desperately into the wash's gravelly floor. It was a death spasm; the man didn't have enough life left in him to keep him dangerous.

Prophet ejected his last spent cartridge and jacked fresh as he dropped to one knee, looking around quickly, awaiting another shooter to step out of a near brush snag or another mouth of the forking wash. When no one showed, and the silence persisted, Prophet rose and walked over to the dead man — a short, broad-shouldered hombre with a sharp chin.

He lay on his side against the wash's sloping bank, his legs crossed. A good four or five days' worth of beard stubbled his cheeks. His mustache was thick and brushy, and it caught the blood dribbling out of both nostrils. He wore a Colt .45 in a black leather holster, and a shoulder gun only half concealed by his filthy spruce duster.

The man's eyelids fluttered, his chest rose once, and then the life left him suddenly. His chest and shoulders fell.

Prophet had seen the man in the group flanking Metalious earlier. The other rider who'd vamoosed east was doubtless part of that bunch, too.

Prophet looked around.

Nothing moved but the breeze. The only sound was the squawking of an oil-desperate wheel somewhere east of town, growing steadily louder as the wagon headed for a mercantile. Finally, backtracking the man he'd killed, Prophet found a saddled horse off where the forking ravine opened up in a bowl in the hills. There was no brand on the mount, which wasn't surprising. Shootists often rode their own trusted mounts, no matter who they were riding for.

Prophet untied the rangy roan from a cedar shrub, looped the reins around the horn, and slapped its rump. The horse lurched off its rear hooves and galloped up out of the wash and turned a slow arc to the east, heading back toward its last remembered meal at the Triple 6 headquarters.

Prophet shouldered his rifle and tramped back past the crumbling church to where he'd left his saddlebags draped over the

Acme's holding corral. E. E. Spalding stood between the barn's open doors, one thumb hooked behind a shoulder strap of his striped coveralls, a quirley smoldering in his other hand.

"What the hell was that all about?"

"Some poor hombre won't be eatin' any more chocolate cake." Longarm stuck the quirley he'd rolled earlier between his lips, plucked the liveryman's quirley from the man's grimy fingers, and used it to light his own.

Puffing fresh smoke, he gave the coffin nail back to Spalding, who narrowed his lone eye at him skeptically but said nothing.

"If you see anyone skulking around over here with a long gun, you let Utter or me know — will you?"

"You got any other orders for me?"

"That should about do it."

Prophet tossed his saddlebags over his left shoulder, hefted his Winchester in his right hand, and headed up toward Brush Street, staying in the middle of the trail cleaving the sun-blistered buildings, wary of more ambushers who might try to pop a shot at him from one side of the street or the other.

When he got to the jailhouse, Utter was sitting at the bottom of his ramp. Louisa was again kicked back in the hide-bottom

233

chair atop the porch, her thumbs hooked behind her cartridge belt. Her empty sarsaparilla bottle stood on the porch floor beside her chair. She and Utter were both staring expectantly at Prophet.

He stopped in front of Utter and poked his hat back off his forehead. "Well, thanks all to shit for the help."

"We were just now discussing if it was old man Playa shootin' coyotes around his chicken coop or you gettin' dry-gulched," Utter said, worrying his shotgun's hammers with his thumb.

"If it was you getting bushwhacked," Louisa offered from behind and above the sheriff, "it was too late to give you a hand. We might as well both stay here and make sure Blanco stayed put."

"It was me gettin' bushwhacked. You can send your undertaker out for another stiff, in the wash beyond the old church."

Utter said, "So Metalious left a man behind, eh?"

"Two. The other flushed like a prairie chicken. No tellin' how many more are skulkin' around the washes and alleys." Prophet frowned at Louisa, who was now sporting a deputy sheriff's star pinned to her poncho. It had been hidden until now by a porch post. "What the hell's that?"

"What's it look like?" she said snootily.

"I gave her Ivano's job," Utter crowed. "She deserves it. You on the other hand are little more than a pain in the ass."

"This pain in the ass just took down a bushwhacker and scared another one off."

"Oh, stop your caterwaulin'," the marshal barked. "I'd give you one, too, but I only got the one. Consider yourself deputized."

"What if I don't want to be your deputy?"

"If you're gonna hang around here makin' sure Blanco don't eat his leg out of the trap, you'll be deputized." Utter leaned forward in his chair, jutting his chin at Prophet. "Which means you're takin' orders from me whether you like it or not."

"Ah, Christ," Prophet grunted. "I can't believe this." He looked at Louisa. "Where you holin' up?"

"Over at the French House." She curled her lip as she said it, as though it were the only place in town that suited such an upper-class little debutante.

"I'm headin' that way for a nap and a whore's bath."

"You go on over to Cora's Rooms," Utter called as Prophet strode westward along the street. "That's more fitting for an old bobcat like yourself!"

The sheriff laughed, delighted at his

humor but betraying his nerves, as well. They were in a tight spot — all three of them. Metalious had about as mangy a pack of bloodthirsty wolves on his roll as Prophet had ever seen, and they wouldn't come at the jailhouse straight on. No, these were wash squatters and alley shooters. They'd likely try to pick Louisa, Utter, and Prophet off one by one.

Probably after dark.

Too late to get Blanco out of town now even if the stubborn marshal of Corazon would allow it. Lead would fly like shit in a Texas twister.

Prophet yawned.

Christ, he needed a nap.

18

"Would you like a room next to Miss Bonaventure's?" asked the portly gent sitting behind his desk under the stairs of the French Hotel. He gave an end of his longhorn mustache a twirl and lifted a faintly insinuating smile.

"Oh, I suppose." Prophet yawned as he dug in his jeans pocket for coins. "She'll probably keep me up of a night with her snoring, but since we're pards an' all . . ."

"You'll be staying until the matter of Blanco Metalious has been settled, I take it."

"You got it."

"Any idea how long that will be?"

"Well, the judge is supposed to be here on Wednesday. So I reckon we'll hang his rancid hide as soon as they can get a gallows built after that. Oh, say, till Friday."

"Optimistic, are you?" the portly gent said, plucking a key off one of the two dozen brass rings on the wall behind him, beneath the rings' corresponding pigeonholes.

Prophet stared at the man until he shyly dropped his eyes to the open ledger book on the halved and varnished cottonwood logs that comprised his desk. "How much for a bath?"

"I don't provide baths here. Mr. Talbot does — just down the street."

"No, thanks then. Just send me up a pail of hot water. A whore's bath'll do me."

Prophet picked up his room key, saddlebags, and rifle and headed for the stairs, stopping when he saw the louvered doors leading off the lobby to his right, flanking the desk. "Food served in there?"

"The best in town."

"Tanglefoot?"

"Of course. After seven o'clock every night except Sunday we have a roulette wheel, and the mayor often hauls in his faro box for those wishing to buck the tiger."

Prophet glanced at the man, narrowing one eye. "What's your name?"

"Green."

Prophet looked into the saloon, where only three men sat around a table playing cards while a barman in arm bands and with thin, pomaded hair automatically arranged glasses into a pyramid atop the bar under the watchful, glassy stare of a mounted moose head. The bounty hunter turned to the portly, mustachioed Green, and narrowed his eye once more. "What's French about this place?"

"Uhh . . ." Green's florid face flushed slightly, and he smiled with chagrin as he flicked a cottonwood seed off his desk with the back of his hand. "Its name."

Prophet turned away from the louvered doors and headed up the stairs. As he turned at the landing, he stopped as a girl came toward him from the steps above, her upper body mostly concealed by the basket load of linen in her arms. As she passed, Prophet said, "Rose?"

She stopped and turned to him. She wore a plain, white-trimmed maid's dress with a white apron, and her brown hair was double-knotted atop her head. Her sun-browned cheeks were flushed, and her eyes were bright from exertion.

"Sure enough, Mr. Green needed a gal," she said ironically. "Right away. Seems he's been shorthanded for a time, and the work has piled up. Anything I can get you, Mr. Prophet? I also fetch food from the kitchen. Room service, they call it."

"No, I reckon I can haul myself down to the dining room later." Prophet frowned with concern. "This kind of work suit you?"

"I don't know," Rose said, a little breathless. "It's a job, and a girl has to eat. I'll be seein' you around, Lou."

Prophet nodded and watched her continue on down the stairs and out of sight. From the lobby, he could hear Green issuing orders to Rose and Rose mumbling her replies. Prophet continued up the stairs and to room nine, and after he'd fumbled the door open and had tossed his gear on the bed, he slid the curtains back from the room's lone window and looked into the street below, untying his neckerchief.

The only movement besides a dust devil or two or breeze-blown trash was a dude in a shabby, green-checked suit coat and gaudy orange trousers riding slowly, wearily into town from the west, two canvas valises hanging from his saddle horn. A salesman of one sort or another. As he angled toward the French Hotel, which was near the edge of town, someone tapped on the door.

"Room service," Rose said.

Prophet unbuttoned his shirt and jerked its tails out of his pants. Unbuckling his cartridge belt, he said, "It's open," and continued staring out the window.

The door opened, and he glanced over his shoulder to see Rose lugging a wooden

240

bucket of steaming water over to the washstand. "I'll let you lift it up there, if you
don't mind."

"Careful, or you won't get a tip." Prophet
tossed his cartridge belt onto the bed with
the rest of his gear.

Rose came over to the window and stood
beside him, looking out. "I heard shooting
earlier."

"Only me ridding the range of another
snake."

"The man in the wagon — was that Metalious?"

Prophet nodded.

"He looked right vicious, if you ask me.
You're gonna need help guarding Blanco
until the judge makes it out here, especially
if you gotta wait all the way till Wednesday."

"You offering your services?"

"I seem rather expert with a six-shooter."

Prophet returned his gaze to the street,
where a couple of punchers in shabby trail
gear were riding toward Brush Street by way
of a side street south of the hotel. Prophet
remembered neither man from Metalious's
group, and while they rode grim-faced and
were obviously hard men, they were likely
just looking for a couple of shots of coffin
varnish and maybe a mattress dance in one
of Corazon's fleshpots to relieve the bore-

241

dom of a Sunday afternoon.

As the riders approached Brush Street and swung toward Prophet's left, he said, "Lots of kids who grow up on ranches know how to handle a hogleg. It don't mean nothin', Rose."

"I wish something would mean something."

She turned and headed for the door, looking a little too sunburned and outdoorsy for the maid's dress she wore even with her hair pinned up.

"Here."

She turned around at the door, and Prophet tossed her a ten-cent piece. She caught it with one hand and looked at it, giving a bashful smile. Her eyes slipped quickly across Prophet's bare chest, a chest that had caught the admiring glances and caresses of more than a couple females in his time, not all of them whores, before she lowered her gaze to the floor.

"My first tip. Much obliged, Mr. Prophet."

Prophet grinned, wanting to try to cheer the girl up a little. If she ever got her memory back, he had a feeling she wasn't going to like all that she remembered, even if hers was just the usual kind of life — a life lived out here in western New Mexico ranch country. A hard, lonely damn life with few frills. She'd be looking at even fewer if she belonged to the dead Tawlin family.

"*De nada,* senorita," he said.

She raised her eyes to his face — they glowed with the light from the window behind him — then backed out, closing the door behind her.

Prophet sighed. He ran a tired hand over his face, then shrugged out of his shirt and let it drop to the floor as he walked over to the marble-topped washstand.

There was water in the porcelain bowl that sat there beside a cracked stone pitcher with a blue ring around its top. He emptied both the bowl and the pitcher into the thunder mug by the bed, then refilled the bowl from the steaming water bucket. He took the threadbare cloth from the peg on the wall over the stand, soaked it and lathered it with the scented purple soap cake that rested in a glass holder with tiny roses painted on it, and thoroughly scrubbed his face and chest and the back of his neck, making sure he dug around in and behind his ears.

That much washing alone turned the water in the bowl black, so he emptied the bowl into the chamber pot, refilled the bowl, then stripped down to his birthday suit and gave his privates, front and rear, a thorough scrubbing. He grunted and groaned with the effort.

Kicking out of his boots, he peeled off his sweaty wool socks, sat on the bed, and ran the cloth over each foot in turn, until each was white with frothy suds, not neglecting the gaps between his toes.

He rinsed his feet off over the thunder mug.

"Whew!"

Nothing like removing a couple of weeks of grime and trail dust to make a man feel human again. But he was still tired. He emptied the porcelain bowl and the thunder mug out the window, hearing the water splash in the street below, then tramped heavy-legged over to the bed. He looped his shell belt and Colt over the bedpost nearest the door beside it, then pulled the covers back and collapsed.

He left the covers off, lying there naked. The fresh, late-summer air felt good against his freshly scoured, pleasantly burning skin.

He rested his arm over his forehead and tried to block out the droning of a late summer fly caroming through the room. Finally, he let go. Sleep tumbled over him, mowed him down like rocks in a slide, hammering him down deep into the depths of warm, black slumber.

A light tap on the door pulled him back

to half consciousness. Immediately, he wrapped his right hand around the worn walnut handle of his Colt holstered to the bedpost. At the same time he noted that the light in the window, stitched with snowy cottonwood from the trees lining the creek, had dulled to the hues of late afternoon. "Who's there?" he asked.

"Me," came the cool, familiar voice through the door.

Prophet removed his hand from the gun handle with a sigh, reached over, and turned the key in the door lock, then lay back on the bed, limbs akimbo, sleep still clawing at him like an unfulfilled woman.

The door opened, hinges moaning. Prophet kept his eyes closed. There was a familiar tread on the floor. He could smell her as she closed the door, fanning him with a slight wind that brought not only her unique smell to him — which he often likened to the smell of jelly beans, for some reason — but that of the trapped air in the hall, rife with smoke, varnish, and human sweat.

Sleep tugging at him, he listened to the sounds she made kicking off her boots and undressing. He was too tired to open his eyes, no longer sleepy but enjoying the luxury of the big bed and the clean sheets beneath his scrubbed, naked body, and the dolor of the afternoon with a cooling breeze whispering through the window.

Birds cheeped faintly.

It was so quiet that he could occasionally hear the faint trickle of the creek over its rocks at the edge of Corazon.

The edge of the bed sank, the springs squawking quietly, and then he felt her hands on his arms, her hair caressing his chest. He opened his eyes. She kissed his belly lightly, sliding her hands slowly up across his chest to his shoulders, and squeezing the slabbed muscles there.

Prophet groaned luxuriously, lifted his big, seasoned brown hands, and slid her blond hair back from her face. She scuttled up his body, her thighs feeling like velvet as she straddled him, grunting softly, desperately, her sleepy hazel eyes meeting his before her tongue flicked across her lower lip.

She stared down at him, her expression oblique, her bare breasts, pale as snowflowers and tipped with rosebuds, sloped toward his chest. "There's going to be some killing soon." Her voice was soft, slightly raspy.

Prophet nodded.

"Why does it make me feel this way?"

With his left hand, he smoothed a wing of her thick hair back from her smooth, lightly tanned cheek. "What way?"

She thought about it, staring at him, her blond brows wrinkling. She shook her head as she whispered, "Hungry."

She pressed her breasts and belly down hard against him, closing her mouth over his.

He left her an hour later, when the sun angling through the window was adobe-colored and he could hear the strains of a Mexican trumpet emanating from the east end of town, near Bayonet Wash and its Mexican cantinas and fleshpots. A guitar sounded along with the trumpet, very softly.

It may have been Sunday, but that end of town never rested long.

Prophet looked at Louisa lying on her side, facing away from him. He leaned over and kissed her slender arm, then rose and dressed quietly, dragging out fresh underwear from his saddlebags. He could hear her breathing softly, deeply as he opened the door, stepped out into the hall, then drew it closed behind him.

She should lock it, but he didn't want to wake her to tell her. Besides, she'd sleep just long enough to replenish herself. She'd likely be back at the jailhouse in a half hour.

There was another man at the desk downstairs — a thin, bald gent in wrinkled shirtsleeves — quickly devouring a huge supper plate of short ribs and potatoes smothered in gravy.

"That the special?"

The man nodded but did not look up from his plate.

Prophet went into the dining room, where Rose was now waiting on the dozen or so men who'd gathered for drinks and supper, a couple grouped near the roulette wheel. He had her fetch him a couple of plates of short ribs while he sipped a whiskey at the bar, then paid her and hauled the plates, covered with oilcloth napkins, out onto the hotel's front porch.

He was just starting down the porch steps when a horse nickered to his right. Stopping and setting his feet once more, he looked east along the trail that shone like vanilla cream as it wound through the darkening scrub over which a soft, blue-and-jade light hovered. The sun was drifting low over the jagged, dark brown western ridges, turning as rich red as the first roses of a southern spring.

Three men came along the trail on trotting horses. Prophet squeezed the plates in his hands as he appraised the three who entered town and rode on past him, two tipping their hats to him, the third giving an oily grin.

They all wore brush-scratched chaps. Two had donned denim jackets against the growing chill while the third sported a leather jacket with small silver conchos on the cuffs and elaborate stitching across the shoulders. They were all armed, and they wore their pistols either high on their hips or low on their thighs, with double shell belts and Winchester rifles protruding from their saddle boots.

As men, they didn't look like much. They were ugly as gobblers. They were a dirty, seedy lot emanating callousness and stupidity as well as an animal brutality.

All three Prophet had seen in the group that had ridden in earlier with Sam "Man-Killin' " Metalious.

They rode off down Brush Street like they had people to see and things to do, heading in the direction of Bayonet Wash. Prophet loosened his .45 in its holster — he'd left his rifle in his room, figured he wouldn't need it until after dark, but maybe he was wrong. Then, carrying one plate in his left hand and balancing the other on his left arm, keeping his right hand free, he tramped toward the jailhouse a block east of the hotel.

The three gunmen had just passed Max Utter sitting on his porch with his shotgun across his thighs. He and the three men standing around him, the liveryman E. E. Spalding and two other townsmen whom Prophet hadn't seen before, were still staring after the wolves. The one who'd grinned greasily at Prophet was doing the same to Utter over his left shoulder.

Then the three disappeared around the dogleg and were gone.

Utter said something to the liveryman, which Prophet couldn't make out from his distance of forty yards or so. The liveryman responded, throwing up his hands while the other two men turned away from the marshal and moved off down the porch steps and into the street, keeping their heads down, sort of truckling under Utter's harsh stare. The two other men were dressed much like Spalding, in patched coveralls and shabby felt hats — one medium tall and paunchy, the other old and swaybacked.

As Spalding followed the other two into the street, heading for the Mecca Saloon back past Prophet on the other side of the street, Utter growled, "You're a chickenshit, Spalding. You're on the Corazon Gallows Committee, you son of a bitch!"

Spalding turned toward Utter but continued walking backward. "You can throw all the rocks you want, Utter, but I done resigned. Better to quit and look the coward than stare up at six feet of dirt."

The liveryman turned forward and followed the other two into the Mecca, whose outside bracket lamps were growing brighter as the afternoon light continued to fade.

"What was that all about?" Prophet asked Utter.

"Those weak-livered lobos refuse to build a gallows for Blanco. Sam sent 'em a message. Told 'em if they started erecting the gallows, they might as well pick out a coffin for themselves over to the undertaker's." The marshal gritted his teeth as he glared at the Mecca. "Weak-livered tinhorns!"

"Well, hell, why don't you just hang ole Blanco from one of them cottonwoods down by the creek?"

" 'Cause we're not lynching the son of a bitch. We're hanging him by order of the judge. Or we will be. Christ, Prophet, were you raised by wolves?"

Prophet handed Utter a plate, which the marshal took with an owly air. "No reason to get personal, 'specially since I brought you some vittles an' all."

Utter set the plate on his lap, atop his rifle, and lifted the oilcloth. "Well, I'll be damned.

Don't tell me you want a raise already!"

The joke seemed to lift his spirits, so, as Prophet sat down on the middle porch step and propped his own plate on his lap, he thought he could broach a subject that had been on his mind but one that would probably be a sore topic for the marshal. "Speaking of the judge . . ."

Utter was already working on his short ribs, using his hands. "What about him?"

"You think he'll make it?"

"Of course he'll make it. Your memory that short? I done told you he's got a passel of soldiers from Fort Stockton escortin' him around three counties. He'll be here on Wednesday. Mark my words."

"All right." Prophet laid into a short rib.

Utter stopped eating to scowl at the back of the bounty hunter's neck. "What do you mean — 'all right'?"

"I mean, all right. If you say so."

"You don't think the cavalry can protect the judge?"

"Obviously you do," Prophet said, chewing. "You know this stretch of sage better than I do."

"Well, that's just plumb loco if you don't think ten soldiers from Fort Stockton, with an experienced sergeant and a good lieutenant, can keep the judge from gettin' greased by old Sam and his brigands. Hell, the soldiers out here are used to fightin' Apaches!"

Prophet didn't say anything as he continued eating the short ribs with his hands and taking an occasional forkful of the gravy-drenched potatoes. He didn't need to say anything. His silence spoke for itself.

The marshal's chair creaked. Softly, he grumbled, "Maybe it wouldn't hurt for you to ride on over to Socorro tomorrow — intercept 'em an' warn 'em."

Prophet split a bone in two and sucked the marrow out of one end of it. "What about them three gun wolves that just rode in?"

"Don't you worry about me."

Prophet was chewing the last bit of meat off his last short rib. "I ain't worried about you. I'm worried about them taking Metalious out of the lockup while I'm gone. I sure would hate to have to ride out to the Triple 6 and snatch him back from his pa, especially when he has such a small reward on his worthless head."

Utter raised his voice. "You don't think I can guard my own goddamn jail?"

Prophet only hiked a shoulder and continued eating.

"You're impertinent."

"If you want me to understand what you're sayin'," Prophet said, licking the last bit of gravy from his plate, "you're gonna have to bend your talk a little lower." He set his empty plate on the step beside him, leaned back, and stretched his long legs out in front of him. "When you're through, I'll take your plate back to the hotel and fetch my rifle. Then why don't you get a little shut-eye? When you're rested, I'll make the rounds, make sure we're only dealin' with three of them Triple 6 shooters tonight."

Behind Prophet, Utter stirred in his chair, making it creak again. Then the man continued eating, tentatively.

"Prophet?" he asked after a time, smacking his lips. "What's your stake in this?"

"Like I said, I sure would hate to —"

"Tell me straight up, damn you!"

Prophet rested back on his elbows, looking out over the darkening town. The music from the direction of Bayonet Wash was getting louder and occasional whoops and bursts of laughter sounded.

Yes, why? There was little money in this venture. He'd probably make a whole lot more if he lit a shuck out of Corazon and continued up into the White Mountains, where the men with the real money on their heads were laying up. The truth was, Utter was a broken man. While the marshal wouldn't admit that to himself — *couldn't* admit that to himself and maintain his dignity and self-respect — it was true.

He needed a hand. And Blanco needed hanging.

"Ah, hell, I reckon I'm just like a ragged-eared old mustang," Prophet said at last. "Don't got sense enough to gallop away from a bad fight."

Utter grunted as he chewed, apparently satisfied by the answer.

19

Carrying three plates of short ribs, the girl who was now seeing herself as Rose Tawlin, though she had little idea who Rose Tawlin even was, pushed through the swing door of the kitchen at the rear of the French Hotel's saloon and restaurant and stopped suddenly as she faced the room of eating, drinking, and gambling men before her.

There were only about two dozen men here, but half were regarding her darkly through webbing clouds of tobacco smoke, as though she herself were something to eat. Obviously, she'd never waited tables before, because such a job seemed as foreign to her as would getting up on a table and trying to sing.

But it was a job, and she needed a job to survive. The owner of the place, Mr. Green, had told her that after the kitchen closed she was welcome to join his other "girl" — the one named Yvette who wandered the room fluttering her false eyelashes — if she wanted to earn some "quick, easy cash." Rose had watched Yvette work, sitting on laps and flirting with the men before finally leading an occasional one out into the lobby and up the carpeted stairs. That looked less strenuous than hustling plates and drinks to the impatient horde before her now, but she doubted she could spread her legs for a living with any more ease than slinging food or singing.

If her feet continued to ache as badly as they were aching now, she'd keep it in mind, however.

Taking a breath and steeling herself for another onslaught of orders for both drinks and food, she strode past the bar on her right, trying not to slip on the puncheon floor covered with tanbark shavings. She hauled the plates over to a table at which five men in shabby suits sat playing cards and drinking and, judging by the three glancing peevishly at her, waiting for their food. She'd thought that one of the men in the saloon tonight might have known her family and thus recognized her and given her one more piece of evidence as to her identity, but that hadn't happened yet. And as thoroughly as all the men in the room had appraised her in their typically goatish male way, if any knew who she was, they certainly hadn't mentioned it.

Either Rose Tawlin hadn't visited Corazon very often when she was home, or she'd been away from home long enough to have been forgotten by anyone in town who might have known her.

She set the third plate down on the table, in front of a man with round-rimmed spectacles and a waterfall mustache but an otherwise clean-shaven face. "Will that be all?"

She'd no sooner gotten the question out of her mouth than she felt a hand on the back of her thigh, sliding upward with lascivious slowness. She could feel the hardness of a ring on one of the man's fingers.

She gave a startled jerk and looked down to see the man with the spectacles gazing up at her, his glasses reflecting the light of the lamp hanging over the table, masking his eyes though not his lips that were pulling away from his teeth.

"Can we talk about this later?" he asked in a syrupy voice she could just barely hear above the din of conversation echoing around the room.

Rose swatted the man's hand away and stepped back, scowling angrily. "Later you can go fuck *yourself,* you son of a *bitch!*"

She knew she'd said enough, but the words were out before she could get a leash on them. "Does your wife know what you do with your paws when you're out with your pards?"

The men around the table laughed — except for the one she'd just scolded. His face turned red, and he quickly drew away from her, dropping his eyes to his plate. Someone grabbed Rose's left elbow, and a man's near voice said, "Jane?"

Rose wheeled to see a short, thickly built man in a floppy-brimmed, bullet-crowned hat staring at her incredulously. He wore double cartridge belts, a pistol in a shoulder rig under a thigh-length rat-hair coat and another in the cross-draw position on his left hip. He had thick, unattractive red lips, and they spread now beneath his tobacco-stained mustache as he continued staring at her, giving her the slow up-and-down over and over again.

"Who?" Rose said.

"I'm Gopher," the man said. Then his brown eyebrows stitched together. "Remember? North of Deadwood?"

"North of Deadwood?" Rose mumbled to herself, casting her thoughts like a fishing line into her past, frustrated at only hooking images from a couple of days ago, back at

Nugget Town. "Are you sure you know me, mister?"

The man released Rose's elbow, and his brown eyes acquired a cautious cast. "Nah . . ." He started to turn away. "Maybe not."

"No, wait," she said, reaching for his arm.

Another man's voice rose louder behind her, *"Rose!"*

She snapped her head around. Mr. Green stood just inside the batwing doors separating the hotel lobby from the saloon/dining room, showing his teeth like an angry cur and canting his head toward a table near the doors to his left. Three more men had just sat down and were leaning forward on their arms, twiddling their thumbs, one spinning his cream Stetson on an upraised finger, obviously waiting for their orders to be taken. The bartender was busy hauling out trays of whiskey shots and beer to the gamblers on the room's far side.

Rose lurched forward, heading for the newcomers. She had to slow down before she got to the table, because a sudden, inexplicable pain suddenly shot through her stomach. It was followed by a wave of nausea so powerful that for a moment she thought she was going to vomit right there in the middle of the saloon, in front of her boss and everyone.

Continuing ahead slowly and trying to fight off the wretched feeling, praying she could keep down what little food she had in her stomach — she'd only eaten a few bites of jerky since breakfast — she stopped at the newcomers' table. Fishing her notepad out of her apron pocket, she said weakly, "What'll it be, fellas?"

"One of you and the short ribs!" said the man on her left, guffawing as though he'd come up with the most original line since humans started walking upright.

When she'd finally gotten their order and was heading back to the kitchen, another wave of nausea washed over her, and she had to fight to keep from dropping to her knees and retching. She pushed through the swing door, set the order ticket on the dry sink for the Chinese cook who was toiling at the big iron range against the front wall, smoking while he seasoned another rack of short ribs, and headed straight across the kitchen to a short hall. She pushed into the hall, past a small storeroom, and through another door and into the alley behind the hotel.

Her guts danced in her belly as, holding one arm across her waist, she headed for the two-hole privy that stood under a cottonwood beside a large pile of unsplit firewood, some of which was covered with a tarp. A cat meowed somewhere near as Rose pulled open the privy's right door, happy to see in the darkness that the smelly place was unoccupied. She lifted the lid, bent her head over the gaping hole, and released the dam holding back the sparse contents of her stomach.

She hadn't eaten much, but she vomited plenty, groaning into the cavernous hole beneath her.

Running the hem of her apron across her mouth, she opened the privy door and stepped out into the night. A raspy breath sounded to her left, and then a man's hand was painfully squeezing her left arm. A hot, sweaty body pressed against her, pushing her savagely back against the privy door with a thud.

She could smell whiskey on the man's breath as he thrust his face close to hers. "Just what in the dung-dippin' hell is your game *now,* Jane?"

"Hold on," Prophet said.

Ten feet to his right, Louisa stopped in the shadows of the buildings on the south side of Brush Street. "What is it?"

"I think I saw somethin' move in that

window there in the stable. Somethin'
shiny."

"Like a rifle?"

"Yeah."

Holding his Winchester up high across his chest and thumbing the hammer back to full cock, Prophet strode slowly out from the middle of the street toward the crumbling adobe stable on the street's north side. This was a dark stretch of Brush Street, a dilapidated part of the business district that was given over to shabby stables and ruins of the town's first businesses, long defunct. No lights here, only shadows that were deepened by the lamps and flares mounted on saloons farther east or west.

This was a no-man's-land, a good place for an ambush.

Prophet sort of sidestepped toward the stable, keeping one eye on the stable itself while shuttling his cautious gaze toward both ends, ready for sudden movement and the hiccup of triggered rifles fired from ambush.

Prophet's boots crunched gravel. He'd removed his spurs to lessen the noise of his footsteps. His breath raked slowly in and out of his lungs as he squeezed the rifle in both his big, gloved hands. Behind him, Louisa stood frozen, feet spread, her own

263

carbine extended from her right hip, her hat hanging down her back by her chin thong.

Prophet pressed his shoulder up against the stable wall, three feet north of the window from which one remaining shutter hung askew. He looked behind him, then ahead past the window. He cat-footed forward, eyes on the window now as he neared it, the darkness within growing.

Starlight suddenly reflected off an object within. Warning bells tolled in Prophet's head, and he stopped suddenly, snapping his rifle up.

Too late.

There was an ear-splitting sound, only to Prophet's surprise as he stayed the pressure on his trigger finger, it wasn't the roar of a rifle. Nor was there the accompanying flash.

It was a raucous bellowing squeal that issued from the window, rattling Prophet's eardrums and sending hot blood jetting through his veins. The mules' eyes appeared just back of the broad, blunt snout that protruded from the window, bobbing, the nostrils contracting and expanding furiously and also faintly reflecting starlight.

Prophet stepped back and released a held breath, letting his rifle fall slack in front of him. The smell of mule, hay, and dung was heavy in his nose now. He should have realized, damn fool . . .

"Sorry, fella," he said between the animal's frightened, angry squeals.

He looked at Louisa. Even in the dark he could read the disapproving expression on her face as she shouldered her carbine and cocked a hip.

"All right," he said. "I reckon I'm gettin' a little nervous. I been bushwhacked from stable windows before, though, and I can tell you it ain't any fun!"

"You wanna go back, let me continue the rounds alone?"

"Don't get sassy."

As they started forward along the street, a sudden gunshot stopped them. The same gun barked again, and then a third time. The shots were muffled, as though the gun had been fired inside a building. A man's ensuing scream was also muffled. He screamed again, only this time the scream was louder, sharper, and then there were two more gun blasts.

These, too, were louder and sharper, as though the man and the gun were now outside.

A woman screamed, a horse whinnied. Another man laughed.

Silence.

"That came from Bayonet Wash," Louisa

said, looking beyond the hunched, crumbling buildings ahead and right of her, toward the southwest corner of Corazon.

"Surprise, surprise," Prophet said.

He started forward.

"Probably just a couple of border toughs mixing it up," Louisa said as they moved slowly but purposefully together along Brush Street.

"Maybe." Prophet shouldered his Winchester, wrapping his right hand tightly around the neck of the stock. "Then, again, we might just have been summoned."

"Yeah, but then again, you're acting like an old woman tonight."

Prophet curled his upper lip. "You just keep your finger on your trigger and an eye on your back trail, Miss Smarty Mouth."

20

The fleshpots and cantinas of Bayonet Wash shone dully in the darkness of the desert a ways outside the town's southwestern edge.

At the very edge of town was an old, abandoned ranch shack of mud and straw, with a collapsed brush roof and an adjoining pole corral. Beyond the ranch was the dry creek bed sheathed in scrub brush, cactus, and willows, and just beyond the creek were the lights of this forbidden part of Corazon.

Prophet and Louisa paused on the wash's left bank, concealed by brush and a spindly cottonwood, and stared toward the lights from where a man's agonized groans sounded — rising and falling and then rising again amongst painful pants and sighs.

Whoever had bought a bullet, which was one of the many things that came cheap on the eastern side of Bayonet Wash, was dying slow.

Prophet pushed through the brush and crossed the creek via a teetering wooden bridge whose boards slumped dangerously beneath his boots. Louisa followed, her black skirt swishing about her legs. On the other side of the creek, Prophet slowed. He and his partner spread out as they made their way toward the tapers and torches that glowed and sparked in the quiet night, cloaking the pale adobe buildings lining the rutted two-track trail in menacing shadows.

Prophet had just seen the figure slumped beneath a hitchrack on the right side of the street, fronting one of the few clapboard hovels mixed amongst the adobe ones. Two torches were bracketed to poles fronting the cantina from which the strumming of a mandolin sounded beneath the wounded man's groans. That it was a cantina was obvious by the several saddled horses tied out front and from the large amount of light emanating from the two front windows behind which shadows slid to and fro.

The slumped figure had one arm negligently wrapped over the hitching post's crossbar, as though trying to pull himself to his feet. His other arm was clamped over his belly, and his legs were curled beneath him. A steeple-crowned sombrero hung down his back. He was cursing angrily now in Spanish and sobbing.

There was the creak of hinges and the thud of boots on a boardwalk. Prophet shifted his gaze left to see a man step out of the cantina and stand there for a moment, holding both batwing doors open as he stared straight out in front of him.

Prophet glanced at Louisa, who arched a blond brow curiously.

The man slowly stepped out away from the cantina doors, letting them rattle behind him as he dropped casually off the board-walk. He disappeared amongst the horses tied there, only his legs showing beneath the horses' bellies in the light from the cantina windows.

He reappeared a moment later. Stopping about ten feet behind the tied mounts, he stared across the street at the wounded man, who gave another ripping curse in Spanish, then dropped his arm down from the hitchrack with a phlegmy sigh.

"Murdering bastarrrrrd!" he shouted, lifting his head again suddenly.

The man standing behind the horses laughed.

Then he lurched with a start, and a gun flashed in his outstretched right hand. The three shots seemed to overlap as the sharp echoes chased each other around the buildings like high-pitched thunder. The wounded Mexican was punched straight back to the ground, arms thrown out from his shoulders, one leg curled beneath the other.

He lay still.

The horses had leaped suddenly when the shots had been fired, and they were still skitter-hopping now, pulling against their reins, as the shooter twirled his smoking pistol, then dropped it with a flourish into the cross-draw holster on his left hip.

He was a short man — his head coming up to just above the horses' rumps — in denims and chaps, and a black vest over a bloodred shirt. As he turned around to start back through the horses toward the cantina, Prophet saw his face for an instant in the window light — a dark red, shadowy mask with a brushy mustache with upturned ends.

One of the three gunmen he'd seen ride into town earlier.

Prophet glanced at Louisa. "Think I'll go in the front, get their attention."

"You want me to go around back?"

"You wouldn't mind?"

Louisa rolled her eyes and sidestepped away from him, disappearing into the shadows between the cantina and a black hulk of a building whose windows appeared boarded.

When he'd given her enough time to find a back door to the cantina, if there was one, Prophet moseyed forward, stepped between the still jittery, blowing horses, and mounted the cantina's splintery boardwalk that teetered unevenly on piled stones. He kept his rifle on his shoulder as he continued forward, stopped, and stared over the tops of the double batwings into the cantina.

It was a seedy, smelly place but with several lamps hanging from the low tin ceiling on wires, so Prophet could see into all the corners except the rearmost ones. A short, plank bar ran along the left wall. A stocky Mexican with sunken, toothless jaws and wearing a stained white apron stood behind the bar, staring back at Prophet grimly.

Along the wall to the right, on the floor, slumped several passed-out Mexicans in charro jackets. Another sat at a table strumming his mandolin while a short, drunken whore in a skimpy red dress danced slow drunken circles with a short Mexican in a canvas jacket and slacks, his long, salt-and-pepper hair flecked with lice.

A couple of vaqueros played poker about halfway down the room, keeping their eyes on their game, while the man Prophet was looking for sat just beyond them and to the left, at a round table with two quart whiskey jugs and three shot glasses on it. A cigar had been put out in one of the glasses.

The man in the black vest and red shirt sat there, both elbows on the table, a hand wrapped around a freshly filled shot glass. His hat was cuffed back off his forehead, and his chin was dipped slightly, upper lip curled angrily. Challenge shone in his eyes.

Prophet stepped slowly forward and hooked a thumb over his shoulder. "Too bad about the bean eater."

"Too bad he was cheatin' at poker. What're you gonna do about it?"

"Well, I reckon I'll have to arrest you." Prophet grinned. "Or kill you."

The man's eyes brightened. Suddenly he was sliding back and leaping up out of his chair.

Prophet hadn't expected the move so he was a hair slow in bringing the Winchester up, and the man's first shot carved a line across Prophet's cheek. Prophet fired the Winchester, and a bottle on the table exploded, spraying whiskey and glass shards into the shooter's face.

He screamed and fired again blindly. The bullet slammed into the batwings behind Prophet, making them clatter and squawk.

The gunman stumbled sideways. Blood streamed from his cut eyes and cheeks. As he brought his big Russian .44 up again, screaming, *"You son of a bitch!"* Prophet shot him twice through the chest.

Blood sprayed from the man's back as one bullet plowed into the wall behind him. One of the bullets tore a meandering path through his chest and exited the top of his shoulder to plunk into the ceiling above his head.

Prophet ejected a smoking spent cartridge, racked a fresh round into the Winchester's breech, and looked around. The cardplayers were on the floor, covering their heads with their arms. The two dancers were still dancing, oblivious of the sudden violence. The bartender was shouting loudly in Spanish and slamming a fist on the bar top.

Prophet turned to him quickly. "Where're the other two?"

As if in reply, guns roared behind the place.

Louisa.

Prophet bolted down the length of the cantina while the bartender continued to berate him in Spanish and the drunk dancers continued to dance. The bounty hunter hurdled the dead gunman and headed for a timbered door in the cantina's back wall.

He did not slow up for the door. As the fusillade continued out back, he put his head down, dropped a shoulder, increased his speed, and hammered right on through it.

The door blew off its hinges. It and Prophet hit the backyard hard, dust billowing.

"Ambush!" Louisa screamed beneath the frenetic barks of rifles and bright gun flashes.

Prophet lifted his head as several slugs screamed around him and hammered the adobe wall behind him, making plaster fly. There was a privy straight back of the place, and one shooter was firing from behind it toward where a wagon without wheels sat amongst rabbit brush and rocks. Another shooter was directing his fire at Prophet, flames stabbing from his rifle resting atop the wagon, while the other was exchanging lead with Louisa, who was apparently hunkered down behind the privy.

At least, he hoped that was his partner. It was too dark to see much but the gun flashes.

Prophet's shoulder throbbed from its impact with the door and the ground. As more lead screamed around him, he rolled wildly to his right and came up shooting, hearing his slugs hammering the wagon. There appeared to be only one man shooting now, the one who'd been shooting at Prophet. As that shooter's rifle licked flames toward the privy, Prophet emptied his Winchester.

There was a grunt and the thud of what sounded like a rifle butt striking the side of the wagon.

Prophet set the empty Winchester aside and, belly down about ten feet from the cantina door, shucked his .45 from its holster and, rocking the hammer back, extended it straight out in front of him.

The wagon sat hunched in the darkness. No gun flashes. No sounds. The privy, too, was dark, Louisa's rifle silent.

Prophet called her name.

"What?" she said in a tight voice.

"You all right?"

A pause and then in the same time voice, she said, "Yeah. I'm okay. Are they dead?"

Just then there was a scrape of brush from beyond the wagon and the faint *ching* of a spur.

Prophet turned toward the privy once more. "You sure you're all right?"

"I'm all right. Just make sure those bushwhacking dogs have been run to ground. They were moving up from behind the saloon, most likely intending to backshoot us both from the front entrance after we'd gone inside."

Louisa sounded indignant, as though she'd been cheated at high-stakes poker, though of course she'd never played the game.

"All right, all right," he muttered, turning to stare over the barrel of his cocked Colt, pondering the situation while worry for Louisa stabbed at him. She might have said she was all right, but she sure as hell didn't *sound* all right.

He couldn't let his guard down, though, until he was sure the other two gunmen were dead.

He got up, wincing at the aches and pains in his hips and shoulders. Leaving his hat on the ground with his Winchester, shoving a lock of disheveled hair out of his eye, he stole into shadows cast by the back of the cantina and the buildings beyond it. When he gained the wagon, moving slowly, Colt extended straight out in front of him, he found one of the gunmen lying dead in a pool of blood still dribbling from the gaping hole in his neck.

The other gunman wasn't there, but Prophet followed the path of his blood, which shone faintly in the starlight, out across a shallow ravine and into the flatland beyond.

The man sat against a boulder, both legs stretched out in front of him, hands in his lap. Prophet could see blood bibbing his chest, which rose and fell heavily, slowly. His rifle lay in the rocks beside him.

"I don't know why," he said in a voice only slightly pinched from pain, "but we never figured on the girl comin' around to the back."

Prophet went up and kicked the man's rifle away, then reached down, grabbed his revolver from his hip holster, and held it straight down in his left hand. He stared down at the man, who looked up at him blandly from beneath the brim of a high-crowned white hat.

His cheeks were bearded, but Prophet couldn't see his eyes. The man's double cartridge belts shone dully under his open denim jacket, moving slightly beneath his bulging belly as he breathed.

Prophet shook his head slowly. "Metalious sure ain't payin' you enough."

The dying man shook his own head and said, "Nope. He sure ain't."

He slumped straight sideways, gave a loud, final sigh, and lay still.

Prophet crossed the ravine and paused.

Louisa's shadow was moving near the privy and grunting with the effort. She seemed to be trying to hoist herself up, using her rifle as a staff.

"For chrissakes!" Prophet jogged over to her and dropped to a knee as she dropped back down onto her right hip and let her rifle fall against her. "Where you hit?"

"The other one."

"Leg?"

"Just a flesh wound. Like the other one. Only, this one hurts worse."

"I knew you were hit."

"Did you put those dogs down?"

"They won't be chasin' any more gut wagons."

Prophet looked at his partner's bloody left leg just above the knee, and worry gripped him. He couldn't tell if it was a flesh wound or not, but even if it was, she needed a doctor fast.

He ripped off his neckerchief.

"Stuff that in the wound while I get you to a sawbones."

Prophet slid his arms beneath her, and, pushing off his knees, climbed to his feet and started to head around the cantina.

"Wait — your rifle and hat."

"They'll keep."

"Put me down and get 'em!"

With a frustrated sigh, Prophet switched course, eased Louisa down while he donned his hat and grabbed his rifle, which she held along with her own as he scooped her up again. He looked through the cantina's open back door to see the bartender dragging the man Prophet had shot toward the doorless opening of the cantina. The bartender was dragging the dead gunman by his ankles, glancing over his shoulder to loudly curse and berate Prophet in Spanish, mostly for the ruined door, it seemed, though Prophet's handle of the man's lingo was of the cow-pen variety at best.

"Go easy, Lou," Louisa said as Prophet jogged across Bayonet Wash. She'd wrapped her arms around his neck, and with one hand she pulled affectionately, reassuringly at his left ear. "I'm gonna be all right."

"Shut up." Prophet ran toward Brush Street. "Jesus Christ, girl — we're gonna have to get you on a *diet!*"

As he and Louisa turned onto the main street, retracing their own recent footsteps, a gun barked three times quickly from straight ahead.

Prophet stopped in the middle of the street and stared toward the jailhouse a block away. Except for the Mecca Saloon just beyond it and on the other side of the street, it was the only building out there with lit windows. There was another *pop!* Two shadows moved on the porch, scurrying down the steps and into the street where a pair of saddled horses stood at the hitchrack, snorting nervously.

"Ah, Christ!" Prophet groaned, starting forward at an awkward run with Louisa in his arms. "Doesn't this town ever *sleep?*"

21

As Prophet ran toward the jailhouse, Louisa flopping like a rag doll in his arms, he saw the two shadowy figures mount the jittery horses, rein them away from the hitchrack, and boot them hard toward the west and out of town.

They disappeared into the darkness beyond the Mecca Saloon, the thuds of their galloping horses dwindling quickly. There was the muffled thud of something — a rifle? — hitting the ground as though carelessly cast away. Several men emerged from the Mecca — hatted shadows in the light of the oil lamps looking around warily, a couple holding drinks in their hands.

"What the hell's goin' on?" one yelled, turning toward Prophet who was angling toward the jailhouse.

"Took the words right out of my mouth," Prophet muttered as he took the porch steps heavy-footed.

"Careful, Lou," Louisa said, turning her head to look through the shack's open front door.

Prophet dropped Louisa into a chair on the porch. "Stay there."

Unsheathing his Colt and thumbing back the hammer with a ratcheting click, he stepped quickly through the open door and to one side. The rusty lamp over Utter's desk swung to and fro, illuminating the fresh gunsmoke webbing in the air in front of the jail cell.

Behind the still closed cell door, Prophet saw boots and dusty tan slacks, though the rest of Blanco was concealed in the cell's shadows. Utter himself was on the floor near his desk, his wheelchair tipped over, the top wheels turning slowly. The marshal was groaning and rubbing the back of his head with one hand while trying to push himself up with the other.

His shotgun was nowhere in sight. The holsters on his wheelchair were empty.

Prophet was surprised the man wasn't dead.

"What the hell happened?" he said, kneeling down beside the marshal and helping him turn onto his hip.

"That girl," Utter said, wincing as he continued to rub that back of his head. He'd been brained good. His eyes kept rolling back in their sockets.

"What girl?"

"The *Tawlin* girl! She came in here offering to fetch me a plate from the hotel. Soon as I turned my back, she brained me with her pistol butt!"

"Rose?" Prophet stared down at Utter, thinking the man must have gotten it wrong. "Why in the hell . . . ?"

Utter looked over his useless legs toward the far end of the office. "Her and some hard case . . . shot Blanco . . . took my keys and . . . took the stolen money out of the cell yonder. Son of a *bitch!*"

Prophet ran over to Blanco's cell, looked in. The outlaw was on the floor, grunting and groaning and moving his legs in agony. Prophet continued over to the next cell and peered through the open door.

The saddlebags had been taken off the cot. They were gone.

His mind reeling, Prophet grabbed the keys out of the lock of the open door, poked one into the lock of Blanco's door, and went in to inspect the prisoner. Blanco was holding both hands across a bloody chest wound and stretching his lips back from his teeth.

"That bastard shot me!" he wailed. "Shot me right through the damn cell door!"

Part of Blanco's left ear was gone. There was another wound in his lower right leg, and blood was oozing onto the floor beneath it.

"Fuckin' bastard shot me!" Blanco shouted, sobbing furiously as he threw his head back and loosed an enraged scream, rocking from side to side and kicking his legs.

"Who was it?"

"Waylon Adams. Waylon 'Gopher' Adams! Get after him — they just left!"

"Shut up." Prophet walked back out of Blanco's cell, leaving the door open. The outlaw wasn't going anywhere. He likely wouldn't be alive much longer. Prophet's weathered features were a mask of confusion.

Rose?

Waylon Adams?

They shot Blanco and stole the loot. Why? Heading where?

First things first.

Prophet got Utter back into his chair and then started toward the porch to help Louisa, but she was already standing in the doorway, leaning on her rifle and looking around with an expression much like Prophet's own.

"So she was bad," she said. "And she

threw back in with one of her own."

"Go after 'em!" Blanco shouted, kicking the front wall of his cell with a ringing bang. "Run that bitch and Gopher down and shoot 'em both!"

"The lobo's got a point," Louisa told Prophet.

Prophet looked down at her leg. Blood was oozing down the outside of her skirt. A thin red line of it meandered across her boot. "It's sawbones time for you."

He bent down and picked her up in his arms. As he started up the street toward the doctor's office, he stopped suddenly. A hunched shadow was shambling toward him, a shabby bowler tilted on his head, a black kit in his hand.

"They get Utter?" the doctor asked in a sleep-gravelly voice.

" 'They' just gave him a headache. Take care of this one first, Doc. Then, if he's still kickin', you better go sew Blanco up."

Prophet brushed past the medico, heading for the man's office. The doctor stared after him, baffled, then, muttering, started back the way he'd come, following Prophet.

Prophet hung around that night to make sure Louisa was on the mend. At dawn, she was sleeping comfortably there in the doctor's back room, her leg cleaned, sewn, and bandaged, so he planted a light kiss on her lips, then went out and saddled Mean and Ugly and a rangy gray that he rented from the livery barn. He walked the horses through town, then booted Mean hard for Socorro, his dust rising in the thin dawn light washing up over the tan jog of craggy eastern ridges.

He followed the stage trail for about four miles, then angled southeast, toward a notch in the ridge. There was a feeble horse trail here that had probably originated as an Indian trace. It was a shortcut that Utter had told him about, one which should save him a couple of hours as it pushed straight through the mountains rather than angling around their southern tip.

His intention was to alert the circuit judge and his army escort about Sam "Man-Killin' " Metalious's gang of roughnecks that would most likely try to ambush the detail somewhere between Corazon and Socorro. It seemed like mighty tough play, attacking a circuit judge as well as army men, but having met Metalious and seen the brand of riders he employed, Prophet felt it was a copper-riveted, lead-pipe cinch that the man would make it.

If the detail commander was as overconfident and arrogant as most young army officers, he'd likely want to stick to his route and rely on his own savvy as well as his men's to sniff out would-be bushwhackers, but Prophet intended to try to convince the man to take the shortcut. Or, at the very least, to send scout riders ahead of the detail.

Following the faint horse trail that hadn't been traveled at least since the last rain, Prophet rode up the notch, then down the other side. At the bottom, he switched horses, and leading Mean by the dun's reins, he followed a canyon between high sandstone walls due south. It was an ancient riverbed with fish fossils showing like broken china in the striated ridge walls.

As Utter's map indicated, there were a couple of runout springs. Prophet stopped at these to let the horses draw water and to take a short blow before he jerked their heads up from the needlegrass lining the springs and continued on.

He followed the canyon for mile after mile, and when he finally came out of it, riding up onto a cedar-stippled plateau, the wind was picking up, hazing the air with grit and tumbleweeds. There was the smell of cow shit and rain. The wind was generally mild, but there was an occasional chill edge to it.

Prophet pulled his hat brim down as he switched horses again and continued riding hard as the wind blasted him with a growing punch.

It was hard to judge the time, as the sun was obscured by blowing sand and weeds, but he figured it was a little before noon when he followed the track back onto the main trail a little outside of Socorro. The outlying shacks slid back away from him on both sides of the stage road. Few people were about, the wind keeping them inside. A couple of businesses were shuttered. The wind whipped the smell of goat dung, overfilled privies, and rotting trash toward him.

Holding his head down and squinting his eyes against the wind-driven sand that lashed his face like steel buckshot, Prophet followed the road past the Wells Fargo office and the Stockman's Bank and Trust. Suddenly, he jerked his spare mount to a halt.

Before him, in the middle of the wide street, was a gallows built of lumber that had turned bronze and silver with age. Three bodies twisted and turned as they hung from ropes beneath the platform, three hard-looking men — two in rough range garb, another in black slacks, dusty boots, and a shabby suitcoat.

Their necks were cocked at weird angles. One man's mouth was open; his tongue was sticking out like a snake poking its head from its hole to test the weather. The ropes creaked; the boots of the men — one of the punchers had kicked his left boot off as he'd died — nudged the gallows' undergirders with soft wooden thuds. Around them, Prophet noticed, the wind was gradually covering the fresh tracks of many onlookers.

Obviously, there'd been quite a turnout for the hangings.

Prophet's chest ached. "Ah, shit," he heard himself mutter against the wind. "Ah, hell — don't tell me!"

"Don't tell ya what?"

Prophet looked to his right. A beefy, goat-bearded gent in a sugarloaf sombrero stood outside the town marshal's office, holding his hat on his head with one hand. His leather vest was flapping around his big belly in the wind.

Prophet booted the gray over to the jailhouse, the shingle of which was swinging on its chain under the peaked porch roof. "The judge make it here already?"

"Sure did." The man looked at the hanged men and grinned.

"I hope he's still here."

"Why, no, no. He came in yesterday. We had the trial for them three rustlers in the saloon last night and hanged 'em this mornin'. The judge and the soldiers was pullin' out just as them fellas' necks was snappin'." The marshal chuckled and rolled a tobacco quid from one side of his mouth to the other. "I'm gonna leave 'em hangin' there a few days, for an example. Rustlin' be down for a few weeks, anyway — you can bet the seed bull on that!" He laughed.

Prophet had barely heard that last. He felt gut sick, stricken. Utter had said the judge pulled into Corazon on Wednesdays without fail. This was Monday. Taking the main stage trail, he was liable to pull in late today or early tomorrow.

The marshal seemed to be reading Prophet's mind as he continued to hold his big hat on his head. "He come early on account of him needin' to get back to Las Cruces by the end of the week for some hoedown with the territorial governor. Say, what's wrong, sonny? You look a mite off your feed."

Prophet looked around at his tired horses, feeling frustrated and helpless. He was tired himself, after that long ride. "He take the main trail?"

"I doubt that army ambulance he rides in

could handle anything *but* the main trail."

"How many men with him?"

"Six. Same as usual. Six bluebellies from Fort Stockton. Lieutenant Ezekial Lewis is leadin' 'em up. There's Clelleant Hamburger and four others."

"How good are they?"

The marshal narrowed one eye. "Say, this doesn't have anything to do with Sam 'Man-Killin' ' Metalious — does it?"

Ah, shit. "Why do you ask?"

" 'Cause a couple of his men pulled in a couple days ago, been hangin' around. One rode out last night . . . just after the judge's detail rode in."

Prophet pondered this quickly, feeling his brows becoming a miniature mountain range. Metalious had apparently posted men here to watch for the judge, in case his other tactics for springing his son failed.

Which they had.

"How far is Metalious's ranch from here?"

"Straight north, on the other side of the San Mateos."

"Shit!" Prophet looked northward as if judging the distance between Metalious's owlhoot camp and the stage road. Too damn close, he concluded. He could have men on the trail right now, waiting for the judge's detail.

"Point me to a good livery stable. I'm gonna need another horse!"

The marshal did, his own gray brows bunching curiously.

Prophet headed for the San Mateo Livery and Feed, where he exchanged the gray for a willowy sorrel. Mean had enough bottom to continue traveling, since he hadn't been ridden for a good hour or so. But Prophet needed at least one fresh mount for relieving the lineback dun farther up the trail.

He wasted no time switching saddles while the liveryman worried aloud about how Prophet was going to get the gray back to Corazon, as the man didn't want to get hanged for a rustler. When Prophet had assured the man that he'd get the horse returned to its rightful owner in due time, and had paid for a day's rent of the sorrel, he climbed onto Mean's back and headed out along the stage road, riding hard.

The wind had picked up, making it so impossible for Prophet to keep his hat on his head that he finally gave up and stuffed it into one of his saddlebag pouches. He continued past the placc where he'd entered the stage road less than an hour ago and urged as much speed as he could from Mean and Ugly.

The horse didn't like the weather any better than Prophet did; the big, ugly dun kept shaking his head and blowing against the dust pelting his eyes.

The trail traced a slow arc from southeast to due north, swinging wide of a spur outcropping of the southernmost San Mateos. It crossed an old lakebed, with black mounds of lava rock jutting up like dinosaur spines from the chalky white alkali dust, though it seemed that most of the dust was in the air, making it so hard for Prophet to see that he squeezed his eyes closed for long intervals and let Mean and Ugly find his own way.

Once they were past the lakebed with its alkali floor, the dust storm seemed to lighten considerably, and Mean gave a relieved whinny and lunged into a faster gallop.

Prophet wasn't an hour beyond the lakebed before he spied the first dead soldier.

22

Judging by the sergeant's stripes on the soldier's wool-clad forearms, the man lying along the edge of the stage road was Sergeant Hamburger. The big man with a thick, bushy, ginger-colored beard lay on his back, stout legs crossed at the ankles. His hat was gone, and his thin, white-blond hair was blowing in the wind around his freckled pate.

A bloody hole shone in his right temple.

The man's Colt Army .44 was still in its holster, which likely meant he'd been taken by surprise. Beyond him to the right of the trail, two army bay horses stood facing downwind, their tails blowing up under their bellies. One's McClellan saddle hung down the animal's side.

Prophet looked around wildly, dread in his eyes. He continued ahead along the trail until he found another dead soldier, a private, amongst deep hoof scuffs that the wind had not yet covered. Just beyond the dead private deep wheel ruts showed where a wagon had recently turned suddenly off the trail's left side and churned up sage as it plowed west over rocks and cedars.

Prophet followed the tracks, finding three more dead soldiers lying twisted and bloody along the ground. One had smashed his head to a red-and-white pulp when he'd apparently been thrown from his horse and onto a rock. He'd been shot once in the chest; another ragged, bloody hole shone in his outthrust right hand.

He'd at least gotten his revolver out, though it was nowhere in sight. His black holster was empty, the flap hanging loose.

Prophet dismounted and let Mean and the sorrel turn downwind as the bounty hunter automatically reached around to grab his sawed-off ten-gauge as he continued following the wheel ruts on foot. The ruts descended a slight grade, turned around a sandstone outcropping, and then continued down the grade once more, where the incline became steeper.

Prophet stopped in his own tracks and stared downhill. The army ambulance lay broken and twisted at the bottom of a sandy wash, two dead horses still in the traces.

Gritting his teeth against the flying dust

and weeds, Prophet ran down the grade, leaped the four-foot cutbank to land flat-footed on the wash's floor, then crouched to look inside the ambulance that had been crushed like a cardboard matchbox under a heavy foot. No sign of the judge. Just beyond the wagon, though, a blue-clad body — probably that of the driver — lay between the two dead horses.

Prophet spied a blood trail leading away from the ambulance and followed it to where an elderly man in a conservative though now torn and bloody black suit lay on the other side of a scrub and boulder snag. The man lay belly down in the sand. He'd been shot through the backs of both knees, through the middle of his back, and then through the back of his bald head.

The tails of his clawhammer coat blew in the wind.

He'd survived the wreck. As he'd tried to crawl away from it, he'd been shot so he'd die slowly, for the amusement of his wolf-like killers. Beyond him lay an open black valise, and beyond the valise, downwind, papers rolled, danced, and fluttered about the sage.

Prophet stared at the papers. He looked down at the judge. Dread was a railroad spike being driven slowly through his stomach to his spine.

Metalious had struck. And he'd had fun doing it. Likely, when he and his gang of kill-crazy cutthroats arrived in Corazon, they'd have an even grander time.

And in their conditions, there was little that Marshal Utter or even the Vengeance Queen could do to stop them.

"Windy night," said the barman of the Mecca Saloon, looking over the polished surface of his mahogany bar at Utter looking up at him from his chair. Utter had a thick, white bandage attached to the back of his head where the Tawlin girl had laid the butt of her old cap-and-ball revolver across it.

The marshal's eyes were sharp from agitation. This whole thing with Blanco had him so far off his feed he didn't think he'd ever be hungry again.

"So it is. Give me a bottle, C. J."

"Tennessee stuff?"

"Why the hell not?"

Utter looked around. The saloon's broad, long hall was empty, all the tables sponged, chairs pushed neatly beneath them. Brass spittoons glistened here and there beneath the softly chuffing and sighing oil lamps.

"The wind keepin' everyone away?" the

marshal asked as the barman rummaged around amongst the shelves beneath the bar.

When he straightened with a grunt and set a corked, amber bottle with the familiar label of etched southern hills on its belly, he smoothed a lock of chestnut hair back from his forehead with a beringed hand.

"Nothin' like the wind for killin' business. Cowpunchers hate wind. I reckon it's because they're in it all day. Even the town fellas stay to home when the wind blows. It depresses my girls."

He cocked his head toward the stairs runnin' up the right side of the room's rear wall. "Both of 'em are piled up in bed with either a headache or stomach cramps."

"Don't bother me." Utter flipped the man two silver dollars, which the bartender grabbed as though he were catching flies. "When I was runnin' down in Mexico with two good legs about a hundred and one years ago, an old Mexican told me that we hate wind so bad because it reminds us of time's passing and our eventual deaths."

Utter leaned forward in his chair to grab the bottle that the barman held over the edge of the bar to him.

"Used to nettle me. Don't no more." Utter stuffed the bottle down between his skinny thighs and began to turn the chair toward the doors. "Let her blow."

He wheeled himself around the tables to the front doors, both of which were closed against the wind, which he could hear moaning out there.

"You want help, Max?" the barman asked behind him.

Utter shoved one of the doors open, which the wind grabbed and slammed back against the wall. "No. Best stay inside, C. J."

"You still got Blanco locked up over there?"

"Of course I damn do!"

The barman leaned over the counter, giving the marshal a thoughtful look as he awkwardly maneuvered himself out the open door and into the blasting wind.

"Why don't you just let him go? Hell, he's headed for a bad end. It'll come to him soon enough. Let him go, and go on home to bed, Max!"

Utter stopped, his chair slanted in the doorway, one front wheel caught on the threshold. The marshal's eyes were big as 'dobe dollars, and his nostrils were pinched. "If I did that, you fool, it'd be like hangin' a big wooden placard around my neck announcin' Corazon is a haven to the wicked and lawless of every stripe. Come one, come all! Rob our bank, and rape our women!

And, oh, by the way — free girls and drinks over to the Mecca Saloon, courtesy of C. J. Boone!"

Utter jerked his chair loose and turned his back to the room. "Damn fool!"

He slammed the door shut behind him.

He sat there for a time, looking slowly up and down the street that was already dark though it was not yet six o'clock. Clouds had blown in earlier, spitting rain. The rain had stopped for now, but the wind was still whipping around and howling like the Devil's hounds. There was a wan, pink-and-lemon glow low in the east, and the few puddles along Brush reflected the light eerily.

No one was out. All that moved was dust and horse shit and the occasional bits of wind-whipped trash and tumbleweeds.

Cursing under his breath — he'd lied about the wind; it still graveled him — Utter wheeled himself to the edge of the saloon's porch, leaned back to lift his front wheels, and eased himself ahead until his big back wheels dropped with a thud down the porch's first step.

Thud! Thud! Thud!

And then he was in the street and grunting with the labor of wheeling himself at an angle across the rutted trace toward the jailhouse on the other side.

His windows glowed with nearly the same color as the feeble sunset. Halfway between the saloon and the jail, Utter stopped, looking south along Brush Street.

A figure, silhouetted against the east light, had moved out from an alley mouth, stopped, then moved back into the alley. Utter stared at the gap between Hackson's Drugstore and Pedro's Barbershop. After a time, he looked around him cautiously. Deciding that his jangled nerves were causing him to see gunmen where there was probably only trash blowing around, he closed his hands around his india-rubber-shod wheels and continued pushing himself toward the jailhouse.

He couldn't help wishing, in the back of his mind, that Prophet were here. But someone needed to ride down to Socorro and warn the judge about a possible ambush, which, he'd finally agreed with the bounty hunter, was fully in the realm of Sam "Man-Killin' " Metalious's capabilities. (Supposedly, there'd soon be a telegraph line connecting Corazon to the outside world, but the stringing of the line kept getting delayed.) If the judge didn't make it to Corazon, this whole thing was pointless. Nothing and no one shy of half an army could get Blanco to the court up in Albuquerque.

Utter wouldn't let the killer free, though. He'd kill him before he'd do that.

Likely, Prophet would get through to Socorro. Just as likely, Metalious's bunch of man-killers was holed up along the stage road somewhere, waiting for the judge's contingent. If Prophet accomplished his mission, Lieutenant Lewis and Sergeant Hamburger would be ready for the ambush, and they'd turn old Sam and his border toughs out with cavalry-grade shovels.

They'd be snuggling with diamondbacks by noon the day after tomorrow, and the judge would be along a few hours later. Potentially, by the end of Wednesday, Blanco could be hanging from one of the jury limbs down along the creek. No need for a gallows! A few hours after that, coyotes would be standing on their hind legs to chew his feet.

Utter smiled at that image as he used the rope to hoist himself up the jail office porch steps.

When he'd hauled himself inside and closed the door on the wind, Doc Blanchard was just stepping out of Blanco's open cell and setting his top hat on his gray head at a learned-man's angle. The doctor closed the cell door with a resounding bang.

"Will he make it till Wednesday, Doc?" Utter wheeled himself over to his desk atop which he set the whiskey bottle.

"That young firebrand has nine lives, I swear. Between him and Miss Bonaventure, I don't know who's luckier. She's been hit in both legs and seems to be doing fine. Blanco's lost about half of all his blood, and I'll be damned if it doesn't seem he'll make it. That bullet in his chest sort of caromed around his ribs and exited under his arm, striking little more than sinew. A rib's broken, but he'll get over that."

"Glad he's on the mend. I want him at least healthy enough to hang. Healthy enough so he's wide awake when he sees Ole Scratch sauntering toward him with his forked tail curled in greeting." Utter laughed as he grabbed the coffeepot off the potbelly stove's warming rack, and filled a stone mug on his desk.

The doctor set his black kit on the desk, in front of Utter, and began buttoning his long, black greatcoat. "That'll be four dollars."

"Four dollars?"

"A dollar for each wound I cleaned. I'm throwing in the exit wound for free. That ear took twenty-six stitches. Another dollar for medication. If he doesn't take the powder I've mixed up, he'll be howlin' so you'll think there's an entire pack of wolves in here." Blanchard grinned. "And I bet this room really echoes."

"Take it up with the mayor!" Utter intoned as he popped the cork on his Old Tennessee. "I don't keep any money around here except my own, and that usually goes to feed myself. If I'd depended on the county to honor my food vouchers, I'd have shriveled up to nothin' by now!"

"You're impossible, Max," the doctor growled as he strode toward the door.

"Thank you!"

The doctor went out and slammed the door behind him. A moment later the door opened again, and the doctor stuck his long, craggy face into the jailhouse, grinning devilishly. "Riders comin' from the south."

He pulled his head back out and slammed the door so hard that the whole room shook and Blanco sighed in his sleep.

23

Utter took a deep draw of his bourbon-laced coffee and slammed the mug down on his desk. He reached over to grab his double-bore from where it reclined against the wall and breeched it to make sure it was loaded. The girl and Gopher had swiped his shotgun, but Prophet had found it where they'd cast it off along the trail at the edge of town.

When Utter had snapped it closed, he set the shotgun across his thighs and turned his wheelchair so that he faced the timbered door.

He pricked his ears, listening.

Blanco snored softly in the cell off Utter's right flank. The coffeepot on the stove chugged. The wind was a monster pressing against the door and caterwauling as though trying desperately to shove it open.

Utter frowned. Had the doc been toying with him?

Then he heard the hoof thuds on the street fronting the jailhouse. A horse snorted and a bridle chain rattled. The sounds were almost inaudible beneath the savage wind, and Utter likely wouldn't have heard them had he not been listening for them.

But there they were.

Riders didn't necessarily mean Metalious's men. But who else would be out on a night like this? If it was really Man-Killin's boys, Prophet was probably dead. And so was the judge.

Which meant Utter was all that stood between Sam and his boy.

The thought was as raw as a panhandle winter.

Utter ratcheted back the shotgun's left hammer, then the right, feeling the eyelash triggers slide out to the middle of the trigger guard, pressing against the marshal's right index finger. They were firm and cool against his calloused skin. Reassuring.

If anything could hold Metalious off, the Greener could.

He waited. The wind moaned. The ceiling timbers creaked. The coffeepot chugged. And Blanco snored.

Utter nervously ran his tongue along the edge of his lower lip. His heart beat a steady rhythm in his chest. Slowly, he slid the shotgun out across his right knee, aiming the double-bore at the door.

The door burst open.

Ka-boommmm!

The tall, hatted figure standing there in a blowing duster flew straight back out across the porch and into the street, as though he'd been lassoed from behind. Another man appeared at the door's right side, his eyes widening when he saw Utter's Greener aimed at him. He pulled his head back away from the door as Utter tripped the second trigger.

Ka-boommmm!

Part of the door frame disappeared along with a large chunk of the wall.

A big man in a long buffalo coat and wearing a low-crowned black hat and smoking a cigar marched up the porch steps. Metalious stepped across the threshold and into the jail office. He held a cocked revolver down low in his right hand.

With his left hand, he removed the cigar from his mouth and smiled. "The problem with them barn blasters is they only hold two shells."

Louisa set her empty teacup down on the doctor's pine eating table.

Something sounded outside beneath the

howling wind. She'd been about to refill her teacup from the kettle on the doctor's potbelly stove, intending to have one more cup before heading over to the jailhouse, as the doctor had wrapped not only the fresh wound in her left leg but the older one in the other leg with crushed mint and parego-ric. But now she turned away from the stove and walked to the west-facing window, slid-ing the faded green curtain aside with the back of her hand.

Amidst the blowing trash and weeds in the street, two riders, hats tipped low on their foreheads, were riding in the direction of the jailhouse. In the stormy afterglow, guns shone on their hips and in their saddle sheaths. A wagon came up behind them, a bulky man in a buffalo coat in the driver's box. A fur rifle boot was strapped to the box's right side, within the driver's easy reach.

Within Metalious's easy reach.

Fury burned through Louisa. It was like a nail hammered through one temple and out the other. Of course, she had nothing personal against Metalious's bunch, but she took her bounty-hunting/killing job more seriously than most.

She whipped around, mindless of the pain in both legs, and grabbed her carbine off the table. She'd already dressed and wrapped her Colts around her lean waist, under her poncho. Now she grabbed her hat off a peg beside the door and was reaching for the knob when the door opened, and the doctor stumbled into his second-story quarters on a violent wind gust.

"Good Christ — it's really blowing out there!" As he started to close the door, he bunched his brows at Louisa. "Where do you think you're going, young lady?"

Louisa grabbed the door out of his hand, pulling it wider. "Out of the way, Doc."

"You don't want to go out there. Metalious and his men are here."

"I saw."

"For cryin' out loud, you've got a hole in each leg!"

The man had stumbled around to berate her further but Louisa stepped out, barely limping, setting her teeth against the tightness in both wounds, and pulled the door closed behind her. She had to take her time descending the stairs — the last thing she wanted was to open up that recent wound and lose more blood — but as she reached the bottom she swung northwestward, facing the jailhouse.

The riders had stopped at the jailhouse's near front corner, the wagon behind them.

Louisa began moving ahead, keeping to the darkness on the street's right side, as the two riders swung down from their mounts and, shucking rifles from their saddle boots, walked one behind the other up the jailhouse's porch steps.

"Oh, no."

She knew what these killers' presence here in Corazon meant about Lou's success at alerting the judge.

Louisa walked as fast as she could but had to stop behind a porch awning post and a rain barrel as more of Metalious's riders came up from behind her, passing her as they joined their boss and the other two men.

She dropped to one knee behind the rain barrel and watched the first two riders — one stepping to the jailhouse door's left side while the other stopped in front of it. He raised his elbows, then a knee, and smashed the bottom of his right boot against the door.

Louisa could hear the crash as the door burst open.

She could also hear the loud blast of the shotgun, see the man who'd been standing in front of the door jerk up and back and hit the street about six feet back from the steps. The two ground-tied saddle horses

310

whinnied and skitter-stepped at the sudden concussion.

The other rider poked his head in front of the door.

There was another blast. Then Metalious, who'd been waiting near the bottom of the porch steps but out of the line of fire from inside, puffing a cigar downwind, mounted the steps with casual arrogance. As he disappeared inside, Louisa racked a fresh round into her carbine's breech. She walked out from behind the barrel, aiming the Winchester at the still mounted riders who fanned out around Metalious's buckboard.

A man's deep voice said behind her, "Where you think you're goin', princess?"

She'd just started to swing the carbine around, when something cold and hard pressed against the back of her neck.

"I'll take that iron," the man said. "Or you'll take a bullet."

Louisa's heart hammered. Could she swing around and shoot this dog before he could shoot her? Of course, she couldn't. If she tried, she'd die. She'd most likely die, anyway, but she'd like to stick around long enough to take a few of these human dung beetles with her.

Louisa let the carbine hang limp in her right hand. The man reached around and, keeping the barrel of his .45 pressed against her side, took the carbine out of her hands and threw it into the street.

A couple of the other riders heard the thud and turned toward Louisa. One smiled. The man who had his gun in her ribs — she could smell his rancid breath despite the wind — pressed his face close to hers as he slipped both her pistols from their holsters, tossing one into the street. He gave the other a quick, cursory inspection, raised an appreciative brow, then stuffed it down behind the buckle of his own shell belt.

He gave Louisa a hard shove toward the jailhouse. Her fresh wound barked, and she dropped to her knees with an involuntary groan, grinding her teeth against the pain.

Inside the jailhouse, Sam "Man-Killin' " Metalious stared down at his son, asleep on the cot. Utter sat near the woodstove. He'd been relieved of his shotgun and sidearms, and now he sat there gritting his teeth as one of Metalious's men held his chair so he couldn't wheel himself to the gun rack.

"Who shot him?" Metalious barked at the marshal.

Utter grinned tightly. "Had us a robbery. Same girl who stole the stolen loot out of the next cell shot Blanco."

"Who's the girl? The *blonde?*" Metalious's

big, dark-complected, bearded face resembled that of a rampaging grizzly. "No one shoots a Metalious!"

"Well, she didn't get the word. And it wasn't the blonde."

"Where's the money?"

"Gone."

Metalious's nostrils flared. He clenched the fist of his free hand, then lifted his gaze to the hard case holding Utter's chair. "Fetch the doc. Tell him to pack an overnight bag. Be quick about it."

The man wheeled and tramped out of the jailhouse.

Metalious looked at Utter. He holstered his pistol then walked slowly, menacingly around behind Utter. He grabbed the porcelain knobs at the back of the marshal's chair and jerked the chair straight back. Utter nearly flew forward and onto the floor but managed to catch himself by the chair arms.

Then he was thrown back in the seat as Metalious spun him around and, yowling like a wildcat, pushed the marshal at breakneck speed through the office, out the open door, and onto the porch.

"Wait!" Utter wailed. *"Stop!"*

Too late.

Metalious had given him an extra-violent shove at the top of the porch steps, hurling the marshal down the steps and into the dark, windblown street. Utter piled up at the bottom of the steps, belly down on the ground, his wheelchair tipped on one side atop him, the big side wheel spinning.

Utter groaned, clawed at the street, his ear ringing.

Metalious shuttled his gaze left of the fallen marshal. One of his men, Burt Lomax, stood near the porch steps, grinning as he held his .45 to the back of Louisa's head.

"Look what I found," Lomax said.

"The blonde!" Metalious laughed malevolently. "Where's that other bounty hunter — that big devil with the Winchester '73?"

"Ain't seen him."

Metalious looked around carefully. He walked down the porch steps, sidestepping Utter, who continued to moan and groan and claw at the street. Continuing to look around warily, holding his cocked Colt out in front of him, Metalious turned toward where the gunman named Bolt was coming with the doctor in tow.

"Any sign of that big bounty man?" Metalious asked him.

"I ain't seen him."

Metalious looked at the doctor, who looked incensed at being hustled out of his

314

warm digs on this dark, windy night. "How 'bout you, Doc?"

The doctor looked at the cocked Colt in Metalious's fist, and shook his head. "He left town."

"I got a feelin' he'll be back." Metalious looked at Lomax. "Put her in the wagon. Tie her up. And keep a gun at her. Doc, you're goin' with us to tend my boy. When he's up and around, back bein' his own self again, I'll have a man run you back to town."

"You can't kidnap me. I've a business to run!"

"Yeah, well, you're runnin' it."

The burly Metalious gave an oily grin. He ordered two of the other riders to fetch Blanco from the jail, then, as the doctor and Louisa were both put up into the wagon, the outlaw leader walked over to where Utter had finally managed to roll onto his back.

The marshal's lips and nose were bloody. His mussed hair blew in the chill wind.

Metalious held his cocked Colt out away from his body, squinting down the barrel as he drew a bead on Utter's forehead. Utter's eyes widened when he saw the .45's large, round maw bearing down on him.

He looked around the gun at Metalious.

He grinned savagely, clenching his fists. "Go ahead."

Metalious held the gun steady. Then he depressed the hammer. "What — and leave Corazon without a proper lawman?"

Laughing, Metalious holstered the .45.

Then, guffawing as though at the funniest joke he'd ever heard, he shambled back to his wagon. Louisa sat on the right side of the driver's box, ankles tied, her wrists tied behind her. The doctor was in the back with Blanco, who sat up on the edge of the tailgate while two outlaw riders spread a buffalo robe on the floor of the box, as per the doctor's reluctant orders.

"Christ, his wounds are gonna open up!" the doctor complained to Metalious.

The outlaw leader climbed into the driver's box, sat down beside Louisa, and released the brake. "That's what you're here for, Doc. My boy dies, you die. You an' this purty little girl! After she done screamin', that is."

Metalious roared.

He turned the wagon around and, his riders mounting up and swinging around as well, headed back along Brush Street. The wind wailed like a thousand angry demons behind him.

24

Prophet had had lousy luck on the trail back from the dead judge and his contingent of murdered soldiers.

His freshest horse, the sorrel, had gone lame after stepping off the trail and into a prairie dog hole. Prophet had turned him loose, as he couldn't be ridden, and hoped the mount found its way back to the livery barn in Socorro. He had to take his time with Mean despite his burning, aching, heart-hammering desire to get back to Corazon as fast as possible.

He wouldn't be going anywhere with a dead horse.

He was walking the lineback dun along the wind-combed trail, making his way through the stormy darkness, when the rattle of a fast-moving wagon sounded from ahead. Quickly, he led the dun off the trail and into some scrub, where he tied him, then shucked his Winchester from the saddle boot.

He hurried back to the side of the trail, hunkered low behind a boulder. The moon was coming up, resembling an old dime behind thin, wind-tattering clouds in the east. By its wan light he could see the riders moving along the trail from the direction of Corazon.

The wagon's clattering grew louder as the jostling figures on the two horses fronting the wagon and on the wagon itself grew larger. As they came within thirty yards, Prophet dropped to his butt behind the boulder and, pressing his back to the rock, swung his body to look around the rock's right side.

The wagon passed in front of him. Prophet blinked, his features hardening into an expression of incredulity and anger.

Louisa rode in the wagon's driver's box beside the big, bearded Metalious. At least one other man was in the wagon box — Prophet saw a high, domed forehead and a thin thatch of blowing, silvery hair. Something else lay humped behind the wagon's low side panel. Probably Blanco. If they had Louisa, Utter was either dead or dying, and Metalious had gotten his son back.

Resisting the urge to run out into the trail, shooting, Prophet tightened his jaws and

318

rolled back behind the rock, thoughts racing. He no longer much cared for what happened to Blanco. His old man could have him. Prophet would even wish him a long, wicked life if he could get Louisa back safely.

When the caravan had drifted out of sight in the darkness, Prophet heaved his weary body to his sore feet and tramped back to where he'd left Mean and Ugly. He'd only started walking the horse about a mile down trail. Mean still needed a rest, as he was standing splay-legged and hang-headed. If Prophet tried to keep up with Metalious on Mean's back, the horse would drop, and the bounty hunter would be stranded out here.

He'd gone as far as he could go without several hours' solid rest.

"Shit," Prophet groused, turning to stare after Louisa.

There was nothing to be done about it. Since Metalious hadn't killed her yet, she probably wasn't in immediate danger. Prophet would find a campsite out here somewhere, rest both himself and the horse, and start after Metalious's bunch in a few hours. They'd likely bed down when they got back to their outlaw ranch, and that would give Prophet time to catch up to them.

"Man-Killin' " Sam's wagon would leave a good trail despite the wind that seemed to be picking up all the dust and tumbleweeds in western New Mexico and hurling them in all directions. The rain seemed to have passed.

He led Mean back away from the trail. In the dull, silver-blue light of the slowly rising moon, he saw a low ridge on the other side of a shallow wash. Reaching the ridge — a long, weathered sandstone spine — he found a natural alcove big enough for both him and his horse.

He scouted the notch to make sure he wasn't intruding on a bobcat or wolf. Seeing only a shredded pack rat's nest amongst the rocks at the back of the place, he led Mean inside and quickly unsaddled him, piling the gear along the base of one wall. He watered the horse from his hat, then fed him a couple of handfuls of parched corn from his saddlebags.

The bounty hunter was so weary himself from the many miles he'd covered over the past several hours, and from the stress of knowing that a notorious, cold-blooded killer had Louisa, that he was fairly groaning and dragging his boot toes as he worked. But he took his time rubbing Mean down with a swatch of burlap and inspecting the horse's hooves for thorns and stones.

He didn't like to admit it, but next to Louisa, Mean and Ugly was his best friend. He depended on the horse nearly as much as he depended on the Vengeance Queen herself, and he took pains to make sure the horse got the best care possible.

It worried him that Mean was so tired that he didn't even try to give his owner a devilish nip. Prophet hoped like hell the dun would be ready to ride again in a few hours.

Finished with the rubdown and hoof-and-hock inspection, Prophet patted Mean and Ugly's hip. "Get some shut-eye, pard. Ready or not, we'll be pullin' out in a few hours. The girl's in trouble again."

Mean turned his head to Prophet, twitched one ear halfheartedly, and gave a somewhat reassuring snort.

Prophet was inclined to forgo coffee and just rest his own weary bones, but the brew would do him good. He wasn't hungry, but he'd gone without food since a rushed breakfast that morning in Corazon, and he had to have something to build his strength back up.

He gathered driftwood from the wash, and some dry leaves and cedar needles, and dug a little pit in the alcove about six feet from the walls on either side of him. The wind kept blasting down over the top of the ridge, pelting him with sand and blowing out his fledgling flames. He continued to coax the fire until it was going on its own, crackling and snapping and nibbling the sun-cured cottonwood sticks.

His dented coffeepot was chugging when a spur rang just outside the alcove. Instantly, the double-bore was in his hands and he was thumbing both hammers back.

A voice said, "Lou?"

Prophet scowled into the howling darkness beyond the ten-foot-wide mouth of the alcove.

"Come closer," he called above the wind. "I got my double-bore cocked and ready to fly!"

Another spur ching. A shadow moved just beyond the notch. The figure came closer until Rose Tawlin was standing just inside the doorway, a long duster that was too big for her blowing about the tops of her stockmen's boots. She wore a hat that was likewise a couple of sizes too big and a blue neckerchief blew around her neck.

She held her hands shoulder high, palms out.

Prophet's rugged, heavy-browed, broad-nosed face contorted into an expression of disbelief.

"I wouldn't blame you if you shot me."

"What the hell are you doin' here, Rose? Or should I be callin' you Jane?"

"It's Rose." The girl took a couple more slow steps inside the alcove and glanced hungrily down at the coffeepot.

"Where's your friend Gopher?"

"Dead." Rose looked at Prophet and licked her lips. She had a sad, lonely expression on her face. Desperation shone faintly in her dark eyes, beneath the wide, bending brim of the weather-stained hat. "He was pestering me, tryin' to get me to bed down with him. Wouldn't take no for an answer. Surprising, how easy it was to shoot him."

Keeping her hands raised to her shoulders but letting the fingers curl back toward the palms, she looked around the alcove. She wasn't studying Prophet's bivouac, however. Deeply perplexed, she was trying to gather her thoughts.

Finally, she let her gaze slide back to the bounty hunter sitting cross-legged beside the fire, his hat cuffed back off his forehead. He was still aiming the double-bore at her belly. "But it wouldn't have surprised you — how easy it was for me to kill a man. Would it, Lou?"

"I reckon not."

"How did you know?"

323

"I saw the wanted dodger amongst those bundled in Utter's desk. He hadn't gone through them yet. I snagged the one with your likeness on it — or, that of alias Miss Kansas Jane, last seen with the cattle rustler and sometime stage robber, Junior Pope."

Prophet frowned. "Your bad memory suddenly shook clear, did it?"

Rose shook her head. "It was gone. Truly. You don't know how terrifying it is to wake up in a strange place and not know who you are. Then it's even worse when you suddenly remember, and everything — all the ugly things about your ugly past, at least the past that started when I ran away from home and started running with Pope — came tumbling back into place. I didn't fall and hit my head again. It didn't happen like that. I was just sitting there across the fire from Gopher Adams — he used to run with Junior, too — and the memories came fluttering down like a flock of Canada geese in a freshly mown hayfield."

Prophet's voice was hard, his right eye narrowed suspiciously. "Why did Gopher give Blanco that case of lead poisonin'?"

Rose, or Kansas Jane, or whoever the hell she was now, hiked a shoulder. "Had some past beef with him, I reckon. I just know Gopher hated him. I take it he ain't dead.

Was that him in the back of his old man's wagon?"

Prophet heaved himself to his feet. Though his angry expression remained fixed, he depressed the hammers of the double-bore. He reached forward and slipped Rose's old cap-and-ball revolver from her holster, and held it down by his side. "You got any more weapons?"

"Just that one. When I shot Gopher I was too nervous to think about his guns."

"I won't frisk you, but I wouldn't make any sudden moves if I was you." Prophet's gaze hardened even more. "What's your game, Kansas Jane?"

"I'm done with games."

Prophet chuffed his disdain.

"I am, Lou. After I shot Gopher, I came back to Corazon hopin' to find you."

"And the loot you'd thought you'd stolen out of the jail cell." Prophet smiled coldly. "I'd like to have seen your face when you saw them saddlebags filled with old wanted dodgers."

Rose looked baffled, shaking her head slowly. "You were that certain I'd try to swipe them?"

"No, but after I saw the circular with your mug on it, along with your phony name, I figured there was a pretty good chance."

"You were setting a trap." It was a cold statement, not a question.

"I hoped you wouldn't spring it. But I was wrong, wasn't I?"

"I didn't spring it. It was Gopher who sprang it. He forced me into his scheme, said he'd tell everyone who I really was, since no one around Corazon had seen me in the three years I was gone from Pa's and Ma's ranch and didn't remember. I didn't want you to know. I wasn't sure then that I even believed what Gopher was telling me, but I knew there was a chance. And . . ."

Rose shook her head again as she crossed her arms on her chest and turned away from Prophet's accusatory glare. "I didn't want you and Louisa to know."

"That wasn't a real good strategy for keepin' it all a secret."

Looking at the alcove's wall and rubbing her arms as though chilled, Rose said, "He said he'd let me go once he had the Wells Fargo and bank loot. It must have gotten around town that Utter was keeping it in his jail. I thought Gopher was just going to take the loot. I didn't know he was going to shoot Blanco." She glanced at him curiously. "Where was the loot, anyway?"

"Where it still is — in Utter's beer cellar. I can tell you that, because I'm not letting

326

you out of my sight until we get back to Corazon. You can have Blanco's cell. The cot's all warmed up for you. Pardon the bloodstains."

She wheeled toward him, a desperate look pinching her eyes and lifting a flush in her cheeks. "Oh, Lou! Won't you please believe and understand me?" She squeezed his left forearm with both her hands. "I want to help you. I . . . I'm not Kansas Jane. I once was. But I don't want to repeat the bad things I've done. Deep down inside me, I'm good. I felt it when I had nothing else but my feelings to gauge myself with. I didn't know it before, because my thoughts were so twisted and clouded by all the boring years on the ranch, with a father who hardly ever let me ride with him to town because he didn't want boys staring at me! And a mother who worked me half to death when she herself was taken to bed with headaches!"

Rose slumped down against the alcove wall, near the fire. She rested her elbows on her knees and stared bleakly into the dancing flames.

"Junior had been riding with Blanco for the past couple months while I was holed up in Amarillo, hiding from the law and running out of loot we'd stole over in

Oklahoma. I never met Blanco. Anyway, when him and Junior were pulling the stage holdup and then the bank robbery in Corazon, I talked Junior into riding over to the home ranch with me."

"Bringin' the beau to meet the folks, huh?" Prophet said ironically, dropping to one knee beside the fire and filling his tin cup with coffee.

"You want to hear the rest?" she asked him shortly.

"Wouldn't miss it." Begrudgingly, he slid the coffee toward her, then dug another cup out of his saddlebags and filled it as she continued.

"I invited Junior because I didn't want Pa to try to force me to stay on at the place. I was done with that life. I only went to see them and my little brother. But we got there a day too late, just after the Apaches struck. Junior helped me bury them." Rose's left eye twitched, and her upper lip quivered slightly. "What was left of them."

She paused again.

"Junior and I stayed in the bunkhouse for a few days. We were staying there together and were fixin' to light out together to join Blanco for the robberies. I was out of money as well as ideas about what to do with myself, with my folks dead an' all. Only,

Junior lit out late one night after I went to sleep. I reckon he wasn't ready for fatherhood."

Prophet frowned at her over his smoking coffee cup.

"It wasn't shootin' that claim jumper that got me sick to my stomach," Rose said.

Prophet continued staring at her over the rim of his cup, chewing his lower lip. Slowly, he nodded. "Bun in the oven." He grimaced and took another sip of his coffee.

"When you found me and I hit my head, I'd been trailin' Junior. I wanted some of that money from the robbery for me and my baby. Claim jumpers crowded me off the ranch."

Rose stared at Prophet as though gauging his reaction to all this as she lifted her own coffee cup in her hands and tilted it toward her mouth.

"You see," she said when she'd taken a sip, "I've got a real good reason to settle down." She took another sip, licked her upper lip, kept her fire-bright eyes on Prophet. "And to make right what I can make right. I figure helpin' you get Louisa back is as good a place as any to start."

Prophet thought it over. It had been a lot to swallow, but it had the ring of truth. A sad, lonely truth. It seemed sometimes that those were the only kind of truths he knew.

He took a deeper swallow of the coffee, then dropped another chunk of driftwood onto the fire. "Better fetch your horse. This wind ain't doin' him no good out there."

As Rose got up and strode out of the alcove, he knew she could be lying about part or even all of it. Gopher could be out there with a rifle. But then, neither she nor Gopher had had any reason to follow Metalious's bunch, unless they'd thought they had the money. That would have been a tall gamble on such a windy night.

No, she couldn't have been lying about all of it. She'd had no reason to lie about the baby, and hell, he'd seen her sick as a dog.

A baby on the way with no father. A mother with no kin to speak of, and with a five-hundred-dollar bounty on her head for armed robberies in Kansas and Nebraska over the past two years.

At least she hadn't killed anyone who hadn't deserved it. . . .

"Ah, hell," Prophet said, giving one of the logs sticking out of the fire a frustrated kick.

25

"Whoaaahhhh, there, you mangy cayuse!"
Sam "Man-Killin' " Metalious yelled as he
pulled back on the reins of the big roan
hitched to the wagon.

Louisa braced her tied ankles against the
dashboard as the wagon jerked to a halt
behind the roan's blowing tail. She bit her
lip against the pain in her left leg. She didn't
think the jarring ride had opened up the
wound, but the knee felt as tight as a
drumhead. Before her, dawn light rippled
like quicksilver on the horse's back and on
the low brush roof of the adobe-brick shack
sitting at the base of a steep, rocky mountain
wall to Louisa's right.

The Metalious ranch, she thought. If you
could call it a ranch. The Triple 6. She
hadn't seen or smelled any cattle on the way
into the box canyon in which the headquarters sat. There were several corrals and a
few outbuildings crouched in the brush

beyond the shack, which, judging by its L-shape, was a bunkhouse, but the place had obviously seen better days. Better days before Metalious's crew of gunhands had moved in, using the place as a headquarters not so much for raising cattle as for stealing beeves and horses and selling them across the border in Mexico.

On the dark trails she rode, Louisa had heard of the man. He was also a vicious killer, as per his name, and a general all-around miscreant. Lou would call him no better than the crust at the bottom of an empty slop pale.

The man needed killing. That was for sure. And Louisa would do just that at the first opportunity. If he didn't kill her, as he'd promised to do eventually, first.

Metalious had set the wagon brake and climbed down the left front wheel and was moving around to the back of the wagon, where the doctor crouched over Blanco.

"How's he doin'?" Sam asked.

"Christ, how do you think after that rough ride? His wounds have opened up. I'm probably gonna have to pull my stitches out and resew his wounds!"

Sam laughed, little concern for his son's well-being in his demeanor. "Just keep him alive, Doc. Keep him alive and let him start gettin' better so he's at least conscious and knows what's goin' on." The outlaw leader turned toward a couple of the men who'd dismounted and were hovering around the wagon while the others led the mounts toward one of the three pole corrals beyond the bunkhouse. "Bob, Luis, take Blanco into the cabin. Put him on my bed. Want my boy to be comfortable."

Sam laughed again.

The doctor grunted as he climbed wearily down from the end of the wagon. "I don't get you, Metalious. What're you talking about — 'just keep him alive'?"

Sam laughed hard and slapped the doctor's back. Then he turned and followed the two men, who'd each grabbed an end of Blanco, toward the bunkhouse.

"What about the girl?" asked a tall man with Mexican features but no Spanish accent, leering up at Louisa from beneath the brim of his flat-brimmed black hat with painted grizzly teeth sewn into its crown. He wore a perpetual, bizarre sidelong grin. "Can I take her first, Boss?"

He spoke with a liquid-sounding lisp.

Metalious stopped at the bunkhouse doorway as the two men carrying Blanco, followed by the doctor, disappeared inside.

"There'll be none of that yet, Clell. I

brought her along as insurance against her big friend with the double-bore gut shredder. And to kill her myself . . . slow." Metalious grinned so that his teeth fairly glowed in the windy darkness against the bunkhouse door. "But first she's gonna cook and clean up this pigsty. You know — to generally do what women are meant to do. Huh, Clell? If I give her to you first, you'll break her neck and make me very angry, amigo!"

Metalious laughed his malicicious laugh. "Bring her." He disappeared into the cabin, in the open doorway of which a guttering lantern light now shone, washing over the board above the door in which the numeral six had been burned three times.

Clell turned to Louisa. "You heard the man." He spread his arms, looking up at her lustily. Louisa saw that part of his upper lip was missing, probably cut off with a rusty knife, for it was hideously scarred, and revealed a grisly portion of his upper gum. Thus the sidelong grin and lisp.

"I'll lift you," he said with a wink.

"You could at least cut my ankles free. Then I could climb down on my own. I'm just concerned about your back, you understand, Clell."

"I could carry you down and *then* cut your ankles free. I would enjoy that more. I appreciate your concern for my back, but you don't look much heavier than a sack of parched corn."

He snaked one arm behind Louisa's back, just up from her rump, and slid the other one beneath her legs, causing the wound above her left knee to bark. With a jerk, he lifted her out of the wagon's pilot box, and although the pain stabbed at her, she maintained a stony expression. He held her there against him, grinning that bizarre grin at her, revealing his decayed gums and the exposed, black roots of several teeth. He slid one hand up under her poncho, gave her left breast a slow squeeze.

Louisa spat in his face.

He slid his arms out from beneath her. The ground came up fast to smack Louisa hard, hammering the air from her lungs. She'd hit the back of her head, as well, and she lay there, trying not to show how much pain she was in but blinking her eyes to clear them.

Clell reached down, slid an Arkansas toothpick from the well of his left mule ear, and hacked through the rope binding Louisa's ankles together. "You and me are gonna raise us a ruckus later. You might even get to likin' ole Clell."

Louisa swallowed, hardened her lower jaw

slightly at the dull pain in the back of her head — it rippled down her neck and into her back — and said in as clear a voice as she could muster with her lungs working at only about one-quarter capacity, "I wouldn't get my hopes up."

Clell straightened and, holding the knife menacingly in his right hand, canted his head toward the bunkhouse. From the open door, Metalious and the doctor's voices emanated.

Louisa sat up. Her wrists were still tied behind her, so she climbed to her feet awkwardly. Clell stepped back warily as she glanced coolly at him out of the corner of her left eye before walking along the path beaten into the sand, gravel, and sage to the bunkhouse's front door.

There was a slight wooden stoop. She stepped over the rotten wood planks and on into the earthen-floored shack. A long table with a scarred top littered with food scraps and whiskey bottles stood before her, a woodstove flanking it. Bunks stood to either side, most of them lost in the hovel's deep shadows.

The air smelled so strongly of old sweat and tobacco smoke that Louisa's gut tightened, and for a moment she thought she'd retch. She'd been around the West a few times, and she'd experienced smells that would choke a dog, but the bunkhouse smelled like an open privy pit.

"I knew you'd come fer me, Pa," Blanco was saying on a bunk at the edge of the light shed by the lantern hanging from a wire over the table. "Sure do appreciate the help."

"Don't talk now, son," Sam said, standing over his son and holding a bottle by its neck in his right fist. "Let the doc tend ya, and we'll settle up tomorrow."

"Settle up?" Blanco said.

"You know — for not involving me in them stage and bank holdups."

"But, Pa, you know how you are. You always wanna run things, and . . ."

"Shhh!" Sam held a finger over his lips, cutting Blanco off. "We'll talk about it tomorrow. Make everything right between us. Tonight, you rest."

As the doctor, sitting in a chair beside Blanco's bunk, began unbuttoning the firebrand's shirt, Blanco said, "Ah, shit! I knew you was gonna be sore. I just knew it!"

Sam had started turning away from the bunk. Now, he turned back, roaring in a deep, savagely menacing voice: "I told you to shut the hell up, Blanco!"

Louisa couldn't see Blanco, as the bunk was in shadow, but she heard him curse and grunt as the doctor administered to him. Sam turned toward her, his big, dark, bearded face still flushed with fury. He pointed his bottle at her. "You git to work, girl! Me an' the boys need supper, and we need it soon!"

"I don't cook," Louisa said with quiet defiance. "But even if I could, it would be a bit hard with my hands tied behind my back."

"You're a girl, ain't ya?" Sam growled, kicking a chair out from the end of the table and slamming the bottle down. "You can cook. At least, you can throw somethin' together better than me or my boys can. And you can clean up around here." He splashed whiskey into a dirty water tumbler, and threw it back. "Clell, keep a gun on her. Don't let her outta your sight. She's a killer! She tries anything, I'll let you take her out behind the cabin. How's that?"

"That's just fine," Clell said, returning his Arkansas toothpick to his mule-eared boot, then sliding a bone-gripped Remington from his thigh holster and kicking a chair out from the side of the table nearest the door. "I think we'd get along right well together. I think she likes me."

"Well, that's because you're a handsome devil," Sam said. Turning to the other two men milling in the shadows around the bunks beyond the doctor and Blanco, the outlaw leader said, "Bob, make sure we got four men on watch all night. You decide the shifts."

"You got it, Boss."

"Me," Sam said. "I'm tired. I'm gonna sit here for a bit and watch the girl cook. I don't get to see that too often."

"Me, neither," Clell said, splashing whiskey into another dirty glass, then reaching into a shirt pocket for a long, black cheroot.

Louisa looked around the makeshift kitchen. The table, the plankboard counter running along the back wall, the shelves above the counter, and the stove were grease-splattered and bloodstained. Even back home in Nebraska, Louisa had never been handy with cleaning or cooking. But there wasn't much else she could do at the moment but appease these men and let them get what dull-witted joy they could at mocking her.

What she wanted to do was kill them as they sat at the table smoking, drinking, and ogling her. She still had two small knives on her person, hidden under her poncho and in the folds of her underwear. But she'd have to bide her time and wait for the right opportunity to use them. Even if she thought she could get away with using them effectively now, with both her wounded legs slowing her down, she'd refrain from doing so.

She was in no hurry to leave this box canyon. If Lou was still alive, he'd be along soon, and then she and the big bounty hunter could take down the entire gang.

She especially wanted to take down Sam and Clell as bloodily as possible, to leave them dying slowly, howling like gut-shot coyotes.

Finished inspecting the mess around her, Louisa grabbed a ragged straw broom from a corner, and raised it like a club.

"Hey!" Clell said, jerking forward in his chair and raising his .45.

"Hold your water."

Louisa swept the broom across the top of the table until all the bottles, glasses, cigarette and cigar butts, and tin cups hit the floor with a raucous clatter and a nasty screech of breaking glass. Clell swallowed as he sank back in his chair, slowly lowering the .45 and looking chagrined as Sam laughed and pointed at him, mocking.

Louisa busily swept the trash from the table out the door, not caring that she'd left a good bit of broken glass behind. She was careful not to limp; revealing that she was gimped up in both legs would do her no good at all. She could imagine such knowledge bringing out the sadism in these killers. As the two owlhoots watched her with a singular mix of wary amusement and guarded fascination, she built a fire in the stove and set about throwing a meal together.

She picked up an airtight tin of tomatoes and slammed it onto the table between Metalious and Clell, who were now playing a desultory game of two-handed stud. "If you promise to cut yourself, I'll ask one of you gentlemen to open this."

Metalious chuckled as he puffed the quirley wedged in the corner of his mouth, then set his cards down, slid a bowie knife from his belt sheath, and used it to cut the lid off the can. Louisa thanked the man dryly, then dumped the tomatoes into a pot that she hadn't bothered to wash out first.

To the tomatoes she added jerky that she found in a burlap sack on one of the shelves, a shriveled potato, and a sprouted wild onion, both of which Metalious chopped for her in lieu of handing over his butcher knife. Since that didn't look like much with which to feed all of Metalious's men —

she'd had trouble counting them but she thought there weren't quite ten of them left — she rummaged around until she found a few chunks of brined pork that she suspected had been sitting there in its oilcloth wrap for quite some time.

She didn't care. She didn't plan on eating the vile concoction, anyway. She would have added rat poison if she'd seen a box lying around, and if she thought Metalious wouldn't catch her at it or force her to sample her own cooking before his men did.

She set the pot on the stove and chunked another log into the firebox.

"There. I think I'll retire to my quarters, if you don't mind."

"What about coffee?" Clell said, looking up from his cards and scowling around his half-smoked cigar. Light from the lamp hanging above the table shone blue in the thick web of wafting tobacco smoke that the cabin's open door did little to alleviate and that was causing Louisa's eyes to water.

It was such smoke as well as drunken male scalawags like the two around her now that kept her out of saloons. Not to mention the fact that she had no taste for liquor of any variety, including beer.

"I only made the stew to silence the

caterwauling," Louisa said. "Make your own coffee."

Clell bunched his lips angrily, closed his hand over his .45 on the table, and began to rise from his chair.

"You make it," Sam ordered the scar-lipped hard case. "She probably don't know how. I bet you prefer milk, don't you, little girl? Goat milk, no doubt."

"That and sarsaparilla."

"Figures."

As Clell grumblingly walked around the table to fetch the coffeepot off a splintered shelf, Louisa drifted back into the bunk-house's shadows, beyond Blanco and the doctor, who continued rewrapping the hard case's wounds.

"You stick around, honey," Metalious ordered behind a fresh smoke puff. "You try to leave tonight, I'll hear you. I sleep light as a rooster. Besides, I got men posted all about the place. If you try to make a run for it, I'll feed you to the whole damn pack at once!"

He laughed.

As Louisa glanced around for a bunk that looked unoccupied and relatively clean, she imagined sliding her knife across Sam "Man-Killin' " Metalious's hairy neck, and her lips quirked with a hard smile.

The smile died when she found a bunk against the shack's right wall. As she drew the bunk's single army blanket up to her neck and rested her head back on the gamey-smelling pillow, her thoughts tumbled to Prophet. The worry that her own dilemma had distracted her from returned, and her stomach dropped hard.

Where was Lou?

Obviously, Metalious hadn't run into him. But sundry other cutthroat packs haunted the broad valley between the San Mateos and the No-Water range. Had he tangled with one of them? Or, if not, would he be able to track her to this devil's lair in time to save her if she could not save herself?

She was living on borrowed time. That was certain. Metalious couldn't keep his men off of her forever, and he probably wouldn't want to. She'd been savaged before, down in Mexico before Lou had galloped to her rescue with a passel of revolutionarios, and she'd vowed she'd never let herself be savaged again.

She'd die first, by her own hand or theirs.

Sooner rather than later her time would run out.

Louisa closed her eyes. She listened to Sam and Clell flip cards onto the table and grunt and spit and hack phlegm and set their whiskey glasses down. They talked little. Outside, there was the occasional horse whinny, and from time to time the men keeping watch on the surrounding ridges called to each other. More than once, riders rode past the cabin — one scout being relieved by another.

Men came and went for several hours, dishing up the stew and pouring coffee and joining the poker game or rolling into their bunks. Finally, somehow, Louisa managed to sleep.

She had no idea how much time had passed, before something woke her. She opened her eyes. The bunkhouse was dark, the air thick with wood and tobacco smoke. To her left, the earthen floor crunched under a stealthy foot. The stench of rancid sweat and horses grew stronger, and she felt the heat of a near man.

A shadow moved beside her. Just as she began to lift her head, a calloused, dirty hand closed over her mouth, pressing her head down against the pillow. A man grunted. She couldn't see him in the darkness, but he was big and brutal, and she could hear his heavy, intense breathing.

Her bunk dropped on the left as he planted a knee on the edge of it and with his free hand fondled her breasts roughly

345

through the blanket. Automatically, she'd reached into her serape for a bone-handled dagger and managed to roll onto her left side while sliding her right hand across her belly, tilting the knife up slightly.

The man who'd been trying to pull her blanket down and climb onto the bunk with her suddenly sucked a sharp breath through gritted teeth. Louisa lifted the haft of the knife slightly, heard the razor-edged tip saw into the denim at the man's crotch — a soft, sibilant sound, like the scratch of a burrowing mouse.

She held the knife there.

The man slowly lifted his hand from her chest. He lifted the other hand from her mouth, and pulled his head back. "Easy," Clell breathed.

The smell as well as the voice identified him.

Louisa continued to hold the knife firmly in her right hand, angled up. Grunting nervously, Clell eased himself up and over the knife and then dropped both feet down to the floor. He turned away and disappeared in the darkness.

Louisa slipped the knife back in the sheath strapped to her thigh.

She closed her eyes.

Buoyed by this one small victory, she managed to will herself to sleep once more.

26

Prophet lifted his head suddenly, grabbed his Winchester almost before he'd even opened his eyes, cocked it, and aimed. His heart thudded. Sitting against the wall of the notch, on the opposite side of the near-dead fire from where Rose lay in her blankets, head resting on her saddle, he peered out the alcove's opening into the darkness beyond.

Rose lifted her head from the saddle, looking around warily, blinking. "What is it?"

Prophet depressed the rifle's hammer. "Thought I heard somethin'. But it's *nothin'* I heard." He set the rifle down beside him. "The wind died."

He'd been sleeping against the notch wall, head on his knees. He hadn't wanted to get too comfortable because he hadn't wanted to sleep long. Louisa would be wondering about him, waiting for him. Needing him. Now he stood stiffly, his butt numb, having fallen asleep, and walked over to the opening and stepped outside.

Silence. Not so much as a breath of a breeze. He stepped far enough back from the ridge that he could see the eastern sky. False dawn was not yet upon him, but the stars just above the horizon were beginning to fade. It was around four, he judged.

"Time to ride, Rose," he said when he'd walked back into the alcove.

Rose flung her blankets aside. She moved as if to rise, then leaned back on her arms, looking straight ahead. Prophet couldn't make out her face in the shadows.

"You all right?"

She nodded. "Just a little queasy, I reckon."

"You seen a doc yet?"

Rose shook her head. "I'll worry about that later. When I've found a place to sink my picket pin."

Prophet walked over and extended his hand to her. She looked up at him skeptically. Then she reached out, placed her hand in his. Gently, he pulled her to her feet. As she continued to stare up at him, her eyes filled unexpectedly with tears, and she threw herself against him and wrapped her arms around him, burying her face in his chest.

Her shoulders jerked as she sobbed.

"There, now," Prophet said, feeling a little awkward but finally reaching around her and giving her an affectionate squeeze. "Everything's gonna be all right."

"I know." Her voice was tight, brittle. She pulled away from him, turned away as though embarrassed, and wiped the tears from her cheeks with the backs of her hands. "I'm just . . . scared."

Prophet held her arm, turned her back toward him. "You ride on out of here, Rose. Go on back to your ranch. It's yours now, with your family dead."

She studied him for a time, frowning, her eyes sliding to each of his own and back again. Finally, she shook her head. "Not yet. You helped me. Now I'm gonna help you."

"Rose . . ."

"You're alone, Lou. Alone against a gang of just under ten. You won't have a chance getting Louisa back without someone to at least create a distraction."

Prophet thought about it. "Is all you got for firepower that old cap-and-ball?"

"I had a newer pistol and a Spencer repeater, but Junior took it when he lit out on me and . . ." She couldn't quite bring herself to say "baby" yet. She looked down at her belly as though there were something alien there inside her.

Prophet squatted by the fire, reached into one of the saddlebags, and pulled out a spare pistol wrapped in a couple of red bandannas. He removed the bandannas and hefted the pistol in his hand — a Smith & Wesson with gutta-percha grips. He rummaged around in his saddlebags again and withdrew a box of shells.

"Spoils of war," he said, flipping the gun in his hand and extending it to Rose butt first. "A .44. Here's some shells for it."

Rose took the gun in one hand, the shells in the other. She looked at each, then narrowed an eye as she glanced up at Prophet towering over her. A faint smile pulled at one corner of her mouth.

"Let's shake a leg," he said with a grunt as he grabbed his saddle and started back to where both horses stood near the notch's back wall.

Rose's skewbald paint stood as far away from Mean and Ugly as he could get in the tight quarters, having obviously been cowed by Mean's evil eye, which the dun was giving even now.

Prophet chuckled. "Glad to see you got your pluck back, Mean." He slapped the horse's right rear hip. "Cussed son of a bitch."

A few minutes later, forgoing breakfast,

351

Prophet led Mean out of the notch. Rose followed with the skewbald paint that had belonged to Gopher Adams. Wordlessly, in the predawn darkness, the stars blazing in the wind-scoured sky, they mounted up and booted the mounts across the shallow wash, the clacks of the horses' hooves sounding crisp and clear in the quiet air.

Faintly, from far away, a single coyote howled.

On the trail, Prophet was glad to see that the tracks of the killers, including the two wheel furrows of Sam "Man-Killin' " Metalious's wagon, had not been so badly eroded by the wind that they couldn't be followed. He knew roughly where the Metalious ranch was located, but being able to follow the trail straight to it would save precious time.

Prophet and Rose alternately loped and walked their fresh horses, stopping once an hour to give the mounts a couple handfuls of water and parched corn. The sun was a vast blossoming rose in the east when Prophet saw the tracks of the wagon wheels swing abruptly off the main trail, making four indentations in the spindly buckbrush, then marking the sand and gravel along a single-track horse trail.

Prophet and Rose rode single-file along

the trail that meandered off across the purpling sage and rabbit brush. The San Mateos rose ahead and slightly left of the trail. A jog of nearer, rocky-topped hills humped straight out from the trail, which, Prophet saw nearly an hour later, angled around on the hill's northwest side. Then it dropped down into a deep, dry arroyo, followed the ravine's far side for half a mile, then swung north again through the apron slopes of the mountains.

All the while he rode, Prophet kept a tense, watchful eye on the brush along the trail, not only on the scout for trail pickets but for Louisa's body. Though the thought was like a log chain in the bounty hunter's gut, there was always the chance she'd been killed. A good chance, in fact, knowing the kind of men she was up against.

Used and discarded.

The farther they rode into the slopes of the San Mateos, the more frequently Prophet stopped and, leaving Rose concealed in a nest of boulders or in a hidden ravine, swung wide of the horse trail to carefully scout the terrain ahead. He didn't want to run into any pickets Metalious might have posted, or, worse, ride up on the Metalious camp itself unawares.

It was almost noon when he returned

from one such scout to find Rose where he'd left her, in a broad, shallow wash on the backside of which three spindly cotton-woods stood, their leaves bright in the mid-day sunshine. Rose sat on a boulder, elbows resting on her knees as she absently spun the cylinder of the S&W that Prophet had loaned her. She'd heard him coming and watched him expectantly as he halted Mean and Ugly on the bank of the wash.

"A couple of sidewinders just ahead."

"You mean the human kind?"

Prophet nodded. "They're guarding a nar-row canyon mouth. The Metalious ranch must be just beyond it." He shucked his Winchester from the saddle boot. "You want to help?"

"That's what I'm here for." Rose stood quickly and slipped the S&W behind the buckle of her cartridge belt.

"It's dangerous."

She scowled at him for mentioning the obvious, then grabbed the reins of her roan and swung up into the saddle. Prophet swung Mean around, and as Rose put the roan up behind him, he followed a notch through chalky buttes spotted with Spanish bayonet and short, wiry, late summer wild-flowers. Back on the horse trail they'd been following from the main stage road, Prophet

354

halted Mean and turned to Rose as she came up onto the trail and stopped beside him, their dust puffing in the still air.

"Give me ten minutes to get around those fellas and get the drop on 'em. Then ride on ahead. You'll see the canyon — just a gap in a rock wall, with a rocky floor. Ride straight toward it. The men are on the right side of the gap. They'll hear you comin' and when they turn their attention on you, I'll pull down."

"You got it."

Prophet dropped his chin and narrowed a doubtful eye at her. "Now, I'm assuming they won't shoot first and ask questions later, Rose."

"They'll see I'm female and hold their fire." Rose shook her head and reached forward to pat the roan's sweat-damp neck. "I'm not worried."

Prophet booted Mean off the trail and through a crease in the buttes, heading in the general direction of a steep, sandstone ridge. When he'd reached the base of the ridge, he swung down from Mean's back, loosened the dun's latigo strap, and wrapped his reins around an ironwood shrub.

He continued ahead along the ridge base, where occasionally he spied mummified bobcat and coyote scat amongst the rocks and weed tufts and along the cut-in base of the ridge, until he came to where the ridge wall curved to his left. He'd seen earlier that the two guards had a cookfire going, and when he spied the smoke rising from a nest of boulders, he stopped, looked around carefully, then continued forward on the balls of his boots.

He kept the snag between him and the smoke that rose in thin white tendrils beyond it. When he'd gained the snag itself, he climbed up carefully, one rock at a time, and stopped at the snag's right shoulder.

Below, one of the two pickets sat on a rock facing a small coffee fire, the flames of which were nearly invisible in the harsh sunlight. He was also facing Prophet though he'd have to tilt his head up at a sharp angle to see the interloper. On one knee, he was tossing a knife into the sand with one hand while holding a blue tin cup in the other. He had a bored, lazy air, shoulders slumped.

Three horses, one black, grazed a small patch of galleta grass on the far side of the trail, in a fold between two rocky bluffs.

Prophet scowled at the mounts. Three? When he'd scouted the bivouac, he'd only spied two. The black must have been concealed by a trapezoid of boulder shade.

Another trail guard stood several feet

away, his back to the fire. He held a rifle in his arms as he stared toward the horse trail that snaked around through the buttes and continued on past him and into the gap to his right, the rocky floor of which shone damp from a runout spring.

The rolling thuds of an approaching rider sounded in the distance, from the direction in which Prophet had left Rose.

"Rider," said the man with his back to the fire, looking left along the trail.

The other man tossed the knife into the dirt once more, then, leaving the knife in the sand and setting his cup on a rock of the fire ring, straightened and turned toward the trail. A rifle leaned against a nearby boulder. As he reached for it, Prophet loudly racked a shell into his Winchester's breech.

"You two fellas wouldn't want to drop them irons and turn around nice and slow, would you?"

Both men froze with their backs to Prophet, the nearest man with his hand angled out toward his Henry repeater. The man nearest the trail, from which Rose's thuds grew louder as she approached the camp, turned his head slowly toward Prophet. He held a half-smoked quirley between in his long, thin lips. His face was so freckled beneath the brim of his torn-brimmed, coffee-colored Stetson that it nearly looked dun colored.

It was also a mask of savage fury.

The other man, frozen in the act of reaching for the Henry, turned his head toward his partner, whose eyes slid to meet the first man's gaze. It was a fleeting, oblique glance.

The eyes of the freckled gent slid back toward Prophet, and his jaws hardened as he jerked toward Prophet's position, swinging his Winchester around and levering a shell into its breech.

Almost at the same time, his partner completed the motion of reaching for his Henry, wheeling on one foot and showing gritted teeth beneath his mustached upper lip. Prophet's rifle belched twice at his shoulder, leaping in the bounty hunter's hands, and both men went spinning, the man nearest the fire managing to squeeze off a shot with his Henry, the bullet spanging with an angry whine off a rock ringing the fire.

As both men lay jerking and kicking their lives away, Prophet ejected the second smoking round and seated a fresh round in the Winchester's breech. Movement on the other side of the trail caught his eye — a man pushing up out of a rocky nest like the one on which the bounty hunter stood. He was dressed in a black duster and black, flat-brimmed hat, and he was lifting a rifle to his shoulder.

An eye wink after Prophet had spied the third gunman, Rose trotted into the bounty hunter's field of vision from his left, her roan kicking up dust along the horse trail. She scowled down at the dead men, only one of whom continued to jerk and flex his hand as though yearning to fill it with a gun.

The black-clad rider lifting up from the rock nest on the other side of the trail swung his rifle toward Rose.

Prophet shouted, "Rose, *down!*"

27

Rose whipped her head around to follow Prophet's gaze, and her shoulders tightened.

He could not take a shot, because she was nearly directly between him and the black-clad gunman. Rose kicked her horse off the trail's far side and raised the Smith & Wesson that Prophet had given her. For a half second, she obscured the gunman with her own body, but Prophet heard the shot and saw the smoke puff atop the rock nest.

Blood sprayed from Rose's back, high up near her right shoulder, and she jerked backward in the roan's saddle. She triggered the S&W into the ground. The roan pitched and whinnied, wheeling angrily, and Rose flew off the horse's left hip, hitting the ground only a foot from the horse's scissoring hooves.

Rose rolled, her hat flying. Dust wafted.

The black-clad gunman was jacking a fresh round into his own Winchester's breech when Prophet, tearing his fervid glance from the wounded girl, drew a bead on the man's middle and fired.

As the Winchester roared, Prophet saw first the red spray against the rocks behind the gunman. Then the man's head jerked back violently. His black hat tumbled forward, bouncing off his chest. He triggered his own rifle skyward and flew straight back into a little cavity in the brush-stippled snag, one leg hanging up on a slightly higher rock in front of him. His hat caught on his right black boot toe as though it had been tossed there.

He bobbed his head, a grimace furling his gray-brown mustache. His shoulders jerked, waving one hand in a death spasm. His smoking rifle dropped with a clatter into the rocks beneath him.

"Rose!"

Prophet lurched forward and hopscotched the rocks to the ground, then leaped the body of the man who'd been tossing the knife. Holding his rifle in one hand, he crouched beside Rose, who'd piled up on the near side of the trail. Dust still sifted after the roan that had galloped back in the direction from which it and the girl had come.

Rose was on her belly, arms akimbo, one

knee bent. Her right shoulder was bloody, and thick red blood oozed down her back.

She groaned as she lay on her side, her face a mask of pain, and looked up at Prophet. "What a fool," she said. "I guess I'm not as good a hard case as I feared I was."

"Maybe not a good hard case." Prophet ripped his bandanna off his neck. "But I reckon you saved my bacon."

She narrowed an eye suspiciously.

"That son of a bitch had the drop on me. You distracted him." Prophet ripped the bandanna in two, wadded up one piece and shoved it into the entrance wound, tamping it firmly with his fingers.

Rose arched her neck and back, and her mouth drew wide in a silent, agonized scream. The blood drained from her face.

"Sorry, girl, but you're losing blood fast," he said, hearing his own desperation in his voice, anxious for Rose but also worried sick about Louisa, knowing that the rifle reports had likely been heard at the Metalious ranch.

He tipped Rose toward him and leaned over her to inspect the exit wound, wincing at the damage the .44 bullet had done to her slender shoulder. Wadding up the second half of the bandage, he said, "One more time," and rammed it into the exit hole.

This time, she merely squeezed her eyes shut and gritted her teeth.

"I'll be all right," she said in a low, razor-edged voice. "Go get your partner."

Prophet stared down at her. He didn't want to leave her. If she died, he didn't want her to die alone. On the other hand, he couldn't leave Louisa with the killers, who were likely onto his presence now. They'd be sending riders here soon.

A wooden rattling sounded from up trail. A wagon was heading toward Prophet. He eased Rose, who appeared only half-conscious now and who hung limp in his arms, in a sitting position against a boulder, so the blood wouldn't so easily drain out of her, then grabbed his Winchester and walked out into the trail.

He frowned toward the sound of the approaching wagon that was still out of sight behind the low, sandy buttes, back in the direction of the main trail from Corazon.

Sitting in a hide-bottom chair on the stoop of the Metalious bunkhouse, Louisa watched a black widow spider scuttle across the rotten floorboards toward where the scar-lipped hard case, Clell, was sitting on the edge of the stoop, feet on the ground.

He was leaning back on his arms, his rope-scarred hands resting on the porch floor. The right hand rested near his walnut-gripped Remington revolver that he was keeping close by in case Louisa made a move.

The black widow, ignoring the pistol, headed straight toward Clell's bare right hand as if it held something the spider wanted.

Louisa, sitting with her chair back against the front of the bunkhouse while the doctor and Sam Metalious were tending Blanco inside the smelly hovel and the other men milled about like bona fide ranch hands on a Sunday afternoon, watched the spider with keen interest.

A faint smile pulled at the corners of her pretty, pink mouth.

The spider stopped just in front of Clell's middle finger, the nail of which was nearly as black as the spider itself. The spider was a female, its round abdomen marked with a tiny red dot in the shape of an hourglass.

The spider seemed to be considering Clell's dead fingernail. Louisa stared at it, the corners of her mouth rising slightly higher as she silently urged the spider on.

Meanwhile, inside the bunkhouse, Sam's voice was rising. Things didn't seem to be going well for Blanco. Sam was severely graveled at his son's having gone out on his own and robbed the stage and the Corazon bank with the obvious intention of keeping the money for himself. He and his gang likely would have headed to Mexico with the loot if Prophet and Louisa hadn't caught up to them in Nugget Town.

Of course, Blanco had been denying this all morning.

His argument was that he'd simply wanted to try a couple of jobs on his own, and he had every intention of splitting the loot with his father and his father's men. But, so far, that argument seemed to be landing on deaf ears. Louisa thought that Sam had gone to a lot of work, and had lost a lot of men, to simply spring his son from jail so he could punish the kill-crazy hard case himself.

But that was the lobo breed for you. Nothing they did made much sense to sensible folks. Louisa had stopped trying to figure them out a long time ago. The only thing for the entire lot of badmen and the occasional badwoman was a bullet or, barring that, a hangman's noose.

The noose was where Blanco appeared to be headed, as three of Metalious's gunmen were stringing a hang rope over a gnarled, long-dead cottonwood in the middle of the yard while three others watched from the shade of the barn, passing a bottle and smoking cigars.

Preparing for a little entertainment.

Their bemused, self-satisfied expressions told Louisa they'd been itching to see Sam "Man-Killin' " Metalious's son hang for a good long time.

The black widow lifted its long, jointed black legs suddenly and crawled up onto the black nail of Clell's middle finger. Louisa lifted her furtive gaze to the back of Clell's head. The hard case was turned toward the hang tree, watching the activity over there with silent interest. He hadn't yet felt the spider on his finger.

Slowly, almost tentatively, it continued across the fingernail, over the first knuckle, and then the second knuckle. Louisa flinched slightly as it continued over the bulging last knuckle.

She glanced at the sunburned back of Clell's unshaven neck. He was still looking toward the hang tree, where two of the men appointed to the task of preparing the rope were arguing over where the end should be tied off.

Clell must have had some thick skin.

The spider stopped just past the middle of the man's hand before he lifted the hand

366

and brought it around in front of him, along with the other one. Louisa saw that he slapped the back of his right hand into the palm of his left one, and jerked with a startled grunt.

The black widow arced out away from him and fell in the dirt.

Louisa began to lurch forward, intending to grab the gun, but stopped. It was too far away. And her left knee was too tight for a quick movement like that. Even if she could grab it, she couldn't straighten fast enough to keep from being turned into human hamburger in a matter of seconds.

"Fuck!" Still clutching his right hand in the left one, Clell straightened, walked out a little ways from the porch, and looked down. "Black widow."

He looked down at the back of his right hand, and fear reddened his scar-lipped features, worry furling his auburn brows.

"Contrary to what most people think," Louisa said from her chair, leisurely tipping back against the bunkhouse's front wall, "the black widow's sting is rarely deadly. The female's, however, can inhibit breathing, which can understandably lead to death in the infirm. You're not in ill health, are you, Clell?" She pursed her lips and favored him with her chill, hazel-eyed gaze. "Just ugly as fresh dog dung."

Clell looked at her, his eyes blazing, his lips bunching in anger. He'd just opened his mouth to speak when the bunkhouse door burst open and Blanco came stumbling through it, sobbing and dropping to his knees at the edge of the porch, dust rising from the rotten floorboards.

"Pa!" he cried. "Now, don't do this!"

Sam strode out behind him and kicked him off the porch and into the yard. More dust flew. Blanco cowered on his knees, wrapping his arms around his belly and sobbing. *"Bastard!"*

"Metalious," the doctor cajoled from the open doorway, holding his black bag in his hand. "I didn't ride all the way out here, keeping that man alive, just so you could kill him."

Metalious stood, his fists on his hips, staring down at his son writhing in the dirt at his feet. "You did a good job, Doc. Damn good job." He turned to the doctor standing on the porch. "I do appreciate it. But I'm damn tired of hearing you yap."

Fear sparked in the doctor's eyes.

Louisa jumped to her feet, mindless of her aching legs. "No!"

Metalious's right hand was a blur of motion as it whipped down to grab the ivory-gripped .45 strapped to his right thigh. *Pow! Pow! Pow!*

The doctor dropped his bag and flew straight back into the bunkhouse, where he hit the table with a thump, then knocked over a chair on his way to the floor.

Louisa looked at Metalious, rage turning her cheeks beet red.

Metalious turned the smoking gun on her, but he did not draw the hammer back. His big chest and bulging belly rose and fell heavily. Finally, he smiled, but the humor remained only on his thick, cracked lips inside his shaggy, black, gray-flecked beard.

Distant gunfire sounded east of the ranch yard. Two quick shots. Sam looked in the direction from which they'd come, as did the other men in the yard.

Louisa's heart quickened as she peered that way, too.

They all stood listening for a time. There were a couple of more shots, then silence.

The others looked at Sam expectantly. He turned to Louisa, licking his lips, thoughtful, then grinned.

"You'll be dead in a few hours, too. Only after you've been the guest of honor at the funeral celebration for my son. In respect for his memory, you understand." Metalious raised his voice and turned to sweep the yard with his gaze. "And because I honor my promise that anyone who double-crosses me dies, including *my own blood!*"

The men around the yard showed their teeth as they snickered or laughed, looking around at each other and then at Blanco sobbing at his father's feet.

Metalious looked at Clell. "Hang him. Slow drop, just like always. Let him dangle there so that he can consider all of his sins before he has his visit with St. Pete. Don't want him forgetting one, now, do we?"

Sam laughed raucously.

Louisa looked down at Clell's gun resting on the edge of the porch. Her heart thudded. Just then, Clell turned to her. He smiled knowingly as he reached down, casually picked up the Remington, and dropped it into its holster.

His stare darkened. He knew she had at least one knife on her. He couldn't say anything because then Sam would know he'd gone against orders last night, visiting Louisa's bunk. Sooner or later, though, he'd have to say something or try to get her hideout pigstickers away from her. Before he did, she'd have to get her hands on a gun.

Clell reached down for Blanco's arm. The young outlaw pulled away and sobbed louder, begging his father for mercy.

"Oh, for chrissakes," Sam said to Clell. "Give him a Dutch rider over there. You're embarrassin' yourself, Blanco. You're embarrassin' not only yourself but me, too. You're just like your worthless mother!" He turned to Clell. "Get a move on. What're you waiting for? Git him hung!"

Clell glanced at Louisa once more, warily. Then, moving quickly, he swung up into the saddle of his horse hitched at the rack fronting the bunkhouse. He removed his lariat from his saddle horn, turned his horse away from the hitchrack, and paid out a long loop, dropping it neatly over Blanco's shoulders. Before Blanco could throw the hondo off his head, Clell took up the slack, wheeled his horse once more, and booted it toward the hang tree.

Blanco was twisted around and jerked onto his belly. He cursed loudly between sobs as Clell pulled him through the dusty yard, leaving a blood trail from his freshly reopened wounds.

Sam turned to Louisa and motioned with his arm, wobbling a little, as he'd been drinking all morning. "Get out there. I don't want you behind me. You got a right sneaky look to you, little girl."

Louisa's mind went to the two daggers

hidden beneath her skirts. She could get to them quickly, through slits in her outer wool riding skirt, but they wouldn't be much good against eight men. Glancing at the long-barreled Colt hanging off Sam's stout, buckskin-clad thigh, she stepped off the porch and moved out into the yard. Sam moved up behind her and gave her a push so hard that she flew forward, tripping over her own feet and the hem of her skirt, and piled up in the dirt.

Both her bandaged wounds barked painfully. She felt the one in her left leg begin to leak.

She whipped her head around and cast a malevolent stare at Metalious, narrowing one eye but saying nothing. Sam only laughed.

"Get on over there!" he ordered, pointing to where Blanco was now being manhandled onto the saddle of Clell's horse and positioned beneath a heavy, barkless limb of the near-naked hang tree. The tree was so old, had been dead for so long, that it looked little more than a large, skinned log poking up out of the ground, with three large limbs extending from its bole.

As Louisa approached it, she glanced around at the guns holstered on the legs and hips of the men around her. The three by the barn were coming up to get a good look at the hanging. If she could nab only one gun and ignore the agony shooting up and down both her legs, she could do some damage before they killed her. However she managed to do it, she had to work fast.

She would not let them rape her.

Lou, where the hell are you — you big, worthless scalawag? If you got yourself killed over there at the entrance to the box canyon, I hope it was painful. . . .

She glanced at Blanco now standing atop Clell's horse, the noose around his neck. The inside of his pants legs were wet. Piddle dripped onto the saddle between his boots.

"Any last words, son?" Sam said, fists on his hips, a drunken grin on his thick, wet lips. . . .

The other men stood in a semicircle around Blanco and the horse, passing a bottle and smoking and looking not only pleased but delighted and maybe also relieved that it was not them up there. Obviously, the hang tree had been put to good use before.

Blanco shifted his boots to keep his footing. Tears dribbled down his cheeks as urine continued to drip onto Clell's saddle. He opened his mouth to speak, stopped, and cleared his throat.

He hardened his voice as he shifted his baleful gaze at his father standing just off the horse's right wither. "Yeah, I got somethin' to say to you, you old bastard. *Fuck you!*"

Sam laughed and nodded at Clell. Clell slapped the horse's rump. The steeldust lunged forward, and the men parted as the horse ran through them and off across the yard, leaving Blanco dangling in the air behind him.

Louisa's heart thudded. Sam was the closest man to her. She'd just begun to edge toward him, when a pistol shot rose above Blanco's choking and the rope's creaking.

Two more shots. Galloping hooves thudded, growing louder.

Louisa peered into the distance beyond Blanco, toward the ridge about three-quarters of a mile away. She couldn't see the gap that led to the ranch, but her heart lightened slightly when she saw a rider galloping toward her. Her stomach dropped again in dread when she saw the black hat and the black duster flaps blowing back behind the man in the wind.

It was the gunman who fancied a black suit of clothes. The others had called him Parnell. He'd been with the two other men, guarding the entrance to the ranch.

He was riding fast, his black image atop his black horse growing by leaps and bounds. He seemed to have some important news he was in a raging hurry to share.

Louisa felt her chest go heavy, her mouth go dry.

Lou had ridden into their trap, got himself greased. She knew it. She felt the brittle chill of it in her bones.

Louisa's legs felt like lead, but she managed to kick herself into a slow, side-stepping maneuver toward Sam Metalious while casting quick, furtive glances at the ivory-gripped .45 jutting from the holster on his near thigh. She kept one eye on the rider, gauging his approach.

When he was within fifty yards and closing fast, head down, the brim of his black hat basted against his forehead, Louisa made her move, bolting suddenly for Metalious's big Colt.

"Hey, wait a minute!" yelled one of the men standing on the other side of Blanco's kicking body.

"Wait, what?" said another.

Louisa held her ground, eyes pinched in confusion.

"That ain't Parnell!" yowled the first man who'd spoken, crouching as he grabbed the two revolvers on his hips.

28

Keeping his head down so that Sam "Man-Killin' " Metalious and his men would believe him the black-clad gunman for as long as possible, storming into the ranch with news about the gunfire they'd likely heard, Prophet holstered his Peacemaker and reached down to slide his Winchester '73 from the saddle boot jutting up from beneath his right thigh.

He cocked the rifle one-handed and brought up his double-barreled ten-gauge that he'd concealed under the black duster that whipped behind him in the wind.

Following the meandering trail, he bounded up and over the last low rise, bringing the ranch yard to within fifty yards of him and moving up fast. The corrals and barn were on the left, a long, low shack on the right. There was a dead tree in the middle of the yard, on the near end. A man hung from it, dancing a bizarre jig as he strangled and jerked this way and that at the end of the hang rope.

Seven men including Metalious stood around the tree. Two were walking slowly toward Prophet, about ten feet apart and one behind the other, frowning and canting their heads this way and that as though suspicious of the rider galloping toward them. The first man had his right hand on the handle of a pistol positioned for the cross draw on his left hip.

Louisa stood near Metalious, her right hand angled out away from her and toward the revolver on the big outlaw leader's right thigh. She'd frozen in midmovement, Prophet could tell, though she and everyone else were bouncing around in front of him as the big black lunged forward along the uneven trail. Her skirts billowed, and her blond hair danced in the breeze.

"That ain't Parnell!" yelled the man nearest him — a thin, rat-faced blond gent with his hat dangling down his back by a thong. He wore skintight fringed leggings and a shirt with Mexican-style piping.

He swiveled his head back toward Prophet, and jerked his revolver from its holster, reaching across his belly with his other hand to grab another. Prophet extended the sawed-off ten-gauge in his left hand, thumbing back each hammer in turn, and aiming the gun at the two men nearest him, both of whom were now slapping leather and lifting iron.

Prophet squeezed the barn blaster's left trigger.

Ka-booommmm!

The first man, who was extending both his revolvers straight out in front of him and glowering malevolently, was lifted three feet up in the air and thrown straight back, triggering both his hoglegs skyward as the double-ought buck punched a hat-sized hole in his chest and belly.

Prophet's wrist ached from the barn blaster's violent kick, but he squeezed the neck of the stock as tightly as he could, and took up the slack in the double-bore's second trigger.

Ka-booommmm!

The second man, stunned by what had happened to the man in front of him, was treated the same way. He fired one of his own pistols into his own kneecap before hitting the ground on his back and turning two violent somersaults toward a horse corral, bloodstained sage and gravel flying up around him.

As Prophet and the big black horse drew within ten yards of the dancing hanged man, the other four or five began cursing, throwing liquor bottles and cigars away, crouching and raising six-shooters. A pistol popped ahead and to Prophet's right, the bullet drawing a hot line across his right forearm. He let the shooter have it, the Winchester leaping and roaring and then its barrel dropping slightly as Prophet recocked it.

As he galloped straight on through the group, two men dove out of his way while Louisa, unable to keep big Sam Metalious from drawing his own Colt, leaped onto the man's back and snaked her arms around his neck, trying to drive him to the ground and get his gun.

As Prophet flew on past the bunch grouped around the hang tree, most of whom, including Louisa and Sam, were on the ground, bullets screamed around his head and thudded into the ground around the black's scissoring hooves. Prophet drew sharply back on the horse's reins, then turned him in a great spray of dust and gravel.

The horse whinnied and tried buck-kicking though Prophet held him on a short leash with his left hand, having let the double-bore drop down his side to dangle there by its leather lanyard.

Two men were down on their knees, bearing down on him.

Prophet ground his spurs into the black's flanks. *"Hee-yahh!"*

As he bounded forward, the extended pistols of the two men on their knees puffed smoke and stabbed flames.

A hot slug tore through Prophet's upper left arm. Sweeping the pain back into a rear corner of his brain, he slipped the black's reins in his teeth and, as the horse galloped back down the middle of the yard toward the hang tree, Prophet held the rifle to his right shoulder with both hands.

Shooting from the hurricane deck was no easy task. He'd fired three quick shots before he finally pinked the elbow of one man shooting at him and blew the hat off the other. He thundered back past the hang tree and the man hanging from it — Blanco Metalious, the bounty hunter noted with vague incredulity — and turned the black once more.

Louisa had Sam Metalious's long-barreled Colt in her hand while Sam himself writhed on the ground beside her, grabbing at a bloody knife handle poking up from his side and bellowing like a poleaxed bull. Extending the Colt straight out in front of her, Louisa triggered lead toward the two men shooting from knees in front of the barn, one holding the elbow that Prophet had pinked down close to his side.

She drilled another, taller man with a hideously scarred upper lip who came running at a crouch toward her from behind the hang tree. He flew back, throwing his gun away, and bounced off Blanco's twitching feet. He piled up at the tree's base, clutching his chest and screaming.

Louisa and the two men on their knees exchanged shots. A couple of Louisa's slugs plunked into the barn behind the men as their shots sliced the air around her or blew up dust at her boots. As one of her slugs slammed the man with the wounded elbow straight back to the ground, the other got up and ran crouching back toward the corral angling off the barn's far side.

Meanwhile, the black had had its fill of the lead storm. It reared suddenly just as Prophet had turned it back toward the yard.

Prophet reached for the horn with his left hand, missed it, and suddenly found himself free-falling off the black's hindquarters, glimpsing the long, silky black tail waving up beside him a half second before the ground smacked his back so hard that the breath left him in a single, loud grunt.

His head spun.

The black galloped back toward the entrance to the canyon, angrily buck-kicking, dust sifting behind it.

Prophet lifted his head and pushed onto an elbow. Louisa was where she'd been before. Her cheek was bloody, and her poncho was torn where a bullet had grazed her arm. She was punching .45 shells from Metalious's cartridge belt while the man lay on his back, breathing hard and clutching his bloody belly.

All but one of the other men were down. The last man was crawling back toward the barn, grunting loudly and wheezing, holding the bloody back of his right thigh.

Louisa looked at Prophet as she shook the spent shells from Metalious's .45 and began sliding in fresh ones. "You all right, Lou?"

"I got a headache."

"Took you long enough to get here. I thought you were visiting the soiled doves in Socorro."

Prophet rose up on a knee and scooped his Winchester out of the dust where he'd dropped it. Brushing dust from the receiver, he watched the wounded man turn and press his back against the barn's front wall.

He, too, was reloading — a redheaded gent with a hook nose and two evil, gray eyes. Two rearing red ponies were piped onto the breast flaps of his bib-front blue shirt. He gritted his scraggly teeth and muttered to himself unhappily.

"No," Prophet said, shaking his head and cocking the Winchester. "But I'm gonna head there soon. Never visited no doves in Socorro, but I bet they have nice ones there."

He drew a bead on the gent sitting against the barn.

The man glanced at him over the gun he was busily punching fresh loads into.

"You're a whoremonger, Lou Prophet."

"Yes, I am, Louisa Bonnyventure."

She smiled at him. He smiled back at her.

The man sitting with his back to the barn's closed front doors flipped his pistol's loading gate shut and spun the cylinder.

With both hands, Louisa extended the big Colt at him, narrowing one eye as she aimed down the barrel. Prophet took up the slack in his trigger finger.

Their guns roared at the same time.

The red-haired hard case said, *"Achh!"* and slammed the back of his head against the barn, the twin side-by-side holes in his forehead glistening in the brassy noon light. He dropped his cocked pistol down between his legs. His shoulders jerked and his eyelids fluttered.

Slowly, he sagged down onto his shoulder and, except for one slightly twitching black boot, lay still. Smeared blood and brains formed a downward curving arc on the wall above him.

Prophet used the rifle as a staff with which to push himself to his feet. He shrugged out of his black duster as he looked around at the seven dead men and Sam "Man-Killin' " Metalious and then turned his befuddled gaze to Blanco, who was now more slowly dancing the same jig as before at the end of his rope.

"It appears," Louisa said as she climbed stiffly to her feet and tossed her hair back behind her shoulders, "that Sam and his son had a rather complicated relationship." She looked down at Metalious, who was clutching his bloody lower left side. "Isn't that right, Sam?"

Louisa angled the Colt toward Metalious and ratcheted the hammer back.

"No!" Metalious covered his face with the backs of his hands, as if it to shield himself from one of his own bullets.

"Hold on."

Prophet canted his head toward where a wagon was coming along the trail from the entrance to the canyon. Gradually, the thunder of its wheels and of the galloping horse in its traces could be heard above Blanco's strangling and the creaking of the hang rope.

The wagon approached, and Prophet saw Rose sitting in the driver's box, left of Marshal Max Utter, who drove with his long-barreled, double-bore Greener across his thighs. Utter had bandaged the girl's arm and gotten her into a sling he'd fashioned from rope he'd found in the back of his wagon, where he was hauling his wheelchair.

Utter reined the coyote dun to a halt, and the wagon squawked to a stop behind the blowing beast, dust sifting around it so that both Utter and Rose choked softly against it and blinked their eyes.

Utter looked at Blanco and then at Sam, who returned the lawman's stare with an incredulous one of his own. The marshal raked his gaze from Prophet to Louisa and then again to Blanco hanging to his left and about six feet off the ground.

"I reckon I could shoot him down, but he'd never live to see another judge."

Prophet cuffed his funnel-brimmed hat back off his forehead. "I reckon you're right."

"Where's the sawbones?"

"Dead," Louisa said.

Utter scowled.

"Sam," he said, "I'll be hauling your ass back to Corazon, in the jailhouse of which, locked up tighter than the bark on a cottonwood trunk, you'll await the next judge. I don't care if it takes a month of Sundays to get another one out here."

Metalious told the marshal to do something physically impossible to himself.

Utter scoffed, shook his head. "You've made a mockery of the law in my town for the last time."

Utter looked at Prophet. "Git him aboard here, will you, Proph? I'll send Lester and his boy out for the doc and to clean up this place and turn the horses loose."

When Prophet and Louisa had loaded Sam into the wagon box, letting his legs hang down from the tailgate, Prophet walked around to where Rose sat, looking pale beside Utter, who was swabbing his face from his canteen.

"You okay, Rose?" He draped an arm around her shoulders and gave her a squeeze.

She nodded and patted his hand. "I'll mend just fine. I'm gonna stay in town and have my baby." She lifted her dusty face to give him a bold, resolute look. "And then I'm gonna go on back to the ranch and raise him . . . or her . . . right."

Prophet kissed the girl's forehead. He swung around and climbed into the wagon where Louisa was already making herself comfortable, resting her back up against the front of the box. Prophet climbed up beside her. Metalious groaned around between them, clutching a neckerchief to his bloody side where Louisa had stuck him with a dagger.

"Everybody comfortable?" Utter said.

"This is the king's quarters, Marshal," Prophet said. "The king's damn quarters."

"Hold on." Louisa looked toward where Clell sat at the base of the hang tree. The scar-lipped outlaw was reaching for a pistol on the ground near his left boot. Blood covered his chest and belly.

He looked at Louisa. He froze. His eyes snapped wide in horror.

"Never did care for you, Clell."

Louisa's extended Colt barked.

Clell fell sideways, bowed his back, then dropped once more for the last time.

Utter turned the wagon around, and they all bounced back along the trail toward the canyon mouth. A hand touched Prophet's cheek. He turned to see Louisa frowning at him as she rubbed a speck of dust from the bleeding bullet burn up high on his cheekbone. She licked her fingers and gave the cut another, rough swab.

"Ouch," he groaned.

"Oh, buck up, will you?"

She grabbed his ear, used it to pull his head toward her, and kissed him on the lips. She pulled away, probing him gently, yearningly, with her hazel eyes. Her breasts rose and fell behind her serape. Smiling faintly, she let him go, rested her head against his shoulder, and gave a deep, relieved sigh.

Prophet stared back over the tailgate at the hang tree where Blanco gave one last twitch. The outlaw's right boot slipped off his foot and tumbled to the ground. The hard case's body twisted slightly, and then his arms fell straight down at his sides.

There was a rush of wings overhead, and Prophet flinched with a start. A hawk, he saw. A big, steel-gray raptor with red bars on its wings and a dark-banded tail. It was coming in fast.

It lighted on Blanco's shoulder and lifted an echoing screech of proprietary delight.

ABOUT THE AUTHOR

Peter Brandvold was born and raised in North Dakota and now makes his home in Colorado and Arizona, traveling around the West. He's written over fifty Western novels under his own name and several pseudonyms, including Frank Leslie. He's also written the *Bat Lash* comic book series for DC, and two screenplays. Drop him a line at peterbrandvold@gmail.com.